A TIME OF DARKNESS

The Circle of Talia Book 2

DIONNE LISTER

Dionne Lister

Cataloguing-in-Publication details are available from the National Library of Australia **www.librariesaustralia.nla.gov**

ISBN: 978-0-9873078-4-2

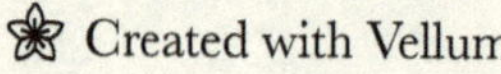 Created with Vellum

This book is dedicated to the three people who have supported me more than any others in the last year. To my husband, who has supported my transition to authorhood by picking up the home-related slack and also accepting I will be in my own little world quite frequently, and to my parents who have been encouraging and have never once said, "You'll never do it." Thank you all for believing in me. I love you.

CHAPTER 1

Zim watched orange embers leap from the funeral pyre as he breathed in acrid smoke. Glowing ash eddied about before sailing skywards on waves of warm air. Symbothial's body, unmade by the fingers of flames, returned cinder by cinder to the mountains protecting Vellonia.

The dragon prince turned to his mother. The queen's silver scales reflected the blaze, and Zim almost expected to burn his clawed hand when he placed it on her arm. "Mother? Symbothial, my beloved cousin, hath made his final flight around our wondrous city. We are the only ones left out here. Everyone has paid their respects and gone. Please, let me take you inside."

Queen Jazmonilly turned sad eyes to her son. "I remember when he first hatched; it was a joyous occasion." Jaz allowed the smallest of smiles to soften her face before anger swiped it away. "I can't believe he's gone, and in such a violent manner. He is the first dragon to be murdered in hundreds of years—

and for what?" She shook her head but allowed Zim to guide her to the mountain that was their castle.

After escorting Jaz to her chambers, Zim headed to his father's private reception room where the ongoing discussion about what to do with Bronwyn and the panther continued. In previous discussions, Agmunsten had hinted he knew more than he could say, and Zim agreed they shouldn't kill the murderers yet, but Jaz didn't concur. If it were up to his mother, the captives would have been put to death before Symbothial's funeral. Zim was glad his mother needed a rest and wouldn't be joining the meeting.

He stopped outside the double doors and breathed in. He knew where everyone stood on the issue, and it wasn't all in the same place. The steel handle turned easily in his giant, scaly hand, and the door opened silently. Zim went through the dimly lit antechamber to his father's main reception room. A chandelier cradling scores of candles hung above a long stone table. The table was the color of honey flecked with ants, the same as the floor and, like much of the furniture in the castle, was hewn from the stone within the very room.

King Valdorryn, Zim's father, sat at the head of the table, an elbow resting on the slab, his chin cradled on one hand while the long claws of the other tapped the polished stone. Zim had never seen him so indecisive. "So, my father and king, what, if any, decisions have been made?"

Zim sat to the right of his father and looked opposite to Agmunsten, who had dark circles under his eyes from the healing he had been administering to Arcon. King Edmund sat next to Agmunsten. Next to Zim sat another dragon—Bertholimous. Bertholimous was Valdorryn's advisor and Master of War; it was his job to train dragons for fighting and to decide tactics in the event of war. He was addressed as either Bertholimous or Master.

The dragon king straightened on his bench seat and looked at his son. "No decisions have been made! I'm losing my patience. We had all come together, Talians and dragons, to discuss the impending gormon invasion, but now we're bogged down on this other matter. We have not decided whether the realmist girl and the panther go free. We all know what Agmunsten thinks. Bertholimous is advising caution, King Edmund does not want them killed, and I can see no clear way ahead at this stage. If I let the girl and panther go free without a very good reason, your mother will never speak to me again. And to tell you the truth, Son, I'm inclined to agree that what has happened is inexcusable." Valdorryn turned his glowing eyes to Agmunsten. "So, Realmist, tell me again why I should not kill the murderers."

Agmunsten's eyes widened at the dragon king's sudden forcefulness, and he tensed his stocky frame. He knew he couldn't drag this out much longer. Agmunsten was a powerful realmist with hundreds of years experience, wiser than anyone, but not invincible, not against a dragon. Bronwyn and Sinjenasta would be dead within days if he didn't provide a good reason for saving them. But how to tell them what he knew without exposing Drakon, the dragon god's role in this? The dragon god would have made it clear by now if he wanted them to know of his involvement.

Agmunsten scratched his head and sighed. "So, my word as first realmist has no sway here? You're not going to just trust me on this?"

King Valdorryn shook his head. "You know I can't. What are you hiding, Agmunsten? Is it worth the life of the human?"

"It may very well be. Are you sure you can't just pardon them on my word?"

"No. Symbothial was a member of the royal family: my family. Not only that, but what message will it send to our enemies? Have you not thought that someone put them up to this? Surely the girl could not have dreamt this up by herself, and we all know it wasn't an accident or self-defense." Valdorryn stared at Agmunsten, daring him to disagree.

"Well, you're right: she wasn't the instigator. I know who was, but I doubt you'll believe me." Everyone leaned towards Agmunsten, and he wished he hadn't said anything. But what choice did he have—if Valdorryn reacted the way he thought he would, Bronwyn and Sinjenasta would die and The Circle's fight against the gormons would be hopeless. Why couldn't that be reason enough for the king? Agmunsten quietly cursed at the power the dragon queen held over her husband. If it weren't for her interference, Bronwyn would be free by now.

"Bronwyn and the panther have bonded. I'm guessing it was the panther who was trying to kill Symbothial, and Bronwyn was only helping."

"Only helping? You make it sound like they were preparing a meal together. She *only helped* murder a dragon, and in Vellonia—the last place we should feel unsafe." King Valdorryn's breath snorted in and out of his nose. Agmunsten worried that if the king opened his mouth again, fire would come lashing out.

Zim spoke into the dangerous silence, "So why did the panther want to kill my cousin?"

Agmunsten cleared his throat. "Maybe you should be asking the panther's name."

"For Drakon's sake, get on with it! I don't have the patience anymore, not while I'm grieving the death of my nephew. If I don't have an answer from you this time, I will order your realmist and her creatura be executed tonight." No one had seen this side of the dragon king before.

Agmunsten's skin prickled in response to the tension vibrating in the room. He inhaled and spoke, "Sinjenasta." The dragons' scales paled; the color seemingly absorbed inwards, fading quickly. This was a phenomenon Agmunsten had heard of but had never seen. Dragons could change color, although it usually only happened when they were highly agitated. The head realmist had heard that during the last battle against the gormons, legions of flame-colored dragons had dotted the sky.

Valdorryn opened his mouth and shut it again. He looked at his advisor and his son. No one spoke. The dragons were hard to read, and Agmunsten had no idea if they believed him or not, although their silence was a good sign.

The dragon king shook his head as if to clear it. He looked at Agmunsten. "Are you saying it's *the* Sinjenasta—the human that Drakon turned into a dragon to sacrifice in the first Gormon War?"

"That's exactly what I'm saying." Agmunsten resisted the urge to shrug the tension out of his aching shoulders.

Bertholimous cocked his head to one side. "But I thought it was just a story, a myth to make the dragons feel indebted to the humans. And besides, a lot of dragons haven't heard the story. I only know because I read it while studying to be Master of War."

"I'm afraid not," said the realmist. "In fact, it's a myth that makes the humans fear your god. Drakon betrayed Sinjenasta. He declined to explain that in order to defeat the gormons, he would have to sacrifice himself. I don't know what he's been doing, or where Drakon has been keeping him, or even why he's here now, but he is, and he's bonded with Bronwyn. I have no doubt that whatever happened was ordered by Drakon." Agmunsten peered at the dragon king. "So, Valdorryn, who would you rather upset—Queen Jazmonilly, or Drakon?"

The dragon king squinted his eyes. "How do you know it's him, hmm? You weren't alive during the Gormon War. How can you know?"

Agmunsten clenched and unclenched his fists. "Bronwyn told me his name and when I questioned him, he all but admitted Drakon was involved. I have ways of knowing when people are telling the truth. Look, Valdorryn, I know this is hard for you to accept—that your god may have wanted one of your own killed. But if I'm right, what does that tell us?"

Zim listened and knew where Agmunsten was headed. He remembered finding that the spires had not been charged properly and Symbothial's reaction when he confronted him. His color returned, but it was with a sad voice he answered the head realmist. "My cousin betrayed us." Zim turned to look at his father. "I know this is hard for you to believe. I didn't want to think it either, but I can't ignore the facts any longer. Symbothial wasn't maintaining the spires properly. It was his job, and we all know how important it is. When I checked them a while ago, the rivers to three of the spires were blocked … more than enough to let any gormons through. When I spoke to him, he acted like it wasn't important."

"That's not enough to condemn him. Maybe he was just being careless because we've been safe for so long; it's easy to become complacent." King Valdorryn's voice trailed off as he lost the energy to make excuses. He had to admit there was only one decision he could make, and he was dreading having to explain this to his wife.

The dragon king sat up straight and looked into Agmunsten's eyes. The head realmist swore he could see small lightning bolts sizzling in the dragon king's dark eyes. "I hereby pardon Bronwyn and Sinjenasta for, for murdering, ahem, killing, my nephew, Symbothial. I'm still reluctant to free your realmist and Drakon's puppet. In fact, I will not free them unless they promise there will be no more killing of dragons within Vellonia. If they can't promise me this, they can stay locked up. Bertholimous, please take Zim and Agmunsten and see to it that this promise is made. If it is, arrange for rooms to be provided for Bronwyn and her panther." Valdorryn stood. "I will see you all tomorrow, if I'm still alive. I'm off to explain things to Queen Jazmonilly."

Agmunsten cleared his throat. "Thank you, King Valdorryn." He swallowed and dared another request. "If you don't mind, I would like to keep Sinjenasta's identity a secret, especially from Bronwyn."

The dragon king nodded and shuffled out, shoulders drooping a little lower with each step. The others looked after him in sympathy, glad it was not their job to advise Zim's mother of the decision.

Bertholimous spoke over his shoulder as he followed his king out the door. "Okay, let's get this over with. Let's see if we can free Bronwyn and Sinjenasta." The Master of War walked quickly. He had many questions for Sinjenasta. What luck—he was about to speak to the only surviving creature of the Gormon War. The information Sinjenasta could tell him may mean the difference between banishing the gormons for the second time or dying in the attempt.

CHAPTER 2

Bronwyn lay in the dark, separated from the cold stone floor by a thick bed of straw. She kept her eyes closed—in the darkness it made no difference—because she had no wish to be reminded of where she was—not that she could forget. Sinjenasta's thoughts intermittently sounded in her mind, but she ignored him, not knowing how to block him from talking to her.

The only way of distinguishing time was by the delivery of her meals. The dragons were generous, considering. Three meals a day were provided to the captives. By Bronwyn's estimation, they had been locked up for six days. They were the longest six days in the young realmist's life. She refused to eat and was beset by nightmares of Symbothial whenever she slept. Each time she woke from one of these vivid dreams, she expected to see the sword in her hand and blood fanning out from the dragon's floating carcass.

"Bronny? Can you hear that? I think someone's coming—and it's not meal time." Despite wanting to pretend she couldn't hear him, Bronwyn listened. Muffled voices seeped through the door, and she shuddered. Was it time to die? Fighting the urge to curl into a fetal position and feign sleep, she sat up, wanting to acknowledge she deserved to die. The realmist would not fight this—she had killed in cold blood and wanted to atone. Maybe, just maybe, she would find peace once she joined the dragon in an endless slumber. Thinking back to when she stood on the cliff, the day this journey started, she regretted not jumping off. If she had, none of this would have happened. She would rather the only person she had murdered was herself. *Gods, I hate you, you stupid coward. This is your fault. Why didn't you jump?* She berated herself.

The door opened, and Agmunsten entered, lamp held out in front. Bronwyn blinked, shielding her eyes with her hand. Agmunsten crouched down and placed the lamp on the floor. He looked into her eyes. "Bronwyn, do you remember me?"

She nodded. "You're the head realmist, Agmunsten."

"Yes. I've been talking to King Valdorryn, and he's graciously agreed to pardon you and Sinjenasta."

"But no. No. He can't." Tears spilled onto her cheeks.

"Did you understand what I said? He's not going to have you killed. You are to be set free, although you must make a promise."

"I understood. But I deserve to die. I helped kill that dragon. I'm a murderer, and I deserve to be punished."

Agmunsten appreciated that Bronwyn felt guilty, and he was glad she did, but he didn't have time to waste. It had been a monumental effort to get Valdorryn to agree, not to mention the secret he had to concede to convince him. Agmunsten's legs shook from crouching too long. He stood and looked down at the girl. "Now listen here. I know you didn't just wake up the other morning and decide you wanted to kill Symbothial. I know Drakon has played a big part in this." He held his hand up when Bronwyn opened her mouth. "Just let me finish. You will have to deal with your guilt. Look at it as part of your training as a realmist. You didn't think it would be a life without killing, did you? For the sake of The Circle, Avruellen, and all of Talia, you need to be grateful you've been pardoned. I want you to get up and promise me you won't murder another dragon."

Bronwyn hesitated. While she struggled to accept what Agmunsten said, hearing her aunt's name was like a slap in the face. Avruellen would not forgive her if she gave up, no matter the reason. And where was her aunt? Was she okay? She stood gingerly, taking a moment to regain her balance. She looked at Agmunsten. "I promise I won't murder any other dragons. I'm so sorry." She cast her eyes down.

"It's okay, child, but remember: I'll be watching you. If Drakon or Sinjenasta asks you to do anything else, check with me first."

Bronwyn nodded and let Agmunsten lead her out of the cell. When she saw that the door to Sinjenasta's cell stood open, she asked where he was.

"I don't know. I'm hoping he's talking to the Master of War." Agmunsten stood beside Bronwyn to see the empty cell for himself. He hadn't expected Bertholimous would have elicited Sinjenasta's promise so soon. The head realmist twirled the end of his beard between graceful fingers and hoped nothing was amiss.

Still tired from days of trying to heal Arcon, he turned slowly and walked towards the stairs that led to the upper levels of Vellonia. "Follow me, Bronwyn. We're going to see the King of the Dragons."

Bronwyn was glad Agmunsten took his time. It allowed her

to observe the grandeur of the intermountain castle and distracted her from depressing thoughts. Rich furnishings, placed at intervals, adorned the halls, but the beauty came from the natural surroundings. Polished stone contrasted with rough. Thin veins of gold slashed a glittery path across the walls, and Bronwyn was reminded of the shimmering skin of the sacred lake. Where she expected to see low, constricting ceilings, there were soaring domes where hundreds of candles burnt in small nooks carved out by the dragons.

Agmunsten stopped, eyes widening. Bronwyn bumped into his back. "Oops. Sorry. I wasn't watching where I was going. Is this where the king is?" The young realmist couldn't see any doors and wondered if the king hid behind an invisible door that operated by power from the Second Realm.

"No, dear. Something's happened. The king will have to wait." When Agmunsten moved this time, it was with the haste of an eager young man.

CHAPTER 3

Agmunsten bustled in the open door, and Bronwyn hung back. She took a hesitant step into the room to see Agmunsten already sitting on a chair by the bed, his hands placed on another man's head; white hair poked out between his fingers. Bronwyn felt a sense of familiarity as she studied the patient. Her musings were interrupted when she realized someone else was in the room.

She turned to see a young man, about her age, staring back at her. A rat sat on his shoulder. Even though she knew she had never seen him before, she was drawn to him. There was something whispering that she knew him. Her blood vibrated in her veins, telling her it was obvious if she just looked. She had a flash of a hulking dragon towering over him, its mouth big enough to eat him in one bite. Bronwyn shuddered. It was the same dragon from her nightmares—the ones that left her screaming out for Avruellen. She blinked, and it was gone.

A raspy voice, barely louder than a whisper, spoke. "Ah,

Bronwyn, meet Blayke. He's my apprentice. And the little fellow is Fang." He paused for a breath. "Do you recognize me, child?"

Brownyn turned to see Agmunsten's hands relaxed in his lap. The other man, the one who had spoken, leaned back into his pillows, but his eyes shone with the brilliance of the symbols of the Second Realm.

Her mouth made an O, and she thrust her chin forward. "You're Arcon! I remember now … from the meeting of The Circle." For the first time in many days, her forehead was crease-free, her worries forgotten for a short while.

He chuckled, "Indeed I am. Your aunt's not here?"

"No." She looked down at her boots.

"Is she all right? Do you know where she is?"

"No, sir, I don't. The last I saw of her was when Sinjenasta took me away."

Arcon sat up and leaned towards her.

Agmunsten stilled Arcon's question with a shake of his head and a hand on his arm. "That's enough for now, Arcon. You and I have things to discuss. I need to tell you what's been going on. The apprentices should be receiving some lessons, I think. And I know just the person, or dragon, to do it." He turned to Bronwyn and Blayke. "Okay, come with me."

"Um, Agmunsten?"

"Yes, Blayke."

"Can we have dinner first? I'm starving."

"Mmm, me too." It was the first time Bronwyn had felt hungry since entering Vellonia.

Arcon laughed until a coughing spasm overtook his mirth. "See what I have to put up with?"

"Hmm, that reminds me," said Agmunsten, "I should introduce Bronwyn to Arie. You can all have dinner and lessons together. Get some rest, Arcon, and I'll be back soon to finish our chat." He sent a mind message to Arie to meet him in the smaller dining hall.

As they walked, Bronwyn asked Blayke, "Have we met before? You seem kind of familiar." Bronwyn smiled. "That's right! You're Arcon's apprentice. Zim ate you at the meeting."

Blayke looked at her, his cheeks red. "Yeah, yeah, go ahead and laugh. At least I didn't murder someone."

It was Bronwyn's turn to blush. "You're right. I'm sorry. I'm always talking before I think. Auntie says it will get me into trouble one day."

Blayke smiled. "It's okay. I'm sorry too. If you don't mind me asking, how did you end up here and, well, you know? You don't have to answer if you don't want."

"It's okay." Bronwyn shivered as she remembered Symbothial's screams. "I was on the way here with my aunt, Avruellen, and Sinjenasta took me away. We came here and bonded; then he had to kill the dragon. I said I didn't want to do it, so he tried by himself. The dragon was drowning him, and I couldn't let him die, so I jumped in and killed the dragon."

"Wow, you make it sound so simple. Don't you feel guilty?"

Bronwyn stopped walking and looked at Blayke. "Of course I feel guilty. What do you want me to say? That I've hardly slept since, that I can't get the image of blood or screaming out of my head, that I wish the dragons would just kill me?" Bronwyn almost screamed the last; pressed by her sides, her hands formed hard fists at the end of stiff arms. She wanted to be back in the cell, alone with her misery and self-pity.

Blayke and Agmunsten stopped. Blayke stared at her with his mouth open, and Fang peeked out of his pocket. Agmunsten walked back to Bronwyn and placed his hands on her upper arms, his voice low and soothing. "Bronwyn, look at me. I know you feel guilty—and so you should—but you can't let it smother your spirit. Killing is part of the realmist's job, probably the worst part. I don't know why, but what you did was something that had to be done in order for Talia to survive. Don't blame Sinjenasta either; he does what he's told. You have my permission to wallow for another day, but then I want you to stop obsessing and focus on what we need to do. You need to build your strength as a realmist. The Circle needs you and Blayke to be ready when we face the gormons. If you're not, we will all die. Self-pity will weaken you."

"I don't know if I can." She searched his eyes for strength she could borrow. She wished Avruellen was there. The occasional dragon that walked past ignored the humans, preferring not to get involved with their trifling problems.

"You're not the only one who's had to kill, I'm sorry to say. How many people do you think I've killed—or your aunt? Do you think she's guilt-free? Look at Blayke. What do you think he's endured to get here? Do you suppose he's made his own mistakes? Had his own guilt to contend with? We all carry burdens, and we all have to endure. Better a few of us feel some guilt than the gormons consume all of Talia. You did what you had to, and those that matter understand. Come on; it's time for dinner." He gently squeezed her arm and led the way.

Agmunsten took them to the smallest dining room of the three in the dragon castle. Two long timber tables sat parallel to each other. Carved into both ends of the rectangular room were hearths Bronwyn could have stood up in. The rough-textured walls had been painted a deep ochre. A row of windows looked out to the valley where the moonlight silvered the trees, and small squares of honey-colored light peeked back at them from scattered dwellings. The ceiling was lower than in many of the other rooms, and Bronwyn estimated that the tallest dragons would have to stoop in order to fit.

Candles in wall sconces bathed the room in a warm glow. At the far end of the room, a boy with shoulder-length hair the color of caramel, and with simple, gray clothes hanging off his reedy frame, sat opposite a green dragon whose scales reflected the cheery flames in the hearth. Bronwyn almost clapped her hands when she saw Sinjenasta lying in front of a crackling blaze; head resting on massive paws, midnight-dark fur shining in the fiery radiance. The panther looked up.

The dragon spoke. "Hello, Agmunsten. I see you've brought some youngsters with you."

Agmunsten's laugh was short. "I haven't just brought them with me. I'm leaving them with you. I was hoping you could take them to see Arcese after dinner. I'd like them to learn about Talia's lifeblood magic you dragons use. I don't know much about it, and we can always use another perspective."

"Of course, Agmunsten. It would be my pleasure." Bertholimous nodded, his giant head moving with a measured grace Bronwyn never would have suspected dragons possessed.

Agmunsten turned to Arie. "I trust you've been behaving yourself?"

"I can't believe you're asking me that. I behave better than you, most of the time."

"Ha! Well, so you do. I'll see you later. I'm going back to talk to Arcon. Thanks again, Bertholimous."

Agmunsten departed, and Blayke climbed onto a bench seat next to the dragon, while Bronwyn sat down next to Arie, both apprentices' feet dangling inches off the floor. "Hi. I'm Bronwyn." She forced herself to look Bertholimous in the eye.

The desire to apologize about Symbothial's murder was outweighed by her fear and shame. Bronwyn thought every dragon must hate her—the girl who was a constant reminder of the dragon's death. She wanted to be anywhere but Vellonia.

It seemed he had read her mind. "I know, Bronwyn." The dragon's deep voice held no malice. Its melodic timbre felt like the soothing caress of a cool stream on a hot day. "I've had a good talk with Sinjenasta, and he explained everything. I would just avoid the queen for a while if I were you, although, she will likely call to see you soon."

Arie patted her back. "Don't worry; we'll make sure she doesn't eat you."

Bronwyn saw Blayke's smile and thought they must be joking—but what if they weren't? The need to vomit became imminent.

Sinjenasta spoke in her mind, *Little cub, fear not. No one will be eating anyone. Take a deep breath. It's okay.* The panther's eyes partly closed in the semblance of a smile.

Blayke spoke, "I'm hungry. How long till dinner?"

"Don't look at me when you say that!" Bronwyn laughed for the first time in weeks, and everyone joined in. Bronwyn felt, unexpectedly, that she was amongst friends.

A dragon appeared at the door, and Bronwyn's heart missed a beat. This dragon was smaller than she remembered Symbothial being (and certainly smaller than Bertholimous), with pale yellow scales that shimmered in the candlelight. Appetizing aromas drifted from the tray she carried, and Bronwyn realized it couldn't be the queen—not serving dinner. She relaxed.

"Ah, Guildelea, thank you." Bertholimous stood and bowed.

She set the tray on the table and placed full plates in front of everyone, including Sinjenasta, who ate in front of the fire. "Eat up, young humans. If you wish for more, let Master Bertholimous know." They thanked her, and she retreated.

Bronwyn again opened her mouth, looked at Bertholimous and closed it, interrupted by Arie who shoved a forkful of meat stew into his mouth and started talking. "Do any of the lady dragonth have hornsth?" A small piece of carrot flew across the table and landed on Blayke's hand.

"Oh yuck! Jeez, Arie. Don't talk with your mouth full." Blayke wiped the back of his hand on his tunic.

"Good observation, Arie," said Bertholimous. "The male dragons have stubs of horns until they reach fifty; then they start growing. We only get one set, so we have to be careful with them. In war times, it's common for many of the males to lose one or both of their horns in battle. It's a testament to the peaceful times of the past few years that most of the male dragons have both horns. Females don't grow them."

"Do dragonesses fight when there's a war?" Bronwyn hoped she wasn't overstepping any boundaries. She wasn't sure what would, or wouldn't, offend a dragon, and seeing as how she had managed to get on the wrong side of one of the most important dragons—the queen—she was mindful not to add other dragons to the list of *Dragons who want to kill Bronwyn. Gods, I hope that list doesn't exist.*

"No. They're too valuable to risk. Things would have to be pretty desperate for us to involve them. Their job is to hatch eggs and keep Vellonia running smoothly."

Bronwyn didn't answer. She looked around as the boys ate, oblivious to what the dragon had said. Typical. The topic didn't concern them: they could do what they wanted, when they wanted. Contemplating a life of hanging around the house, doing nothing but hatching eggs and serving dinner was not Bronwyn's idea of fun. Since starting this journey with Avruellen, her eyes had been opened to a life of possibility and adventure. Although there were some moments she would rather forget, she had experienced some of the best times of her life. She wondered if the dragonesses were happy with their situation: who knows; maybe they were.

After some boisterous chitchat, they finished dinner, and Bertholimous rose. "Okay, humans, it's time to go to work. I'm taking you to see one of our realmists—Arcese, Princess Arcese."

Bronwyn was almost happy—for just one minute—that she wasn't going directly to the queen, until she realized one thing. "You mean she's the queen's daughter?" Bronwyn paled.

"Yes, she most certainly is. Let's go."

As they walked out, Bronwyn dawdled at the rear. Sinjenasta caught up and nuzzled her hand. *It'll be all right. I promise.*

She looked at him and spoke aloud, "I might feel better if it didn't sound like you were trying to convince yourself."

The nausea returned, and Bronwyn wondered if she would survive her first lesson with the dragon princess.

CHAPTER 4

Verity rode Puddles, her mud-coloured horse, and Boy rode beside her on a pony. He had never ridden prior to coming to the castle, and he didn't trust animals. Verity had taken him out riding a few times since Prince Leon had departed, but Boy refused to ride a large beast, only agreeing to go when Verity picked out Chalk—a small, docile pony that Boy was actually beginning to like.

The sun shone, warming the day. Security had increased around Bayerlon since the king had left, and Queen Gabrielle had reluctantly agreed to let Verity ride outside the protective city walls. Verity's nagging had won out, and the queen sent four of the more experienced castle guards with her daughter and Boy.

Verity breathed deep of the fresh air outside the city, shut her eyes and turned her face to the sun. The warmth made her content, and she thought of her tabby cat who loved to sit on her bed in the morning sun.

Boy interrupted her basking. "There's a good place for our

picnic over there." He pointed to some well-spaced trees that marked the entry to the forest. "Remember the place you showed me the day Leon left?"

"Oh, yes. That's a great idea. I was thinking of that myself. Okay, last one to the trees is a pile of horse dung." Verity kicked her horse into a gallop, her laughter and fair hair streaming out behind her. Boy kicked his pony, but they both knew he would never win. Winning this race wasn't his objective anyway. Perculus had sent Boy a message a few days ago, followed by one last night. Today was the day Leon had warned him to watch for.

He reached the trees and slowed his horse to a walk, relaxing his hands from their vice-like grip on the reins. Verity's brown eyes were bright, her smile broad—Boy couldn't help but smile back. He enjoyed spending time with her, and found himself staring more than he would've liked. She had taken to teaching him the alphabet and numbers—knowledge he never would have gained in his old life. On the occasions she'd caught him staring, she'd giggled and tousled his hair before saying how she would have loved to have a little brother.

They negotiated the narrowing track until they came to the clearing. A circle of lush grass stretched from tree to tree. Verity and Boy dismounted. One of the guards had the picnic hamper strapped to his horse. "Is this spot all right, Princess Verity?"

"That's perfect. Thank you, Reglan."

The gray-haired soldier spread a rug on the ground and placed the picnic basket down before returning to his horse, and protective duty. The princess took the food out of the basket, scooping out freshly-picked strawberries; a loaf of bread that contained dark pieces of salty olives and sprinklings of herbs in its doughy embrace; tomatoes; and a chunk of a fragrant, orange cheese—a delicacy made from the milk of the plack, a long-haired, larger relative of the goat. Placks originated from mountains in the north but couldn't survive the warmer climes of Veresia. The cheese had to endure at least a week of travelling before it reached Bayerlon.

Boy's mouth watered. He sat. Verity sliced the bread into thick pieces and did the same with the cheese and tomato. They chewed in silence and listened to the chirping of fat, round blue jays. The princess spoke, "Do you miss Prince Leon?"

"Um, not really, Princess. It's fun to hang out with you and learn stuff. Sorry you got stuck with me though." He let his fringe fall over his eyes, not wanting to see if she really felt "stuck" with minding him.

"Don't be silly, Boy! It's been fun having company that's not so much older than me. I'm not allowed to spend time with normal people—by that I mean people who aren't trying to teach me, protect me, or get something out of me. It's nice to just chat with someone who has no ulterior motives, other than having fun." She smiled the smile that set off butterflies in his stomach.

He peered through his hair. "Do you ever wish you weren't a princess?"

She thought for a minute. "Hmm, sometimes. It's a lot of work, and having to be nice to everyone all the time can be tiring too. But you know, when I see the beggars at the bottom end of the city, I know I'm lucky. Other girls dream of having what I have. How could I not be happy? Being lonely is a small price to pay. Who knows? Maybe one day I'll make a difference to people's lives, a real difference."

"I hope you do, Princess Verity."

They finished lunch, and as they packed their things away, the birds stopped singing. Heavy silence settled. The two guards who'd stayed in the clearing looked at each other before Reglan spoke, "Princess Verity and Boy, get on your horses."

He was already untethering Puddles. Verity ran towards him and mounted. She was not used to panicking but knew to listen when she was told.

Screams penetrated the clearing. Regnus and Brooklyn drew swords and mounted. Regnus slapped the rump of Verity's horse with the flat of his blade. "Brooklyn, ride with her. Go." Before Regnus rode in the opposite direction, he turned to Boy who stood, confused, next to Chalk. "Boy! Ride to the castle. Make sure Princess Verity gets there, and tell Captain Gaston to reinforce the garrison and shut the city gates. I have a bad feeling about this. Go, Boy. Go!" Regnus rode the opposite way, the hairs on his arms standing up from unseen energy.

⬥

Queen Gabrielle paced the throne room, too agitated to sit. Why did everything have to go wrong when Edmund was gone? She supposed things probably went wrong when he was here too, but he was experienced at dealing with the complexities and politics of everyday life—he possessed more patience than she.

"So Perculus, tell me again why I can't tell Duke Fortescue to pay the back-taxes he owes. The money will go a hell of a way to paying the food bill for the orphanage for the next two years." She placed her hands on her hips and narrowed her eyes at the rotund advisor.

He smiled his oily smile, the patronizing one where his

lips remained closed and his head tilted to the left. The queen wished she were a dragon. She so wanted to breathe fire and watch Perculus disintegrate. Gabrielle opened her mouth and, disappointed when no fire materialized, closed it again.

"Well, my queen, if you understood the tax system, you wouldn't have to ask me that question."

"I don't have to understand the tax system. I have an advisor. You are the advisor, aren't you?"

"Ahem. Yes, and you should just trust I know what I'm talking about."

And there was the problem. She didn't trust him. Gabrielle contemplated how she could make his life more difficult, when two men rushed into the room. They stopped and bowed. Dirt smudged their faces, their clothes were ripped, faces unshaven, and their hair was the consistency of straw. Recognizing the two men, she quickly hid her surprise and didn't know whether to be happy or sad. One wore a coat that marked him as the captain of Edward's bodyguard. He spoke. "Forgive us for the intrusion, my Queen. I need to speak to King Edmund. Now."

"That's all right, Pernus. What are you doing back here? Has something happened? Is Leon…?" It was difficult to look concerned rather than excited at the thought the prince might be dead.

"Not that I know of. I would prefer if we spoke in private, with the king."

"Follow me." Gabrielle took one step forward, and Boy ran into the room, sliding on the tiles and careening into Fendill.

"Whoa. Careful, young man."

"Sorry, sir." Boy untangled himself from Fendill's gray robe and looked at the queen. He spoke through quick breaths, "They've taken Verity." The queen froze and felt as if she couldn't breathe.

Pernus leant down and grabbed the child's arm. "Who are *they*? Answer me. Quickly!"

"The… they were wearing gray clothes, and their faces were covered. I saw them try and grab the princess, but Brooklyn stepped in. He injured one, but there were four, and one made some kind of magic. They made a lightning bolt come from the sky. They killed Sergeant Brooklyn."

"Where did this happen?" Pernus kneeled in front of Boy, keeping hold of his arm.

"About two miles from the castle. I rode Chalk as fast as I could. I'm sorry." Boy remembered Verity's screams. She was the first person who had been truly nice to him. He had betrayed her.

Pernus dropped his arm and pushed Boy towards Gabrielle. "Take him to your room and make sure he stays safe. He's our only witness. Come on, Fendill. We need to go. Now." The men ran out.

Wading through her shock, the queen spoke to the first-year guard who had run after Pernus when he'd arrived. "Find Captain Gaston and send him to my chambers. Hurry." She turned to Perculus. "And you. You tell Duke Fortescue he has one month to pay what he owes. If he doesn't, we will confiscate lands to the value of what he owes us. Is that clear?"

Perculus pursed his lips and retrieved his sly smile. "Of course, Your Majesty. If there are repercussions, I trust you will tell Edmund they were your fault."

Speaking through clenched teeth, Gabrielle growled more than spoke, "Get out before I lose my patience. I would hate to have to explain to my husband how his advisor ended up in the dungeon." Turning her back on him, she knelt down to Boy. "Did they hurt my daughter?" She held her breath.

"Not that I could see. She was struggling and screaming. But when they carried her off, she didn't look hurt. I didn't hang around in case they grabbed me."

"That's okay. You did the right thing."

Tears glazed Boy's eyes, and she put her arms around him. When Boy's tears came, the queen couldn't tell, but they were from guilt. If Leon killed Verity, he would never forgive himself. If he told the queen what he knew, she would never believe him—he'd probably end up in the dungeon, not to mention creepy Perculus would probably kill him. Boy cried on the queen's shoulder. He didn't want to tell her the truth—they had knocked Verity unconscious. He remembered her limp body, her head and arms bouncing as one of the gray men carried her away. His tears came faster. What the hell had he done?

CHAPTER 5

Princess Arcese, her pearlescent pink and green scales shining delicately in the candlelight, watched as Bronwyn concentrated. Sweat beaded on the realmist's forehead as she tried to grasp the warm Talian energy, or as Arcese had called it, natural energy. It coursed through her veins—ancient power born of subterranean lava flows and the pressure of rock on rock that seeped through miniscule fissures in the invisible membrane that held Talia's lifeblood in its belly.

The trick, which was proving hard for Bronwyn and Blayke, was to separate the power vibrating through their blood and find an outlet for it. One could only hold a small amount of natural energy in their blood before it became dangerous. Experienced dragons, for no other humans had been taught to use this magic, were able to draw power while simultaneously channeling it to whatever use they chose. The advantage to natural power was that you could store a small amount to use later, but the feeling of the power thrumming in your veins was distracting and increased body temperature, which, for humans, could prove fatal if kept up for too long.

"Okay, Bronwyn. Stop concentrating for a minute. Focus on what you want to do with that energy."

Bronwyn looked at Arcese, marvelling at the light, soothing notes of her voice, and drank in her iridescent beauty. "Can I make myself look like you?"

"Like a dragon? No, that's beyond your capabilities."

"No, not my whole body—just the color."

"Hmm, yes, I think you could. There's two ways you could do it. They would both have slightly different effects. The first way would be to create colored light between the layers of your skin. That would probably create pulsing, muted colour. The other way would be to create invisible scales with the right properties to refract the light to the color you wanted."

"The second way sounds a lot more complicated."

"More complicated but more effective, although I think you should try the easier option today." Arcese smiled, and Bronwyn shivered—she knew not to be afraid, but there was something about looking at so many sharp teeth.

Blayke, Arie, Fang, and Sinjenasta watched as Bronwyn shut her eyes. Bronwyn imagined the color of the princess's scales and the pearlescent pink and green embedded in her skin. The vibration and heat in her blood rose to the surface of her skin until she felt a swelling pressure. Blayke and Arie gasped. Bronwyn opened her eyes.

"Oh, gods!" Mouth open, Bronwyn stared at her arms, not believing the hue glowing underneath her now-translucent skin. She spoke in a mind voice only Sinjenasta could hear. *You never taught me how to do this with the natural magic.*

"Wow, you look like some kind of weird candle." Arie

stepped forward and touched Bronwyn's arm. "You feel like a toasty fire. Has anyone got something they want to roast?"

"Ha, ha. Very funny. I'm not that hot. Arcese, is that the energy coming out of me?"

"Yes, Bronwyn, and now it's fading. The power you were holding is now used. Eventually you'll learn to draw and dissipate the power simultaneously."

Everyone watched as Bronwyn ceased being a human lantern, the radiance evaporating until nothing remained. Arcese turned to Blayke and Arie, "Okay, you two. I think it's your turn."

Arie and Blayke looked at each other, grinning. "Princess?"

"Yes, Arie."

"I want to try the more complicated way, but I don't think I'd be able to do it all over my body. Can I try it just on my hand? I think I need some of the energy I'm holding to examine your scales and see what they really look like—you know, the miniscule bits that make them refract light in a certain direction."

"Yes, Arie, you could." Arcese watched, bemused; she doubted a young human would have the intelligence to successfully perform what he was attempting.

"Let me do mine first, Arie. I want to watch when you fail." Blayke laughed and lightly punched his friend in the arm.

"Ouch." Arie feigned pain and rubbed his arm while grinning.

Blayke drew a deep breath, closing his eyes and letting the air flow out of him as he pictured dirt and rocks. He opened his eyes to the sounds of "Ooh," from Bronwyn and Arie.

Bronwyn spoke, "You look like a kind of rock man. You even look like you have a rough texture." It was Bronwyn's turn to touch Blayke's arm. "I can still see it's you, but if you were standing in the caves below us, I don't think anyone would be able to see you." As soon as she mentioned the caves —the place she had murdered Symbothial—she cringed. Arcese looked at her, although Bronwyn couldn't guess what she was thinking.

"That's what I was going for. Remember when that bird and snake tried to eat us, Fang?"

Don't remind me!

Bronwyn smiled when she realized the rat had spoken in her mind. When she looked at Arie, he nodded, indicating he, too, had heard. Bronwyn spoke. "You guys were almost eaten? That must have been a big bird and big snake."

"It was when we bonded. I turned into a rat. We almost died." Blayke shuddered. "If we could have camouflaged ourselves, it would have been a lot less dangerous." The layer of dirt and rock that appeared to coat Blayke dissolved.

"That was rather clever, young realmist. You have the beginnings of something useful. I would continue practicing. After Arie attempts his little trick, we will draw the same amount of power as before. When you are good at dissipating it quickly, we can practice drawing a larger amount. You need to find your limits, but we must do it carefully. I'd be in trouble if I let one of you cook yourselves." Arcese wasn't surprised when no one laughed.

Arie shut his eyes, mouth barely moving as he spoke near-silent words. He opened his eyes and they all watched as his thumb and index fingers wavered and disappeared. By the time everyone gasped, his fingers had reappeared.

"Did I just see what I think I saw? Or rather didn't see?" Blayke moved to Arie to more closely inspect his hand.

"It appears you did." Arcese marveled at Arie's unexpected

success. How had he done that? The dragons had never figured it out, although they hadn't spent a lot of time researching invisibility since they had no real enemies on Talia —up until the first gormon had reappeared, anyway. "You are going to share with us how you did that Arie, but before you do, I must insist that what we've just witnessed remains a secret. No one is to tell anyone of this. Am I understood?" She focused dinner-plate size eyes at each realmist in turn. Everyone nodded, and Bronwyn shrunk back. She would be the last person to go against a dragon's wishes after her recent experiences.

"So, Arie," continued Arcese, "how did you do that?"

Part of Arie wanted to keep it his secret, something only he knew how to do, but the proud part of him wanted everyone to know how clever he was. He shifted from foot to foot. "Um, I'll tell you on one condition."

"And what would that be, young human?" The dragon princess stood up straighter, and even though her gaze had further to go to reach the boy, distance didn't diminish its desired effect.

"Ah, um. I'd like the procedure named after me."

Bronwyn laughed. "So if we're going to do it, we say, *I'm going to do an Arie*?"

"Yeah, I suppose." Arie smiled. "If we're all agreed, I can tell you how I did it." Everyone nodded. "I used the natural magic as a kind of magnifying glass and looked at how Arcese's scales linked together. I pushed the power out of me. I don't know any other way to describe it. It felt like I was pushing them through tiny holes in my skin. When I felt like it was coating my skin I told the energy on each side of my hand to imprint on the other side what would be behind it."

"What? Can you speak Verdonese please?" Bronwyn wiped a stray strand of hair off her face.

"Okay. Um, if I put my hand in front of your face like this," Arie said and put the back of his hand up to Bronwyn's face, "I asked the energy to tell the energy on my palm what it saw and for the energy to show that picture on my palm. So I wasn't really invisible; I just looked very much like the background."

"So kind of like my camouflage thing, but way more advanced?" Blayke asked.

"Yep. But it took heaps of energy, and I don't know how it would work if you were running. I don't know if the energy could keep up with the background."

Arcese stayed quiet, thinking. This discovery could help them. She wondered if it could be done with Second Realm magic as another way of hiding their symbols, a way that would not take as much energy. Arcon's near-death episode had shown how long one could shield. There may come a day, very soon, where their ability to hide from the gormons would be the difference between surviving and not. It was clear she would have to stay with the boy and work with him—she didn't want to risk him overdrawing the power or risk her acquisition of this important knowledge.

"Okay, everyone, it's time to draw more of the energy. I want you to draw a handful more than you did last time—and that is an imagined handful." She made the point to avoid any silly questions on how they were supposed to measure it. Humans could be rather daft at times.

As Arcese watched, they did as they were told. When Blayke released the power, he imitated his first camouflage. Bronwyn created a ball of light that hovered above her upturned palm, and Arie practiced his invisibility spectacle: this time he managed to "hide" his whole hand.

"He, he. I'm getting better." Arie's wide grin fell. "Oh, no. Something's happened."

"What do you mean? Did the power hurt you?" Bronwyn rushed over to inspect his hand.

"No. Agmunsten sent me a mind message. We're all to meet in the king's reception chambers as soon as possible."

Blayke looked stricken. "Is Arcon all right?"

"I don't know. He didn't say why we had to rush—just that we had to."

"Follow me." Arcese led the way, her huge tail swishing from side to side as she hurried along the corridor, a band of worried realmists in her wake.

CHAPTER 6

On entering the king's reception chambers, Bronwyn hung back, trying to hide behind her friends. Symbothial stayed next to her, although he drew attention rather than helped—it was hard to go unnoticed when you had a giant black head with fangs to match.

Blayke sighed in relief when he saw Arcon seated at the reflective stone table. Arcon managed a wilted smile. The dragon king sat at the head of the table. Blayke took the seat between Arcon and Agmunsten while Arie sat on the other side of Agmunsten. Bronwyn sat as far away from the king as possible, with Arcese sitting protectively between them. That didn't stop King Valdorryn casting grave glances at Bronwyn. She suddenly found the colored streaks in the table fascinating.

Agmunsten cleared his throat. "Okay. We're all here, so I'll start."

Arie spoke, "But where's King Edmund, and Zim?"

"That's why we're here. King Edmund has received news

from home that his daughter has been kidnapped by Prince Leon."

Arcese, Sinjenasta, Blayke, and Arie all started talking at once. Agmunsten held up his hands. "Shhh." The chattering continued. "I said QUIET!" Silence and chagrined faces surrounded the table. "Now, because of what's happened, Zim has been generous enough," he said, nodding at Valdorryn, "to fly King Edmund back to Bayerlon. We have a crisis. Leon has murdered the Inkran king and intends on taking the throne for himself. We're not sure what his motives are. Before kidnapping Princess Verity, we might have thought he was trying to gain favor with Edmund; however, the more likely scenario is that he will move against his brother."

"This has changed our plans considerably. The meeting we wanted to have here won't be going ahead. The Inkran situation will have to be sorted before we can defeat the gormons. The prophecy we've been following for the past five-hundred years specifically states that *if, when the gormon hordes on Talia do descend, division exists in the folds of her land, blood will run and thou shalt see, the blood of humans and dragons run free. If, however, there is no divide, the gormon hordes may be turned aside.*

"And we have another problem." Agmunsten looked at Bronwyn. "Do you have the quartz Avruellen gave you?"

"Yes." She fingered the chain around her neck and worked the quartz free so it dangled down the front of her tunic. The stone, with the stain of blood within, appeared unremarkable.

"Well, we need to finish activating it. Zim will be returning in a couple of days with Blayke's half, and we'll have to do the first activation here. As you know from yours, Bronwyn, it's very dangerous. Because Arcon is recovering, I've asked Arcese if she'll join us, and she's agreed. We're aware the gormons breached your activation so we'll be looking out for that this time.

"Time is fast approaching when the second part of the activation of both pieces of quartz is to take place. For this, and the final unlocking, we will need the aid of a special tome. This book is not in our possession. We need to find it before the next full moon, which is in nineteen days. I've sent your aunt to get it, and she's been stymied by bad weather. I always thought you needed to be there when she found it, but when you were diverted here, I assumed I'd misinterpreted the prophecy. I might ask her to wait for you."

Bronwyn's eyes lit up, and she sat straighter, forgetting the dragon king for a minute. "Really? We could *all* go?"

She could barely stop herself from jumping up and down, but she knew she wasn't exactly in the good books at the moment and didn't want to provoke the dragons.

A small smile curved out from under Agmunsten's beard. "I'm thinking you and Sinjenasta could go with Blayke and Arcon. You'll have to wait three days for Zim to return and for Blayke's piece of quartz to undergo the first unlocking stage. I think Arcon will be strong enough to travel by then."

Bronwyn could contain herself no longer: she jumped up and ran to the other side of the table and hugged Agmunsten. "Oh, thank you. Thank you so much."

Agmunsten cleared his throat and carefully removed Bronwyn's arms. "Ahem. Thank you, my dear. Please refrain from such excitement—it's not becoming for a realmist."

Bronwyn smiled at the blush on Agmunsten's cheeks, and even King Valdorryn chuckled at the head realmist's discomfit. But when the king spoke in a voice without mirth, Bronwyn flinched. "So, Bronwyn, the queen and I would like to have a talk with you and your creatura."

Bronwyn turned and stared at the black dragon. Her smile evaporated faster than water in a boiling pot. Thoughts fought for dominance: *Oh, gods, they're going to lock me up again, but no, they won't, or why would they have let me out? Maybe they'll kill me when nobody's watching? They couldn't do that or we can't beat the gormons.*

Sinjenasta's voice cut in. *Bronwyn, shush! They're not going to kill you. Calm down.*

"Sinjenasta's right, Bronwyn. We're not going to kill you." King Valdorryn turned to Agmunsten. "Finalize your plans and let me know in the morning. It's time I took these two dragonslayers to see Queen Jazmonilly." The king gestured towards Bronwyn and Sinjenasta. Bronwyn winced while following the dragon king out. Sinjenasta nudged her from behind as she battled unwilling feet. She wondered if she really would ever see Avruellen again.

CHAPTER 7

Klazich absently picked at his teeth with a sharpened ulna—courtesy of his last meal. He looked across the table at his brother. Squinting and blinking did nothing to improve the hazy view. The Third Realm wavered and shaded reality like a suffocating nightmare—nothing appeared clear. Feldich's outline was revealed to him, and he could *almost* look into his eyes. He curled his clawed hand into a fist, resisting the urge to slam the table.

Feldich sipped from the glass of bevanda, his favorite mix of blood and acidic lake water, and burped. Many gormons had died trying to adjust to the acidic water when they were first banished to this dim, nowhere realm. "Ha, Brother. I might have just hit upon the only thing I'll miss from this stinking realm. I suppose we might be able to acidize Talia's water once we're there. What do you think?"

"Whatever you want." His raspy voice suited the gloom. "Right now, I couldn't care less. If we don't get out of here by the full moon, we'll never get out. I don't fancy dying on this shitty, gods-forsaken excuse for a realm." Klazich placed the bone in his mouth and crunched down, snapping it in half.

"How long have we got?"

"The next-best window through the corridor is Talia's next full moon. Embrax calculated that's in sixteen First Realm days. He'll watch the moon's symbol as it grows brighter."

"Only one corridor will be open?"

"Yes. I know it's not ideal. We'll all end up where High Priest Kerchex is. It will take longer to spread out and crush those usurping parasites. But we will do it. I won't rest until every filthy human and dragon is dead." Placing the rest of the bone in his mouth, he chewed, grinding the fragments into splinters. He hated the humans. He hated the dragons. Talia had once belonged to the gormons, and it would again.

Klazich stood, walked to the window and looked out. The dusty, bland landscape stared back at him through distorted, perpetual twilight. He craved clear sight. A hundred different hungers gnawed at him, but none could be sated here. He accessed a memory passed to him from his ancestors. Green grass, tickled by a warm breeze, waved around the legs of juicy, fat cows. No gormons in the Third Realm had ever seen green, or grass. The Third Realm palette consisted of gray, brown, and black. Light acted differently here. Anything worth appreciating was leached of beauty, not that gormons had much use for such things.

Feldich joined his brother as he gazed at the eyesore that was their imposed home. "I've done a head count. One-thousand-and-fifty-three humans remain. We are one-hundred-thousand gormons. Some will starve before we leave."

Klazich growled. "I know that, idiot. We've already quarantined the older gormons. The killing will start tomorrow so there is still meat on their bones. When the two thousand are eaten, we will eat the humans."

Feldich looked at his brother, the leader of the gormons. *If only I were quicker out of the egg*, he thought. He had some ambition but realized he wasn't as smart as Klazich, and sometimes he preferred to sit around and do nothing. He begrudged his brother the extra food but not the work.

"Have you checked the progress of the Gate?"

"Yes. It will be ready in time—early, in fact."

"How many can go through at once?"

"Four at a time." They looked at each other. Neither needed the miasma to clear to grasp what the other was thinking. The gate would only be open for a certain amount of time—whether that was ten minutes or two hours, they didn't know. How many of them would not make it?

"Prepare the order. Strongest first. The few eggs we have will have to be left behind. Now go and tell Vark. Get organized. Report back to me in two days." Klazich turned his back in dismissal. There was no way to tell night from day in the Third Realm. They watched the waxing and waning of Talia's moon in the Second Realm.

Klazich used his mind to call Embrax, his Realm Master.

Yes Klazich? Embrax's mind-voice contained a hint of annoyance.

Am I interrupting you, brother? Klazich's tone was like shards of glass grating a gormon's leathery skin.

Ah, no. Forgive me, Malevolent Father. I was trying to calculate the gate's duration. I feel like I almost have the answer. What can I do for you?

That's better, Embrax. Do not forget yourself. We can't all go through the gate. They weren't telling the other gormons. There was no need to start a panic. Gormons were likely to start killing each other to guarantee their own place through the corridor to Talia, and with their skill at serving out death, there would not be enough gormons left to conquer Talia. Klazich would not risk failure—not when the Third Realm would be the outcome for the loser.

Get High Priest Kerchex.

Yes, Malevolent Father. I'll let you know as soon as I have contact. Will that be all?

Yes, Embrax. Klazich let the link die and thought of High Priest Kerchex. When the gormon priest on Talia wasn't feeding, he was using his powers of compulsion to plant seeds into the minds of a whole town of humans. When the gormons went through the corridor to Talia, their bodies would not come with them. They would come out in the cave where High Priest Kerchex waited. The only way they could leave that cavern was in the bodies of humans. They would be vulnerable until they metamorphosed. Secrecy was their weapon. He chuckled, his mirth spilling over his black lips like dripping blood. Sixteen First-Realm days to go. The countdown had well and truly begun.

CHAPTER 8

Bronwyn stood in the stone doorway to Queen Jazmonilly's chambers, reluctant to breach the threshold. A necklace of delicate snow-star flowers traced the frame's edge, carved and painted white, so realistic that Bronwyn thought she could smell the syrupy nectar. Sinjenasta stood protectively in front of her, and Bronwyn wondered at his lack of fear. The young realmist chewed her fingernails and considered if she could draw enough of the natural power to make herself invisible: a crooked smile broke through her anxiety for the briefest of moments.

A sharp "tap tap" sounded from an inner room—clawed footsteps drawing nearer. Sinjenasta's tail twitched, and Bronwyn gripped the doorframe to keep from running out. King Valdorryn entered first, his black girth seemed to fill the high-ceilinged room, and Bronwyn felt like even the air had retreated in his presence. She gulped two desperate breaths. Sinjenasta spoke in her mind, *Stop it, young cub. I won't let anything happen to you.* He turned from the king, and his luminous eyes met Bronwyn's. She let go of the stone and grabbed the generous fur at the nape of his neck.

King Valdorryn's commanding voice drew their immediate attention. "I would like to introduce to you my wife, the light of Vellonia, Queen Jazmonilly."

In spite of herself, Bronwyn's mouth fell open. Silver scales glimmered in the candlelight like the sun firing lustrous diamonds on the harbour on a brilliant day. No dress could be more beautiful, no scene more breathtaking, than this creature who possessed an elegance Bronwyn would have thought impossible for someone so large. Bronwyn curtseyed.

The regal dragon flared her substantial nostrils and cast a stern eye on the young woman. After an uncomfortably long silence in which Bronwyn chewed the nails off four fingers, the queen spoke. "So, what have you to say for yourselves?"

Sinjenasta spoke, and his words, to Bronwyn's chagrin, were not chosen carefully. *We are sorry if our actions have upset Your Majesty, but we did what needed to be done. I will take full blame, as the realmist was doing what she could to save her creatura. We all know instinct can be overwhelming at a time like that. I suggest you find it in your heart to forgive us, Queen Jazmonilly, for we acted in Talia's best interest.*

Sinjenasta settled his furry bottom on the floor, calmly lifted a paw to his mouth and fastidiously licked in between the leathery pads.

Small spikes on the back of the queen's neck rose, punctuating her words with a dangerous energy. "You are not in a position to *suggest* anything. Why did you kill my nephew?"

King Valdorryn rubbed his nose on Jazmonilly's shimmering neck. "Please let it go, love. We can't bring him back, and I know you have delved into their hearts and see no danger or malice there. If Drakon has let this happen in our own home, you know it was for a reason."

"What reason, my king? I see no good reason to kill my beautiful nephew. He was a good dragon. There are so few of us left, and the future appears grimmer by the day. Why did he have to die? Why? I want answers. Someone needs to be punished." Her nostrils flared in and out, over and over. Danger filled the room, and Bronwyn feared Jazmonilly would incinerate her husband, closely followed by the murderers.

"Enough!" A thundering voice resonated around them. Bronwyn jumped, but recognized the voice. "Jazmonilly, my daughter, you will not punish anyone. Is that clear?"

The dragon queen, realizing Drakon had spoken, managed not to faint as she had last time he had made an appearance. When she replied, nose haughtily raised, Bronwyn couldn't believe her courage. "So, you're the culprit. Why did you kill my nephew? Aren't there few enough of us as there is? What god kills his own creations?"

"I have my reasons, none of which I care to explain. That is all." As suddenly as he had appeared, he disappeared.

Jazmonilly buried her head into Valdorryn's neck. Bronwyn stared at the ground. The dragon queen's sorrow was unexpected and something the realmist didn't want to witness. This creature she had feared was as vulnerable as she in some ways. The mighty dragons, the fiercest beings on Talia, their allies in the coming war with the gormons, were not as invincible as she thought. Suddenly the gormon threat seemed more menacing.

Bronwyn trusted in her aunt and The Circle. She knew the gormons were coming, but felt it was a matter of course—they would fight them, win, and go back to doing whatever it was they had done before the invasion. Realization of the danger had alighted, and it wasn't a feather touch: it came with the weight of ten dragons, and Bronwyn knew, for the first time, that life was uncertain, as was Talia's future. She flinched from the thought, but it was there now, and hiding would not make it disappear.

Bronwyn stepped from the doorway and went to Queen Jazmonilly. She spoke through lips that felt frozen. "I'm sorry for killing your nephew."

Jaz lifted her head and looked at the small human.

"I didn't want Sinjenasta to die, and I didn't want to kill the dragon, but it was a choice, and I did what I had to. I see your nephew in my dreams and in my waking thoughts. I hear his screams and see his blood. I don't know why it happened, but I do know Sinjenasta wouldn't lie to me. He said Drakon had ordered it." Bronwyn stepped closer and shocked everyone by attempting to circle her arms around Jaz's belly— the only part she could reach.

The queen laughed: out of shock or amusement, no one could tell. "Are you embracing me?"

"Yes. I'm sorry for your pain. In my world, when someone is hurting, this is what we do." Bronwyn let go and looked up at the silver dragon.

Sinjenasta shook his head and shared a look with the king, neither believing what they saw. If the panther had his old hands, he would have rubbed his eyes. The thought brought a yearning to be human, and he held a painful breath as he watched Bronwyn. It had been hundreds of years since he had touched a woman with his human fingers, had looked in a mirror and seen a man staring back at him. He had believed himself accepting of his life by Drakon's side, but now a tremor loosened foundations built on reluctant necessity.

Jaz smiled with a closed mouth—she found humans sometimes mistook a toothy smile as a threat and figured it had something to do with her bountiful, sharp teeth. "Eventually I will find out why Drakon saw fit to murder one of his own, but I will let it rest for the moment. I won't say I'm accepting of what happened to Symbothial, and I am still upset, but I do forgive you, Bronwyn, and Sinjenasta. I can imagine you have been placed in a situation where no decision was favorable. You have my pardon."

"Thank you, Queen Jazmonilly. I appreciate your forgiveness." Bronwyn curtseyed again, and the panther bowed his head.

King Valdorryn spoke up. "Now that's all sorted, I think it's time you two were off to bed. I'm sure you have a lot of work to do with my daughter while you're here. I understand she's teaching you the secrets of Talian magic."

"Well, she's teaching me. Sinje already knows how to do it." Pride in her creatura shone in Bronwyn's delicate smile.

"Ah," said Valdorryn, "that's to be expected, I suppose. Oh, how the world moves on without me. I can't remember the last time I ventured out of Vellonia." He sighed.

Jazmonilly patted his arm. "We like it here. It's not like there's anything to see out there that's superior to our beloved home; is there?"

"No, love, you're right. Anyway, enough of my complaining. You two have a good night's sleep, and we'll see you tomorrow."

Sinjenasta and Bronwyn thanked the dragons again and left. "I told you everything would be okay, didn't I?"

"Yes, Sinje, you did. Thanks for being so strong. What would I do without you? Hmm. Actually don't answer that question. I wouldn't be in this mess in the first place: I'd be somewhere with my aunt. I hope she knows I'm okay."

"Agmunsten will tell her, and I'm sure Drakon would have let her know. And I should have told you this before, but don't tell anyone Drakon talks to us. You never know what secrets are revealed by seemingly harmless words."

"Oh, okay. Sorry. I won't tell anyone anything. I thought it was a good thing you're related to Drakon somehow."

Sinjenasta coughed and said nothing. Bronwyn had a lot to learn.

❧

Two days had passed. Realmists and creaturas reclined in the cool grass of Vellonia's valley, under the retreating afternoon sun, awaiting Zim's return. Blayke breathed honeyed spring fragrances and snapped verdant grass blades between slender fingers. "Arcese is such a slave driver."

"I'm not complaining. Just look at everything we've learnt."

"You would say that, Arie," said Blayke. "You're the fastest learner I've ever seen—not that I've seen much." He laughed.

"You've got that right, lad," Arcon's blue eyes crinkled at the corners.

"Ha, ha, you're *so* funny," Blayke quipped, overjoyed at having his uncle back from the edge of death. Arcon's strength grew daily, and after the latest review from Agmunsten, it had been decided they could leave Vellonia in another two days. Blayke's brow furrowed when he remembered what he was trying not to think about—tonight they would have to undertake the first stage of the unlocking for his piece of quartz. When Zim arrived, he would be carrying the mineral that held a drop of blood—whose or what's blood, no one knew.

Bronwyn quickly rose from her position resting back against Sinjenasta. "I think I see Zim!"

Her eyes squinted into the azure sky. The others looked up.

"How can you tell it's him? That dragon's too far away to tell anything." Blayke placed a hand at his forehead, shielding his eyes from the glare.

"I don't know. Maybe it's not him, but I think it is."

Arcon stood and observed everyone watching the dragon's gliding descent. When he had finally woken the other day and seen his nephew sitting by his bed, enormous relief washed over him. That none of them had died seemed a miracle. Talia still had a chance, although with Leon's greed and stupidity, it was yet to be seen whether they would stand united before the gormons arrived.

He looked at dark-haired Bronwyn and thought it a miracle that no one had asked questions. Well, they may know soon enough, but he wasn't about to tell anyone their secret. Maybe when they caught up to Avruellen, the truth could come out. Goodness knew Bronwyn would have many questions, and her aunt would be the best person to answer them.

He flexed his fingers and felt an ache he knew would take a few more days to dissipate. Shielding for so long had almost killed him, but it had saved Blayke. He would have to teach his nephew how to do it. Maybe there was a less dangerous way to shield using Talian magic? He would have to ask Arcese.

"See, I told you it was Zim." Bronwyn's comment jerked Arcon out of his reverie. He saw the black dragon that was almost upon them. It was now clear it was the prince.

Zim, sixty feet from the ground, swept in an arc parallel to the valley floor, beat his wings down with gusting, powerful strokes and dropped the last fifteen feet to the ground, crushing the flowers unlucky enough to be growing underneath. "Ah, I have a welcoming party." His teeth-revealing smile caused the younger realmists to shiver. "So, you must have missed me?"

"Don't flatter yourself. We needed some fresh air after being cooped up inside that mountain. We hadn't even realized you were gone." Agmunsten winked.

"Well then, you don't want to receive the news I've brought, or the pendant I carry. Never mind; there are others who love me." Zim sniffed and carefully wiped an invisible tear from his eye with the back of a clawed finger.

"He's as good an actor as you, Arie. We should have shows and start charging. I knew there was an easier way to earn a living than being a realmist." Agmunsten rubbed his palms together, while Arie rolled his eyes.

After everyone greeted Zim, they retreated into Vellonia to meet with King Valdorryn. It was time to plan, and then it would be time to bless the piece of quartz that would help decide Talia's fate.

CHAPTER 9

Bright candlelight reflected off the polished stone, and Blayke looked briefly at his faint reflection on the walls. Sweetly-scented smoke wafted around him before it curled into small vents at either end of the ceiling. The room was bare, save for a wooden bowl, which was the size of two cupped hands, sitting on the floor in the middle of this small, underground chamber.

As Avruellen and Augustine had done for Bronwyn, Agmunsten and Arcese had warded the perimeter and stood—Arcese hunched over in the restricted space—waiting for Blayke to take his position by the bowl. Blayke felt sweat on his palms. He looked down into the vessel and saw a chain and amulet, similar to Bronwyn's, resting on a bed of herbs. Agmunsten grabbed Blayke's left hand while Arcese slipped a leathery, clawed hand around his right, engulfing it.

Agmunsten looked at Blayke. "Are your hands always this sweaty?"

"No." Blayke swallowed; smiling through his fear was too hard.

"It will be okay, lad. I can see you're thinking about what happened to Augustine. If you pay attention and do your job properly, as we discussed, we won't be in danger. Arcese and I are strong, and I have no doubt Drakon will help us. Are we all ready?" Agmunsten looked from Blayke to Arcese, who nodded.

Blayke hoped Agmunsten was as wise as his white beard suggested. He breathed in deeply and concentrated on the warmth from the head realmist's hand and the cool roughness of Arcese's large palm. They were standing close together, yet Blayke felt exposed, like he was standing out in the open, by himself, surrounded by Morth and his bandits. He focused on the amulet and what it signified and pushed aside his vulnerability—he knew it was there but chose to ignore it. It was time.

Agmunsten's voice was deeper than normal as he intoned the rites. "We stand here today to unlink a piece of the chain that binds our salvation. I order you, Blayke, to link with Erme, the water corridor to the Second Realm.

Blayke tightened his stomach muscles against the rush of power as it filled him.

"Realmist Arcese, I ask you to link with Quie, the fire corridor to the Second Realm." Even Agmunsten held his breath. This was where it had gone wrong last time, and Augustine had not known until it was too late. He waited for some sign from the dragon that he should continue. Arcese closed her eyes for a moment. In the seconds before she opened them, Blayke thought his resolve would snap—he wanted to run from this room and never look back. The air felt charged with energy, and goose bumps freckled his arms and legs.

When the dragon opened her eyes, Blayke thought he saw fear, but it was so brief he may have been wrong. She nodded to Agmunsten, and he let out his breath. "I now link with Zaya, the corridor to the gods, and I seek the blessing of Drakon, god of the dragons." Agmunsten's voice had been measured until now, but Blayke heard the tension in his elder's voice as he spoke faster. It was as if he wanted to get it over and done with before something untoward happened. Blayke hoped, for the hundredth time that day, that none of them were about to die.

"Do you agree to unlock this piece I present, thereby enabling the possibility of humans and dragons to defeat our oldest and bitterest enemy?" Agmunsten looked to the ceiling as if he could see past the tons of rock above, to the heavenly abode of the dragon god. Arcese and Blayke looked at the bowl. Blayke squeezed the hands of his fellow realmists a bit tighter. The air shimmered, and momentary dizziness swayed the young realmist.

"Ah, so it is you, humans, but with one of mine. Greetings, Arcese, my child."

"Greetings, Father." Arcese bowed her head in respect.

The shimmering air pulsed with Drakon's voice. "I will help, but there is a price you must pay. It is a price set by the Realms, and a trifle compared to what you will lose if you don't."

Agmunsten stood taller, bracing himself to take the news on the strongest shoulders he could offer. "Tell me the price so we may get on with this blessing." Blayke wondered what the price would be, and knew, from the head realmist's voice, it would be a big one. He shut his eyes and drew a deep, calming breath.

"Listen carefully, and repeat this to no one. When the price is asked, you will have one chance to act. If you hesitate, the chance will be lost, and so will Talia. The two you must sacrifice are…."

All three realmists paled, and Blayke blinked back tears. When Drakon finished speaking, the energy flowing to the channels ceased, and as Blayke reached down to gather the quartz in his shaking hands, he wished he were an innocent child once again. He didn't know how to carry this new burden and thought death would be so much easier. His fingers touched the pendant, and he fell to his knees. Agmunsten and Arcese stood in silence as Blayke knelt on the floor and wept.

Agmunsten covered his face with his hands. They had survived the blessing of the quartz, so why did it feel like they had failed?

CHAPTER 10

Bronwyn hadn't thought she would be sad to leave Vellonia—since she doubted she would ever leave at one point—but found herself wiping her eyes as she said goodbye to the king and queen and all the dragons she'd met since coming here. The dragon she had spent the most time with, Arcese, was the one who was most difficult to say goodbye to. Standing on the shore of the underground lake, they embraced, and Bronwyn wanted to never let go. Even though Arcese's leathery scales were not soft, she felt peace in the large creature's arms. In the short time they were there, this dragon realmist had taught them all much about earth magic—knowledge that would be invaluable in the weeks to come. Arcese's calm and kind nature had captivated Bronwyn. The young realmist wished she were more like the dragon.

Bronwyn stepped into the boat and sat behind Blayke and Arcon. Sinjenasta jumped in after her, making it rock so violently, she grabbed the side. He lay in the back of the boat.

A strap uncoiled from the floor to secure itself over the panther's back. Once all were harnessed safely, the boat glided away from the edge of the bank. Their belongings were being flown out by one of the dragons and would be waiting when they reached the outside.

Looking at the water, Bronwyn could see no evidence of Symbothial's murder. Such a violent, sad moment—the ending of his life, and no sign to suggest it had ever occurred. If only she could erase it from her mind as easily. *I won't forget you, Symbothial, and I'm sorry.*

Bronwyn turned and waved until the boat rounded a bend and she lost sight of her friends. "I think I'm going to miss Vellonia." After a minute, when no one responded, she spoke again, "What about you, Blayke? Are you going to miss it?"

He had been unusually quiet after the blessing of his amulet, and nothing Bronwyn asked could pull a reason from him.

"I will, for sure, if only because it could be the last peaceful time we get to have. I'm not looking forward to what's out there." Bronwyn didn't have an answer, as she suspected it was true. Arcon stayed silent and tried to figure out what was upsetting his nephew. He had never seen him like this, and Fang had no ideas either. Maybe it was just that he was growing up and realizing the nature of what lay ahead. Maybe his distaste of killing was affecting him.

The boat jerked as the speed increased. They all held on— even Sinjenasta extended his claws, trying to gain purchase on the timbers underneath him. This time the boat didn't drop, but circled, faster and faster, until Bronwyn thought she might vomit. Finally, the boat shot out of its whirlpool, spearing towards a hole barely bigger than the boat. The young realmists gripped the boat with strained fingers, and Bronwyn shut her eyes, not wanting to see the moment her head would bash against the rock of the hole that looked too small. She had tried to bend over and put her head on her knees, but they were travelling too fast—the force of the air keeping her upright.

As they passed from Vellonia like a cherry pip spat from a mouth, Bronwyn thought she felt a rock lightly graze her head; then the warmth of the sun reached her through the cold wind of their flight. The boat hit water and slid to a halt, drenching Blayke and Arcon in the process as a sheath of water, upset by their landing, washed over the front of the vessel.

Bronwyn opened her eyes as her belt unclasped. "Oh, look: our horses!"

In her excitement, she stood and almost fell from the boat as it rose out of the water to hover next to the top of the riverbank.

Settle down, young cub. I don't feel like fishing you out of the river today, Sinjenasta chided.

The group stepped off, one by one, and Bronwyn took extra care not to embarrass herself further, although she couldn't resist running to Prince. She stroked her fingers along his nose and hugged his neck. "Oh, I've missed you so much. I thought I'd never see you again."

She nuzzled her face into his, becoming reacquainted with the dusty fragrance of sweat mixed with hay that she loved.

"It's just a horse. Why do girls get so excited over horses?"

Arcon answered, "I can't say why, lad, and let me tell you: there's a lot of things you will never understand about women. I think you should just get used to it."

"How come you're not married?" Blayke had always wondered but never asked.

Arcon, one foot in a stirrup, hesitated, clearly taken off

guard by the question. He raised himself into the saddle and looked to the sky. "Oh, look at those dark clouds. I think we might get some rain today."

"Nice try at avoiding my question. Come on; you have to tell us."

"I don't really, but what the Third Realm. I'll tell you a bit about my life as we ride, but don't expect it to be exciting." He chuckled. A lot had happened in his life, but it had happened so long ago, he sometimes felt it had happened to someone else. The memories he pulled from the depths were cloudy, and it saddened him that he couldn't picture the faces of the ones he had loved the most. "Many, many, many, many years ago, when I was twenty, I met a young lady. Her name was Marcie. We met at the Bayerlon Spring Fair. She had hair the color of fiery autumn leaves, and her green eyes enchanted me the first time I saw her."

Bronwyn, Sinjenasta, and Fang all listened eagerly as they rode. Bronwyn cried when Arcon told them how, after they married, as Marcie gave birth to their first child, she started bleeding. Arcon had just begun training as an apprentice realmist. There was nothing he, or the midwife, could do. Both Mother and Baby Boy died. Arcon had married again, when he was a lot older, but never had children—the memory of losing his son was always too painful, and he realized after becoming a realmist, that he would outlive his children if he had them.

"I don't really want children, but I hadn't thought about getting married. Does that mean we should choose other realmists?" Bronwyn asked.

"Don't look at me."

"What? I wasn't looking at you, Blayke, you idiot."

"Idiot? Gee thanks."

"Well, if you don't want to be called 'idiot', don't say stupid things. And, I might add, thanks for the insult. What would be so bad about marrying me?" She looked straight at him, her eyes alive with challenge.

He looked at Bronwyn. He couldn't deny she was striking, with long dark hair and large gray eyes, and he would be lying if he said he hadn't noticed her "assets." But there was something he couldn't name, something that meant she didn't excite him. He studied her closer: the shape of her square jaw, prominent cheekbones, straight nose—all were familiar. Blayke stopped his horse, not sure whether to be happy, angry, or both. The question was out before he had a chance to reconsider. "Arcon. Are Bronwyn and I related?"

Now it was Arcon's turn to stop. The question he had been waiting for, and dreading, had come earlier than expected. Over the years, he had rehearsed his answer and decided the direct approach would be the best. "Yes."

Bronwyn had halted, staring at Blayke. Sinjenasta stood beside Bronwyn's horse. Fang climbed onto Blayke's shoulder and rubbed the top of his furry head against his partner's neck in a gesture of support.

Bronwyn looked at Blayke with a new perspective, and she cursed herself for being so caught up in her own dramas that she never noticed the similarities. Although he had green eyes and was taller than her, their features were similar, even the way he held his head while waiting for an answer, as he did now, slightly to one side. *Zebla's hounds! Are we really related? How are we? Is he, is he, oh gods!* The words rushed out of her mouth, "Arcon, tell us. Who are we?"

She had waited a lifetime for an answer, and her heart beat

faster in anticipation. So many nights she had fallen asleep imagining what her mother and father looked like. Did she have sisters or brothers? Then something other than joy intruded, something she hadn't anticipated: fear. Was she ready? Would she like who her family was, or were they murderers, greedy, or horrible?

"All right, but don't fall off your horses, or run away. Before I tell you, I need your promise to try and understand why we couldn't tell you." Both nodded, willing to promise anything to know part of who they were. "You are brother and sister: twins, in fact." The news was met with a sharp intake of breath from all but Sinjenasta and Phantom.

It surprised Arcon that a weight lifted as he spoke. He had never enjoyed keeping secrets—they eroded inner peace, especially when the information had the potential to hurt those you loved. So many times he had opened his mouth and almost said something without meaning to. Now he didn't have to worry. There it was.

The two young realmists sat atop their horses, mouths open. Bronwyn's reins lay forgotten across her horse's neck. Blayke stared at Arcon, not knowing where to begin. He reached up and absently stroked Fang's back. Finally, he broke the silence. "Why were we separated? Why did it have to be a secret?"

"The Circle knew you were important for Talia's future, and we couldn't risk anyone knowing you were alive. If someone did find out, we thought separating you would mean if worst came to worst, at least one of you would survive. We took you from your parents as soon as you were born. Your mother held you, and, when you were taken away to be cleaned up and settled, we told them you'd died."

Bronwyn's voice grew louder with each frantic question. "Surely they asked to see the bodies? And what about Avru-ellen? You kidnapped us! Who are our parents? Are they still alive?"

She thought of all the questions her aunt had fobbed off over the years. She was angry she had not sometimes asked what was in her heart in order to spare her aunt's feelings, when it seemed, now, her aunt had no feelings to worry about in the first place. When Bronwyn looked at her brother—her twin brother, no less—she saw a friend she was only just getting to know: they were practically strangers, so much time lost. Bronwyn had always felt something was missing, and now she knew what it was.

Arcon spoke with a gentle voice. "We put you to sleep with power from the Second Realm to make you both still and quiet. We slowed your heartbeats until they couldn't be felt and gave your skin a blue tinge. I also had to tamper with your parents' minds so they easily accepted what we told them. I'm sorry we had to do it that way, but if we hadn't, there would be a good chance you would have been killed for real. At least this way, you will see your parents again."

He mentally kicked himself at the last, because he wasn't ready to answer questions about who their parents were. They couldn't be told yet and needed impartiality to do what needed to be done. There would be people who would have to die on their way to defeating the gormons, and Blayke and Bronwyn's actions would decide the outcome. If they knew the truth, it might stop them doing what they should. Not to mention they'd want to race to them right now, when there wasn't time.

"So, Uncle, who are our parents, and who are you to me, really?"

The last question hurt Arcon in a way he hadn't thought was still possible. He had loved the boy like a son, and he was his great (a few times over) uncle by blood. He knew that revealing this secret would have repercussions, but he didn't think they would pain him so much. Well, the boy's trust in him would have to be sacrificed for the time being—better that than Bronwyn and Blayke finding out this news at an inconvenient moment, like while fighting a gormon.

Arcon dismounted and walked over to Blayke. He looked up at his nephew. "Blayke, I am your real uncle, if a few generations removed. I know this is a lot to take in, and I don't think this was really the right time and place to tell you, but it needed to be said. I love you like a son and always will." He turned to Bronwyn. "Bronwyn, your aunt is your aunt; she is also my sister. We are both responsible for taking you from your parents, but please understand, we had no choice. I know she loves you more than anything in this world, so please don't be too hard on her when you see her."

Arcon mounted his horse. "We have to get moving. We'll talk more about this tonight when we're not sitting on horses. As for your parents, you will see them soon, but not just yet." Arcon raised his hand to still Blayke's question. "Not now, lad. I'll tell you all you need to know soon enough. Right now, Avruellen's waiting for us, and there's no time to waste. Who's having the first turn at warding our symbols?"

"I will," volunteered Bronwyn.

"Okay then. Hop up behind Blayke and hold on around his waist. We'll do shifts of eight hours each. Blayke can go after you, and Sinjenasta can do the night watch. I'll take first turn tomorrow."

"Is it safe for you to do it again so soon?" Blayke's concern was echoed by Phantom's hoot.

"I think so. I feel strong enough, and it will only be for a short time. I'll be fine." Blayke narrowed his eyes and frowned, but Arcon just turned his back on his nephew, kicked his horse and moved off at a walk. Once Bronwyn was settled behind Blayke, they followed Arcon in silence. It was going to be a long day.

CHAPTER 11

After saying goodbye to their fellow realmists, Arie spent the day exploring the valley, while Agmunsten met with Zim, Arcese, Bertholimous, Warrimonious, King Valdorryn, and Queen Jazmonilly. No other dragons would be trusted with more than they needed to know. Zim didn't know who Symbothial had betrayed them to, but so much about his cousin's behavior didn't fit. They couldn't afford to open themselves up to more betrayal.

"So it's agreed then. My sister, Arcese, and I will fly Agmunsten and Arie to Bayerlon to help King Edmund retrieve his daughter and get Prince Leon under control. We may need your help Bertholimous, if we go to war with Inkra." Zim shifted on his bench seat, wishing he were not talking of war, although Prince Leon and a few thousand humans were not going to be much of a match for the strength and tactics of an army fortified with dragons—unless….

"I know what you're thinking, Zim," said Agmunsten, "but I don't think Leon will have any gormons, or anything else, at his disposal. I think he may have one realmist, but I can't be sure.

"Better to be safe than sorry, as they say." Bertholimous looked at Warrimonious, his second-in-charge. "We'll keep in touch, every night. I'll have Arcese ward our conversations. If one of us doesn't check in, we should assume something has happened."

"Then what?" asked Warrimonious.

"I don't know. I suppose it depends on the situation."

"Excuse me. I hate to interrupt, but that doesn't sound like much of a plan." King Valdorryn looked from his master of war to his captain and back again.

"Have you got a better one, Sire?"

"Hmm, no. It's been an extremely long time since we've had to deal with war. I'm a bit rusty: we all are."

Agmunsten spoke. "I'm going to send for one of the teachers and four students from The Academy. I think it's time you shared your Talian natural magic secrets with more realmists. We'll need the advantage when it comes time to fight the gormons. Have you got anyone here who can teach them?"

Arcese looked at her mother and smiled. "My mother is quite good, actually."

"Well, I don't like to brag, but I can hold my own with my talented daughter. I'd be only too happy to share some of our secrets with them."

Agmunsten stifled a cough when he saw the queen flutter her eyelashes. He hadn't even realized dragons had eyelashes —and just when he thought he'd seen everything. "Good; it's settled. So, I think it's time to get to bed. We have an early start tomorrow."

King Valdorryn listened, all the while tapping his claws on the table. When he spoke, his voice had taken on the edge of menace Agmunsten heard after Symbothial had been murdered. And he looked straight at the head realmist. "If it comes to war, you keep my daughter out of it. Do you understand? I won't have any of our female dragons fighting, and certainly not my daughter." A tendril of smoke escaped his nostrils and drifted towards the ceiling.

Agmunsten combed thick fingers through his beard. "I wasn't planning on sending her to war, Valdorryn, but we may have to before this gormon thing is finished."

Valdorryn leaned forward and pointed a clawed finger at the realmist. "If I hear my daughter has been used to kill anyone, or has been put in the way of danger, I will be forced to take action."

"I am inclined to agree with the king. No wife of mine is going to war. It's my job to protect her—not the other way around." Warrimonious looked at the realmist, then at Arcese, who stared back at him with a look that would have sent a lesser dragon scurrying out of sight.

Agmunsten didn't want to provoke the king, but in the current situation, they needed all the man and dragon power they could get. The head realmist stood, but was, of course, still shorter than the seated dragon king. "I will promise to do my best to keep her out of it, but I will never say never, and neither should either of you if you want to see the gormons sent back to the Third Realm. This war isn't about choices; it's about have-to's. I will do what I have to, and if you don't like it, you can kill me later. Good night."

He strode out of the room without waiting to be dismissed. Silence followed him.

Sunrise came late to the valley—the sun had to clear the mountains, and today there were clouds to contend with. When Agmunsten roused Arie, a light sheen of rain coated the window. The boy was surprised to be woken. In his excitement, he vowed he wouldn't sleep, but sleep he had. He padded over to the washbasin and shocked his face to alertness with a splash of cold water.

"Put your shoes on, have breakfast, and relieve yourself, then carry your bag up six flights from here, to the level with black arrows—the launching level. I'll see you there."

"Gee, thanks for reminding me to go to the toilet. I never would have thought to do that all by myself." Arie put his thumb in his mouth and sucked.

"No need to get smart. There's no good telling me you need to go when we're 2,000 feet off the ground."

"Can't we just be like the birds and do it on unsuspecting ground dwellers?" Arie chuckled.

"You might find it's a bit cold and precarious perched on a dragon flying at speed. That's the last place I'd be pulling my pants down."

"Too much information. Now all I can picture is your wrinkly behind. Okay, I'm going to have breakfast before I lose my appetite."

"You started it." Agmunsten shrugged and ruffled the young boy's hair as they left.

After forcing down his breakfast on a stomach infested with butterflies, Arie made sure he went to the toilet. When he was done, he ran up all six flights of stairs, sliding his fingertips along the smooth stone walls as he went, his full bag jangling about on his back. He had dreamed of flying on a dragon ever since he was a small boy at home when his mother would tell him bedtime tales of brave warriors riding fierce dragons. It didn't seem real that he truly would be high above the ground on Zim's back in a few minutes. His face flushed with more than his exertion when he reached his destination, over ninety feet above the valley floor.

Agmunsten greeted him at the top of the stairs, "Come this way, lad." Arie noticed his mentor wore a heavy, black, tight-fitting cloak and thick, yamuk-skin lined boots, the sky-blue wool encircling the top of his calves. It took several minutes to walk the entire length of the hallway. When they reached the dark stone wall at the end, Agmunsten reached down to a bundle on the floor. He picked up a fawn-colored coat and handed it to Arie. "Here, put this on. It's going to be very cold out there, and do your hood up too."

Arie let his bag slip to the floor before sliding his arms into the luxurious coat. He was pleased to feel that the yamuk-skin wool lined the coat too. He buttoned it up and fastened the hood over his head, tightening it under his chin with soft ribbons that poked from the bottom of the rim of the hood. He couldn't help but shut his eyes for a moment, like a contented pussycat.

"Enough of that, lad. Are you ready?" Arie could see even Agmunsten's eyes glistened with childlike anticipation.

"You bet! Have you ever ridden a dragon?"

"Nope. This will be my first time." He grinned and rubbed gloved hands together. "Oh, and there should be gloves in your pocket. Put them on. One word of warning, lad: dragons are not horses, or inferior animals. Treat Arcese with respect and don't tell her where to go. Listen to any instructions she has and obey immediately." Arie nodded, his hair rubbing against the plump wool in his hood.

The boy turned at the faint, yet familiar, click, click on the tiled floor. Zim reached them and smiled, a minute stretching of black lips, exposing only a few teeth. Arie looked at Agmunsten, and asked, "Do you ever get used to that?"

Agmunsten barked a short laugh. "Eventually."

"What did I do?" Zim pretended to be offended. "Maybe I should just smile all the time and you'd get over it soon enough … if you didn't die of fright first." Zim winked a huge eye.

"You'd better stop that, Zim, or our boy will be running back to the toilets." It was Agmunsten's turn to wink.

"Sorry I'm late." Arcese joined them, and Arie noticed, for the first time, that each dragon had a harness that wrapped behind front legs, or arms—Arie never knew what to call them and was too scared to ask—to their backs and another strap around their bellies behind their wings. Attached to these straps was a saddle. Both dragons looked uncomfortable wearing them; Arcese gave a slight torso twist intermittently— it looked like she was trying to adjust, or banish, the unwieldy contraption.

"Are you okay wearing those?" Agmunsten knew this was asking a lot of the dragons. The other reason they didn't like wearing saddles is that thousands of years ago, before dragons dominated, a harsher race of humans—predecessors to the Inkrans—had lived in consort with the gormons. They had control of the dragons and enslaved them, forcing them to wear similar saddles. The dragons had toiled: working the fields, building things, whatever the humans and gormons could compel them to do. This was at a time when the natural magic had been unknown by the dragons—Drakon had transported the dragons to Talia, thinking it was a safe and rich land, not realizing the gods of the Inkrans had other ideas. The old stories were lost to most dragons, and Drakon hadn't explained to the realmists the knowledge and power the

Inkrans used to have. The dragons just knew it signified a darker time, a time of shame and imprisonment.

"We do what we have to—you said it yourself. You won't hear us complaining. The only thing I'll ask is that you hold on tight. There is a strap on the saddle," Zim shuddered as he spoke, "that you put over your lap—it should help you stay on." He looked at his sister. "Are you ready, Princess?"

Arcese laughed. "Yes, Brother."

It had been many years since he'd used that affectionate term with her, and she was glad to be reminded of their childhood. "Shall we?"

They turned to face the end of the corridor, and Arie wondered what they were doing—there was no door or window. Zim walked and placed his hands on the solid stone. He shut his eyes and concentrated. When he removed his hands, the wall slid sideways with a sound like a giant grinding his teeth. Arie guessed the stone had disappeared into a recess.

A ledge ended four feet in front of the opening. The valley spread before them; acres of lush grass shaded near the river by majestic trees. The rain had ceased, and the clouds were clearing; rays from the sun spilled over the western peaks to illuminate the valley floor. Two dragons were out on the thermals, gliding and playing, deftly swooping low before rising up to where eagles nested. Arie stood, hypnotized, while the breeze caressed his face, its spring-scented fingers trying to wriggle beneath his hood. He stepped closer to the edge, not wanting to miss anything, not wanting to forget. Agmunsten grabbed his arm. "Not so fast. That's a long way to fall."

Arie shook his head, disengaging the stupor. When he grinned, Agmunsten basked in the unfettered and untarnished joy of the twelve-year-old. "Don't worry; I wasn't going anywhere."

The opening in which they stood was not wide enough for them all. Arcese spoke. "Arie, please come inside and climb onto my back. It's time we embarked. I imagine King Edmund is eager to receive us."

Arie walked in and settled his pack on his back. He patted the dragon's neck. "Sorry Arcese, and thank you for allowing me this privilege."

"You are welcome, young Arie." Arcese crouched down and braced herself for the boy to climb on. She knew it wouldn't hurt—she would hardly feel the weight of his skinny body—but the feeling of being commanded or forced by another was something she feared. Maybe it was in her blood, a genetic remembrance from ancient times. Her eyes closed as Arie placed one foot in the stirrup.

Arie reached up to grasp the edge of the saddle; even crouching, as she was, Arcese was tall. He heaved himself on and flung his leg over, stepping his other foot into the stirrup hanging over the other side. After he strapped the leather belt over his lap, he looked for somewhere to hold on, as there were no reins—the dragons had not agreed to that. "Arcese? Where can I hold on?"

"Place your fingers under my scales. Your gloves will protect your fingers from getting cut, and my scales won't fall off." Arie found two scales, just behind either side of the dragon's shoulders. Each scale was about the size of a man's hand. Arie leaned forward to burrow his fingers under them. He noticed Arcese's subtle scent, a mixture of damp earth and fresh rain, and wondered that he'd never noticed it before. Of course dragons would smell like something; he'd just never imagined what it could be, and if he'd been asked to imagine, he probably would have expected they'd smell like horses or smoke. He was glad he would have been wrong.

Confident he was seated comfortably and had something to hang onto, Arie looked over at Agmunsten climbing onto Zim, the older realmist moving smoothly, showing nothing of his age. When Agmunsten was seated and had found his grip, he turned his head and looked at Arie. "You good to go?"

"Yep." Arie nodded sagely once, a gesture he'd seen his father do many times when discussing important matters with the village council. He gripped the scales tighter when Arcese shifted beneath him as she stood.

Arcese spoke to him, mind to mind. *Okay, Arie hold on. If you feel like you're slipping or getting tired, make sure you let me know quickly, as it takes time to land, and I'd hate to lose you.*

He could hear the mirth in her mind voice at the last, but that did nothing to calm his nerves.

Arie felt Arcese's smooth gait as she walked backwards. Zim followed her, not stopping until they were some twenty feet from the opening. Arie watched as Zim started running, his stocky, powerful legs accelerating at a pace the boy would have thought impossible. When the dragon reached the opening, he kept going, and Arie held his breath. Half a second before Zim launched off the ledge, he threw his wings out and glided away, quickly reaching a thermal and rising, instead of falling, as Arie had feared. Arie giggled when Agmunsten's fading *Woohoo* of joy reached him.

The boy fell silent when Arcese crouched slightly before exploding into a run. The opening sped towards them, and Arie leaned closer to Arcese, digging his fingers in as hard as he could, his adrenalin-filled body tense yet excited. Vellonia's walls disappeared as they were birthed into fresh air, and the dragon leapt off the ledge. Arie forced his eyes to stay open—either he would die or fly, and he wanted to watch, no matter what was about to happen—he didn't want to have to say, when asked about his first flight on a dragon, that he had kept his eyes scrunched shut.

Even sheltered behind Arcese's strong neck, Arie felt the wind tug at his hood. He was forced to squint his eyes against its assault as tears blurred his vision—he dared not try and wipe them away. And then, suddenly, he could open his eyes as the dragon caught a thermal, slowing, yet still rising. Arie kept his grip strong but cautiously looked down. When the momentary dizziness cleared, Arie gasped at the valley shrinking beneath them. They were climbing fast, now almost in line with the top of the tallest peaks surrounding Vellonia. The massive trees and buildings in the valley were no more than different-colored blots on the green landscape, and the river was a slim serpent silently wending its way through the unreal scene.

When they cleared the mountains, Zim stayed his northerly course, and Arcese pumped her wings twice to catch up to her brother. When she drew next to him, Agmunsten turned to smile at Arie and spoke into his mind, *So lad, how did you like that?*

Arie was so excited that he started speaking out loud. "It was fantastic! I can't believe I'm flying!"

Agmunsten interrupted in his mind. *Arie, lad, I can hardly hear you, what with the wind and my hood covering my ears. Speak to me in here.*

Agmunsten, more confident of staying on the dragon's back than Arie, let go of Zim's scales and tapped his head with a finger.

Oops, sorry. Is that better? Agmunsten nodded. *I was saying that it was the most incredible thing ever, and I can't believe I'm flying. The land looks so strange from up here; it's like I can see patterns I couldn't before, kind of like one of mum's tapestries. If my parents could see me now, they wouldn't believe it.* He shook his head and grinned.

Agmunsten watched his protégé and took heart in the boy's momentary happiness. He hoped Arie would see his parents again one day, because if anything happened to him he would never forgive himself. Out of all his apprentices, the old man thought he liked Arie the best. The boy was a quick learner, laughed at Agmunsten's bad jokes, and it was obvious he had affection for the head realmist. Agmunsten felt renewed pressure: they had so much to lose, and the gormons had so much to win.

Zim interrupted his thoughts. *It won't be easy, but we'll do it; we'll rid Talia of those monstrosities. They're an abomination, and we have Drakon's help. That has to count for something.*

That's what worries me, Zim. Why is Drakon the only one willing to help us. Where are the other gods? According to our limited records, they didn't intercede last time, either. What do they know that we don't? What has Drakon done that they don't communicate with each other?

Maybe nothing, Agmunsten. Maybe your gods have abandoned you. I wouldn't complain since Drakon is there for you when your own gods aren't."

"He's helping but he's helping because he wants to save his dragons. It wouldn't be the first time he's used humans for the dragon's gain.

I love you, Agmunsten, but please don't insult my god. I have my limits, you know.

Sorry, Zim. Just thinking it through out loud. I mean no offense, but you have to see what I'm saying. I think there's more to this gormon invasion than we know. Let's hope we don't need to know what that is to survive the coming war.

Don't worry. Everything will be fine; you'll see. Both of them knew Zim was stretching things with that statement, but Agmunsten stayed silent, trying to give hope to the lie.

As they flew towards Bayerlon and King Edmund, Agmunsten turned his mind to the problem of Leon. The "gods" theory would have to wait because Leon was the dragon's claw in their side right now. Agmunsten sighed as he tried to figure out how to tell King Edmund they would have to go in and kill his brother as soon as possible if they had any chance of saving the princess—if indeed she was still alive. *Hey Zim?*

Yes, Agmunsten.

Are there any warm islands we can go to at this time of year? I think I need a holiday. Zim laughed as they flew towards war, his black scales absorbing the early morning light.

CHAPTER 12

Gabrielle stood staring out of a northeast-facing window, absently playing with the heart-shaped gold locket at her neck—a present from Verity on the queen's last birthday. She looked, although not seeing, in the direction her daughter had been taken—towards Inkra and her evil brother-in-law. At least Edmund finally knew what Leon was capable of, but what a hard way to learn. Gabrielle prayed for the millionth time that her daughter was alive and unharmed, and she wondered if she should have told Edmund about what Leon had done to her—maybe he would have believed she'd been raped and would have dealt with Leon then. Now it was too late. Verity might be lost to them forever. Her face paled to white, and mute tears followed a worn path down her cheeks.

"Excuse me, Your Highness?" Verity turned and looked down at Boy, who held a bouquet of bright-yellow tamsin lilies. They were one of the first flowers to bloom when the snow of winter subsided. He raised his arm and smiled when Gabrielle accepted them with melancholy fingers. She held the blooms to her nose for an instant before calling Sarah to put them in some water.

"Now, Boy, come sit with me and tell me all about your lessons." Boy had been sitting in on Verity's lessons, and since she had gone, the queen had insisted things be as normal as possible—it gave her hope that Verity would return. Every night Gabrielle went to bed and hoped to wake up the next morning to find it was all a bad dream. Waking up was the worst; in the time when the last mist of sleep cleared, and the first remembrance of why she didn't want to wake up insinuated itself upon her consciousness, her heart felt constricted, and she wished it would stop beating. The only thing that got her up was her husband's assurances they would see their daughter again, that she needed to be strong for when Verity returned. She tried to stay strong for Edmund too, knowing that not only had he lost his daughter, but had also suffered the stab of betrayal from his only sibling—he was wounded almost beyond cure.

Boy fidgeted under the queen's questioning. Each day the guilt gnawed on him until his insides felt like an infected sinkhole of puss. But he couldn't confess—confession meant death, and he wasn't ready to die, at least not until he had figured out a way to make things right. It was an effort to keep quiet about what he knew, especially when he saw the dark circles under Gabrielle's eyes and the wet sheen that constantly coated her cheeks. He prayed every night that Verity was alive—Leon couldn't be that evil, could he? Boy shuddered.

"Are you cold? Do you want a coat?" The queen's concern astounded him—he was nothing, had always been nothing, and if she knew what he had done…. Before he could answer, a scuffling of boots and tumult of voices sounded in the hall outside. The queen jumped to her feet, hope lighting her features. She rushed to the door, meeting King Edmund as he came in; Zim, Arie, Arcese, Agmunsten, Fendill, and Pernus came marching behind. "Oh, my. Welcome, welcome." Everyone bowed to Gabrielle. She embraced the dragons before greeting Agmunsten and Arie with a kiss to both cheeks. Arie noticed Boy standing behind the queen, gaping at the dragons.

"Hi, Boy. Didn't think I'd see you again so soon. Do you want to show me the rest of the castle?"

"Sure." Boy tore his eyes away from the giant beasts and managed a small grin. He thought spending the day with Arie was much better than spending it wallowing in regret. "I know the perfect place to start."

Agmunsten nodded to Arie, and the boys ran out.

Edmund spoke, "I think we should adjourn to my private reception. I want to get things sorted by tonight. We've had some time to get the army ready, thanks to Pernus's quick actions before I returned. If we decide, we will be ready to march out in two days. Anyway, I don't want to discuss this here. Let's go."

Gabrielle watched her husband lead the others away, and a small spark of hope kindled at his straight-backed confidence. Finally something was happening, although it could end in war if Leon didn't back down. Her short laugh sounded more like a snarl as she thought how silly her hopes were—*of course he won't give in. He is Leon, and his brother is going to kill him either way. He has nothing to lose.* How many soldiers would die so she could save her daughter? She knew she should feel selfish for condemning many families to heartache so she could assuage her own, but no matter what others may think of her, she would get her daughter back. She would kill Leon with her bare hands if she had to. Shaking her thoughts off, she made her way to the kitchen—there was a counsel of war to feed.

They sat around the spiderwood table, its dark-red timber crisscrossed with gossamer threads of white. The spiderwood tree was rare and the timber difficult to work with, but any furniture made with it lasted for hundreds, if not thousands, of years. The table had occupied this room for twelve generations of King Edmund's family—he drew strength from it, feeling the support of his ancestors, imagining what they had endured so the Laraulen family could retain the throne.

"I will ask Pernus to fill you in on where we're at." Edmund sat at the head of the table. Pernus stood.

"We've sent scouts ahead with Fendill, who is no longer Leon's realmist. They'll report back on the weather and the situation. I've drawn a map of what I can remember of the layout of the city and castle, which is more than I thought." He rolled out the map on the table's burnished surface and stopped the corners from rolling up with silver-colored paperweights—they looked like smooth river pebbles with the Laraulen family crest of a snow-covered oak engraved on the top.

"Your training's coming in handy." Edmund was proud of his man and at this point, extremely grateful.

Agmunsten interrupted, "I hate to say this, Edmund: I never trusted your brother, but I don't think I expected him to be so ambitious and ruthless as to kill the Inkran king and kidnap his own niece. This has taken us all by surprise. It's safe to say we can't put anything past him, and I need to ask if you've given thought to what happens after we catch him."

This was as delicate as the head realmist could be—there wasn't time for subtlety.

Though the king looked tired, there was no mistaking the icy shards of fury embedded in his eyes. "He will be tried and executed upon our return. He is no longer my brother, and no one is to address him as such. He is the 'blackhearted betrayer.'" Edmund's composure slipped with each word: his face reddened, and he gripped the edge of the timber table, his fingers bent and strained with anger. "He has betrayed more than my family or Veresia; he has risked Talia for this. He knows the prophecies. How would he think to unite Talia like this?"

Agmunsten turned a thick obsidian ring around on his middle finger. "Maybe his arrogance has finally given way to insanity. You know he's been on the edge for a few years. They say jealousy is a curse, and it seems Talia is about to learn the truth of it."

"If I may go on?" Pernus drew their attention back to the map. "As I was saying, this is what I could remember of Inkra and the palace. The red doors I have marked out are those working on what I can only assume is Second Realm energy. The only people who can open them are those with knowledge of Second Realm power. Fendill can explain it in your terms when we catch up to him, Agmunsten. So, we need realmists with us when we go in.

Something else we've been worried about is the snow—it slows things down, and if we get stuck out there with dwindling supplies, the 'blackhearted betrayer' will win without even trying. We have to be smart about this." Pernus turned to his king. "I know you want this over with yesterday, but it's going to take a few more days of planning before we can move. I have a couple of ideas I need to discuss with Zim,

Agmunsten, and Arcese. My feeling is that this will be a war more about Second Realm power than might, but even then we don't know what resources the 'betrayer' has. King Fernis is gathering his army—he has Elphus with him—and Queen Alaine, from Wyrdon, will be ready in two weeks, although they're staying put until they hear from us." Pernus stopped talking when servants entered the room with trays of fruit, cold, spiced meats, and freshly baked bread.

Agmunsten hadn't eaten breakfast and was quick to speak at the sight of food. "Okay, roll up that map Captain; it's time to eat. My ears don't work well on an empty stomach."

The realmist at least elicited wan smiles from the highly-strung audience as they set aside planning while they ate and considered the situation. When they finally emerged the next morning, grainy-eyed, they had two plans to choose from, and neither was perfect. Either way, they would leave in few days with an army ready to fight. Whether any would return was a question they didn't ask—no one wanted to know the answer.

Pernus sat in his saddle and frowned at Perculus, the king's advisor. He was grateful they'd managed to keep him out of their plans for Leon. Edmund realized he was Leon's man, but they didn't let on they knew. They set up a "fake" counsel of war and fed him false information. It was impossible to hide the dragons, so they covered by saying Zim and Arcese were there to give advice and had been forbidden to go anywhere near the war—which was partly true. They considered killing Perculus on the road, but if he was still in touch with Leon, it might alert him to what they were doing. The fat man couldn't ride well, and as his horse trotted to the gates, his chins jiggled and his stomach slapped on his thighs as he jounced around. Pernus and Edmund considered betting on how long it would take him to fall off.

When Perculus, and his soon-to-be sore bottom, cleared the gates, Pernus surveyed the twenty new king's bodyguards. They had lost a large number of elite soldiers to the swords of Suklar's murderers. When Pernus returned, his first task, other than relaying the horrifying news, was to find twenty of the best men from the army. One of the men he chose was Chisholm, the young soldier who had survived the massacre, because he would know what to expect, and he followed Pernus around like a loyal puppy. The veteran tolerated it because he knew what it was like to owe someone, and he was a good soldier—certainly someone he could trust. The girl they had brought with them, Karin, was under close watch, although free to roam the castle and its grounds as she pleased. She was learning Veresian and proved to be a capable student. Karin and Chisholm were still enamoured of each other, and she was seeing him off with a wave and a tear.

After Karin went inside, so she wouldn't cry in front of everyone, the queen explained, Pernus prodded the soldier. "She's reserved, lad. You're not even going to get a hug?"

"You know where she comes from. They're not into talking in public, let alone hugging. And besides, we said our *proper* goodbyes earlier." His cheeks reddened. Pernus nodded, unsuccessfully hiding his smile behind pursed lips.

The captain didn't have a special someone to say goodbye to—it's not that he didn't like women; he just didn't see the point of marrying and leaving a widow with ten kids when he was killed in battle. He had chosen his job and the Laraulens over love. Gabrielle smiled, watching as Pernus gathered his troupe—he seemed oblivious to the stares of two of her staff and at least two eligible young nobles. Even the queen couldn't deny that his imposing physique, chiseled face, and commanding manner were enticing. She spoke to Sarah. "We'll have to get Pernus a woman when he gets back. It's such a shame to see such a good man go to waste."

"Indeed, my lady." Sarah giggled.

King Edmund strode over and swept Gabrielle up in strong arms. He leaned his face down and looked into the green eyes he loved so much. "We'll get her back; I promise." He caressed her smooth cheek with his thumb and kissed her lips.

"Just make sure you come back, too." Their kiss this time was almost frantic: a promise. The soldiers averted their eyes, not wanting to intrude on this moment that was more than their king and queen saying a common goodbye—it was the goodbye of a soldier and his lover when both knew it could be the last.

The clop of hooves on the flagstones as the soldiers left the palace courtyard was to Gabrielle a lonely sound; it was the sound of her husband leaving for war.

The queen turned, and Sarah followed her inside to where Agmunsten, the dragons, and Arie sat. Two tables had to be brought into the larger reception room to accommodate Zim and Arcese. Arie, Boy, and Agmunsten sprawled on an upholstered lounge that featured blue and white stripes—the Laraulen colours. They stood and bowed. Gabrielle sat, and Agmunsten returned to the seat next to her. "Are you all ready?" she asked.

"Yes, my queen. We're leaving tonight. Darkness will hide our whereabouts. We should reach Klendar in three days—a lot earlier than King Edmund. We're hoping this will be over with before the army even gets there. Sending the army out is a ruse that will hopefully fool Leon into thinking he has more time. With a bit of luck, we'll have Princess Verity out of there before Leon knows what's happened."

Gabrielle's jaw tightened. "I prefer the name Edmund has chosen."

"As you wish." Agmunsten nodded. "In any case, I don't think old Blackheart just woke up one morning and thought, 'I might go and kill the Inkran King today.' If he's had this planned for a while, there could be other spies in the castle. Do not trust anyone, and if anyone asks, Zim and Arcese have flown us back to Vellonia."

Gabrielle nodded. "I'm going to miss you. At least I'll have Boy and Sarah to keep me company." Boy kept the disappointment from his face. It's not that he disliked the queen, but he wanted to *do* something to help get Verity back, and staying with Gabrielle was a constant reminder of his betrayal. He wished he could ride on the dragon with Arie; that was something he dreamed of but dared not ask—those dragons had sharp teeth.

Boy looked at the queen. "Is it okay if I say goodbye to Arie now? I don't feel too good."

"Oh, no. Are you sick? Come here." Boy kneeled at the queen's feet, and she touched his forehead with the back of her hand. "I don't think you have a temperature. Maybe it's something you ate. Very well. Say goodbye now and go and have a rest."

Boy embraced Arie. "It's been fun. See you soon, I hope."

"Me too. It's a shame you can't come to Inkra." Arie looked hopefully at Queen Gabrielle. She shook her head.

"I won't risk another child, and if I had my way, you'd stay here too."

Arie shrugged at Boy. "Sorry. I tried. I'd better shut up before I'm stuck here too."

"I miss out on all the fun." Boy sighed before bowing to the dragons. "It was an honor to meet you, Sir and Lady Dragon."

Zim laughed, a deep vibration Boy felt as well as heard. "You can call me Zim, and my sister is Arcese. We're friendly, you know." He winked, and Boy smiled.

"Bye." With that, Boy shuffled out and made his way to his room where a packed bag waited under his bed. He didn't like lying, and he knew the queen would be angry when she found he was gone, but that was a small thing compared to what he'd already done. He would help get Princess Verity back if it was the last thing he did.

After the queen left them, Zim spoke in the realmists' minds. *I've scried Boy's symbol. There's something about him I don't trust. If we need to know where he is in the future, I'll be able to find him.*

Arie felt he had to defend his friend, *He's okay. He's had a tough childhood, which he won't really talk about, but I can't see him being a danger to anyone. He's loyal to the queen because Leon saved him somehow.*

And that just supports what I'm saying. Where does his loyalty lie, hmm? With Leon, or the king and queen? Wasn't he there when Princess Verity was taken?

You're not suggesting…. Arie's eyes widened.

Agmunsten rubbed a finger across his brow and spoke aloud. "He's right, Arie. If it smells like dragon poo and looks like dragon poo, it probably is dragon poo."

"I beg your pardon?" Arcese pinioned Agmunsten with dangerous dragon eyes.

"Oops, sorry. Forgot you were there."

"I don't know what's more insulting." Arcese folded her

scaly arms and swished her tail back and forth like an angry cat.

"Sorry, Arcese; you know I was only joking, right?"

"I'm not known for my sense of humor, Realmist. Watch I don't burn you to a crisp." Agmunsten's mouth twisted down as he contemplated whether he was about to become charcoal, and then Arcese laughed—the smooth, musical laugh Arie loved. Zim's chuckle vibrated the chair on which the realmists lounged.

Agmunsten looked sideways at Arcese. "Hmph."

"Laugh it up, old man," said Zim. "It could be the last one you have for a while."

"Thanks for reminding me, dragon boy." Agmunsten smiled at his own joke. "I'm hungry. Where's lunch?"

"I'm looking at it," said Zim, staring at Agmunsten. Agmunsten pretended to be horrified, eliciting more laughter.

Zim was right—what they were about to do was dangerous, and even if they came back alive, no one wanted to be the one to tell the queen that Verity was dead. Agmunsten let the laughter wash the negative thoughts away. They would get there in time: yes indeed, they would.

CHAPTER 13

After travelling for five days, Bronwyn was tired and grateful to be eating a dinner of stewed vegetables and slightly-stale bread. She looked around the camp, first at Sinjenasta who shielded their symbols, then at Blayke and Arcon as they ate a dinner consisting of vegetable stew and dried beef.

"How come you eat meat? I didn't think any realmists would eat meat." This was a point she wanted to bring up before, but felt she hadn't known them well enough.

"It tastes good," Blayke replied.

"But what about the animal? Surely after bonding with Fang, you can see animals have feelings and thoughts, just like us? Would you eat a person?"

"Of course not. What do you think I am?"

"My brother." She couldn't resist—after so long with no sibling, it felt good to use the word.

He grinned. "Ha, so I am. I'm still not used to it. I'm kind of sorry we didn't get the chance to grow up together; it would have been fun to have someone to tease."

"I'm sure I would have won most of the arguments." Bronwyn beamed.

"Nah, I would."

"No, I would."

"Stop it, children!" Arcon laughed. "If you want to make up for lost time, do it when I'm not around—I'm too old to listen to children arguing." It had been an awkward couple of days after telling them his secret, but eventually both teens had forgiven him. Arcon had been so relieved when he was certain Blayke still loved him that he had quietly cried. His old heart was not as impervious as he thought. He soaked up the feeling of familial camaraderie like a cat sunning himself on a sun-bleached porch.

Blayke, who was sitting next to his uncle, put a hesitant hand on his shoulder—open affection was something they didn't regularly practice. "I want you to know that even when I meet my father, I'll still think of you like a dad. You've been more than an uncle to me. I know it wasn't my dad's fault he didn't bring me up, but I know you love me. And even if I am still a bit angry when I think about what happened, it would kill me to lose you." A crooked smile and a pat on the back was all Arcon could manage without crying. Blayke knew his Uncle was sad and looked away.

"That was beautiful." Bronwyn smiled and leaned against Sinjenasta. The panther nuzzled her arm, and Bronwyn sneezed.

"Gee, Bronwyn, since I've known you, you've had a cold," Blayke observed.

"I have, haven't I?" She thought for a while. "The first time I remember sneezing and sniffling was in Vellonia, right before, well, you know." She thought that killing Symbothial would forever be a painful memory.

Arcon spoke. "So it started just after you met Sinjenasta?"

"Yes."

"Bury your face in Sinjenasta's fur."

"What?"

"Rub your nose and face in his fur," Arcon instructed. Bronwyn turned around, placed her arms around her creatura and sunk her nose into his shiny, black fur. After a moment, she sat up, and a barrage of sneezes assaulted her. She wiped watering eyes.

"Well, that settles it," said Agmunsten.

"Settles what? Achooo!"

"You're allergic to Sinjenasta."

"What? That can't be right; he's my creatura." Sinjenasta sat up, blinking, and Bronwyn wore a horrified expression.

Blayke laughed until he, too, had tears in his eyes. "Dragons' balls! Who's ever heard of anyone being allergic to their creatura."

Bronwyn sniffed. "It's not funny. That means I can't go near him unless I want to have watering eyes and a red nose all the time."

"And sneezing is not conducive to sneaking," said Sinjenasta.

"No, it's not," Fang agreed.

"So what in the Third Realm am I supposed to do?"

"I'll see what I can come up with. If I don't have any remedies, your aunt might know what will help—she's always been better than me with herbs."

"Don't worry, Bronny. You can still love me from afar." Sinjenasta winked.

"Ha, ha. Very funny. Why can't you be allergic to me?

Why is it that people are allergic to animals, yet you're not allergic to us?"

"Just lucky, I guess." Sinjenasta licked a giant paw and cleaned his face.

"I think Drakon should help; he's the one who made us bond."

Blayke's voice held bitterness Arcon had never before heard, "Drakon's help comes with a high price—avoid asking him for anything."

"That's a bit harsh."

"He's right, Bronwyn. Sometimes it's better living with the gormon you know." Sinjenasta's mind voice sounded resigned.

"Hmph. All the sneezing's made me tired. I think I'll turn in." She felt sorry for herself that she couldn't snuggle up to Sinjenasta whenever she wanted—he'd become a comfort since she'd been separated from her aunt and best friend, Corrille. She burrowed farther into her bedroll, her back to the small fire, and shut her eyes. The sooner she fell asleep, the sooner it would be time to start on the last leg of their trip. She would see Corrille and Avruellen again tomorrow afternoon— a time she longed for, and dreaded. Arcon hadn't told Avru- ellen their secret was out, and Bronwyn had no idea how her aunt would react. Bronwyn had many questions to ask and would be angry if they weren't answered. As much as she would be happy to see her aunt, she was also ready for a battle of wills, which up to now was something she had never won against her aunt. She fell asleep listening to the soft murmur of Arcon and Blayke's conversation—whatever happened tomor- row, she was finally part of a family. No one was going to take that away from her again.

Avruellen woke happy—well, as happy as one could be when gormons were skulking around Talia. Today she would see her niece again. She couldn't scry for Arcon and Bronny— Agmunsten had warned her they would be shielding on the way, so she had to wait the old-fashioned way. It would be a relief to see them. Even though Carpus was a quaint enough town, she couldn't shield herself for so long without dying from the effort, and creaturas didn't have the skills to shield— that seemed to be a gift given from the gods to humans—so Flux couldn't help. As a result, she felt like the lone gozzle-berry pie at a culinary festival for hungry people—it was only a matter of time before the gormons, or whoever had been watching her, would stick their claws in. Her one consolation was the true dream she'd had last night. She dreamt of Bronwyn rubbing her face into the giant panther, which was odd. The image only lasted for a minute—long enough for her to see Bronwyn sneezing uncontrollably; she hoped she wasn't getting a cold. Avruellen knew they were due sometime today, so she dressed with an enthusiasm she hadn't felt in a while.

She strolled the length of the town and back again, trying to project an air of calm, but when she'd finished, not only was she not tired, she was bored. Even though it was dangerous, Avruellen decided to walk towards where her niece would be coming from and meet them on the way. She called to Flux, telling him to meet her one mile from Carpus.

As Avruellen walked the well-worn dirt path, the ferocious winds that, on her arrival, had raked the yellowing shafts of grass until they lay flat upon the ground, had dissipated to a steady breeze that bent the long blades to a sighing crescent. The overnight change in the weather had come as a surprise after the constant thrashing upon the coast—*how fortuitous,* she thought. The captain she had spoken to previously would be ready to sail in the morning, then. Avruellen and Arcon would have one day to catch up before they sailed. She bit the inside of her cheek as she thought about the news she had to share— just thinking about it made the hairs on her arms stand on end.

A high-pitched squeal broke her thoughts. She turned to see Flux trotting towards her, his orange-and-white muzzle peeking above the flax-colored stems. He howled again.

When he reached Avruellen, she crouched and embraced him. "What's all the noise about?"

I felt like howling. I'm restless. It's nice to howl once in a while. He twitched his ears a few times—a sign to Avruellen he was happy. *I can smell Bronny. They're not that far away.* He led the way.

Flux's *not far away* was farther than Avruellen anticipated. After walking almost two miles, from the top of a rise they saw three horses in the distance and a black outline that was half as big as the horses; it was a shape Avruellen remembered well. She resisted the urge to run, but it seemed Bronwyn didn't have the same discipline—one of the horses broke away from the group and galloped towards Avruellen. "It's her," Flux confirmed after sniffing the air. Avruellen clasped her hands in front of her and bit the inside of her cheek again. When the horse neared, she could see it was Prince. Bronwyn, confident and glorious, sat in the saddle, dark hair streaming out behind. Avruellen hadn't smiled that wide for a long time.

In one fluid motion, Bronwyn reined in Prince and dismounted, running into Avruellen's arms. Avruellen hugged her close and kissed her forehead, breathing in the fragrance that was Bronny mixed with horse. "Ah, my child. When you were taken from me, I thought I'd never see you again."

Bronwyn squeezed her aunt then stepped back. "I thought I'd never see you either. I have so much to tell you and…" Her smile evaporated. "And you have a lot to tell me, I suspect."

The older realmist knew, then, what Bronwyn meant. "How did you find out?" Arcon and Blayke reached them. Avruellen looked at Arcon, "Did he tell you?" There was no malice, only weary acceptance and a letting go of tension as the rope binding all her secrets slid undone. "It seems we have much to talk about."

Arcon swung his leg over and jumped down. "So many aches and pains. These old bones aren't what they used to be."

"You look okay to me," said Avruellen as she stepped towards him, and they embraced; she was careful not to dislodge Phantom, who slept on Arcon's shoulder, his face burrowed beneath a wing. "It's been too long. And this must be Blayke." Blayke gave a short bow and grinned.

"Pleased to meet you, Auntie."

"What a handsome young man." Avruellen nodded, pleased. "And this must be Fang." She took his paw between her fingertips and gently shook it in greeting, after which she turned to Sinjenasta. The realmist matched gazes with the giant cat before speaking. "So, this is Drakon's beast. I hope you've been taking good care of my niece?"

I think I've done a good job, although she is stubborn. How did you cope all those years?

Avruellen laughed, a sound she hadn't made in weeks. "So, you feel my pain. Hmm, I think you and I are going to get along just fine."

Bronwyn rose from hugging Flux. "Okay, I know I'm so wonderful you just can't stop talking about me, but I'm hungry. I'm sure you can take us somewhere nice to eat and finish the conversation. Let's go." She linked her arm with her aunt's while Arcon led her mount. The lament of the breeze as it played amongst the grass and gnarled bushes gave a whispered accompaniment as they strolled towards Carpus. In the excitement of the reunion, Arcon forgot to mask their symbols in the Second Realm. By the time he realized, it was already too late.

CHAPTER 14

After reassuring the owner of the Seafarers Inn that the giant black panther with her was tame, Avru-ellen settled everyone in their rooms. The humans had a chance to freshen up before eating, and now the group took lunch in the timber-paneled, private dining room of the inn, except for Phantom, who slept in a room upstairs. Sinjenasta lay on the floor under the table, shielding their symbols while everyone ate. In order to shield properly, the realmist doing the shielding had to be close enough that their energy could reach the people whom he was shielding, because the symbols in the Second Realm had to be close together. Instead of the realmist taking the energy from the Second Realm to use in the First Realm, their symbol was acting in the Second Realm. It was almost like hiding everyone with one blanket—the realmist could only channel so much power through his or her symbol, and the power to cover so many symbols was not easy to hold onto. The smaller the area they had to cover, the easier it was.

"I thought creaturas couldn't shield?" Bronwyn just realized Sinjenasta should not have been able to do what he had been doing for the last few days.

"He's a special case, because he has the connection to Drakon." Arcon lied—he wasn't ready to tell Bronwyn that her panther actually started life as a human and was eagerly waiting the day he could return to his original form. They had enough trust issues to deal with.

Blayke changed the subject, speaking around a mouthful of baked fish. "Nice cutlery; is it silver?" Everyone stared at him.

"What? Since when have you taken an interest in cutlery?" Arcon asked, and Bronwyn laughed.

Blayke blushed. "I don't know. I guess it's just nice to be eating somewhere civilized for a change. Remind me never to appreciate anything in front of you again."

"I understand you, even though I have no interest in cutlery," said Fang, his whiskers twitching in a ratty giggle.

Bronwyn leaned over and gave Blayke a quick hug. When he looked at her, surprise on his face, she smiled. "Hey, big bro, I can do that now. I'm the annoying little sister you never had."

"How do you know I'm older?" Blayke turned to Arcon. "So, who did come out first: me or Bronwyn?"

"You don't expect me to pay attention to stuff like that. I wasn't even in the room."

"It was Bronwyn." Avruellen answered, her voice tight with emotion. Bronwyn looked at her, all the hurt she had pushed down gushing upwards, stinging her throat with its acid.

Her gray eyes darkened, like an approaching storm. "How could you hide that from me for all these years? Every time I asked a question, you knew, but you let me think I had no one, that my parents didn't love me, that I was no one. How could you? Do you even have a heart?"

She was standing, looking down at Avruellen, who sat across from her, fork frozen halfway to her mouth. The only sound in the room was muffled laughter from the common room downstairs.

Avruellen placed her fork on the table, letting both hands rest on either side of her plate. For the first time in her life, Bronwyn looked into her aunt's eyes and saw not anger or guardedness, but sorrow and apology. Avruellen held her gaze. "I know you didn't mean that last comment."

Bronwyn swallowed. "No, I'm just angry. Sorry. But why can't you just answer my question? Arcon explained why you had to do it, but that doesn't stop me feeling hurt. Do you know how many times I asked myself over and over who my parents were? I would have given anything to see them, even once. I never really knew who I was, and you saw that, but you said nothing. Surely when I was a bit older you could have explained it to me; I would have understood. And now, when you have the opportunity to explain, you can't even admit that what you did has hurt me."

Avruellen stood and left without saying anything. Bronwyn looked at Arcon who frowned at her. "What? Why are looking at me like that?"

"I know you have questions you need your aunt to answer, but you've had a few days to adjust. We've dropped this on her today. Give her time to adapt."

"Oh, great, so I have to give in as usual because you're both older and are out to save the world. It's for my own good and I should just shut up and be thankful I don't even know my own parents. Well, not anymore." Bronwyn thrust her chair back, the tempest in her eyes showering Arcon with rage before she stormed out.

Bronwyn ran down one flight of stairs to the ground floor and out the front door. She sprinted blindly down the main street, anger driving her onward. As she ran, shopfronts turned to houses, which eventually turned to scrub. The street shrunk into a narrower, sandy road that gradually descended as it led north. Bronwyn, puffing, slowed to a walk. Her surroundings came into focus. She noticed she wasn't far above the harbor.

She found a flat rock and sat down, staring out to sea—a view she hadn't seen before. Avruellen's home was inland, and they had never travelled anywhere that Bronwyn could remember. Gulls coasted high above the water—occasionally she would see one dive, hurtling beak-first into the ocean, to appear soon with a mouthful of what she assumed was fish. She breathed in the briny air and delighted in the tang that filled her nostrils.

"Nice view, isn't it?" Bronwyn turned. A well-dressed man wearing polished black boots and a brown vest smiled down at her. As he reached for her, the sleeve of his white shirt slid up, and she noticed an unusual symbol that appeared to be burnt into the skin on the underside of his wrist. She didn't know what it was, but the symbol made her shiver. It was the last thing she saw before her vision shrunk to a pinhole, and darkness called her home.

Sinjenasta's eyes snapped open. He crawled out from under the table and turned his yellow orbs on Arcon. He spoke into Arcon's mind. *What in Drakon's name just happened? Bronwyn's symbol pulled out of the shielding and now it's gone.*

Arcon's face drained of color. "Blayke, go and tell Avru-ellen that Bronwyn's gone missing. I want you to go to the south end of town and look for her. Sinjenasta and I will go north. Hurry."

Sinjenasta sat and raised a paw. *Wait. Let me pick up the scent. There's no point wasting time and energy when I can pinpoint which direction she went.* The panther trotted out of the inn and turned left. *She's gone north. Blayke, stay with Avruellen; we don't want anyone else to go missing.*

Sinjenasta jogged down the street, Arcon at his side. When they reached the rock where Bronwyn had stopped, the trail turned east, towards the water.

Arcon noticed blood on the ground and tested it between his fingers. "It's still wet. Is it hers?"

Sinjenasta sniffed. *Yes. But it's not much. Maybe they hit her over the head?"* He started in the direction of her trail. *"I wouldn't be surprised if they've taken to sea. We may have to hire a boat. I'll need you to do the talking.*

The panther, with urgent steps, made his way down the gradual incline towards the docks, Arcon behind, battling to keep up on the uneven, pebble-strewn path.

As Sinjenasta sauntered to the end of the long timber wharf, sailors and merchants ran to get out of the way, and Arcon was reminded that to everyone else, the giant panther was a lethal nightmare come to life—Arcon was glad he was on their side. On reaching the end, both stared out to sea. They watched as two ships, one larger than the other, sailed out of the harbor, one tacking to sail north, the other contin-uing east. "I don't suppose you can follow the scent over the water?"

Not usually, but I might pick up the trail if the wind is blowing in our direction. I don't like our chances; those ships are too far ahead. I think you've got some investigating to do.

Arcon retraced his steps back along the wharf and stopped at the first ship where an overseer was supervising the unloading of live yamuks and cows. The overseer gesticulated with his pen, punctuating each number as he counted. He wore a too-big shirt, and his wispy hair refused to sit politely on his head, sticking out at odd angles and making him look like a slightly demented orchestra conductor. "Excuse me, sir?" He kept counting, so Arcon spoke louder and waved a hand in front of his face. "Hello. Excuse me."

The man shook his head as if startled out of a daydream and held his hand up towards two leather-skinned men who were facilitating the unloading. "Stop!" he shouted. He looked at Arcon, blinking rapidly. "Can I help you?"

"Yes. Sorry to bother you while you're in the middle of everything, but did you see who was on the last two ships that left the harbor? I'm looking for a young woman with long dark hair. I think she would have been being carried."

"And what's your business with this young woman?"

"She's my niece, and she's been kidnapped." Arcon didn't think it would do to make up stories at this stage, and he hoped the terrible situation would create enough sympathy that anyone would be eager to help.

"How much is the information worth?"

Arcon rolled his eyes. "You're kidding, right?"

The overseer attempted to smooth down his hair, which sprang up immediately and dashed any hope he had of looking serious. "No, I'm not kidding. How do I know you're telling the truth? If you're desperate enough, you'll pay."

Arcon sighed heavily. "How much?"

"Two silvers." Arcon would usually haggle in a negotiation

—it galled him to pay more than something was worth—but in this case, the information was worth the cost and more. It didn't stop him being disappointed that no one was willing to help just because it was the right thing to do. He reached into his pocket and found two silvers.

The supervisor jangled them in his palm, feeling the weight. "Your niece is on the smaller vessel—the Rapture. A fellow, who goes by the name of Morth, carried her. He arrived this morning and was quick to hire the first boat he could get."

"Was he alone when he arrived?"

"No. He had a cranky, older woman with him and another young girl. Couldn't tell you who they were, though. I saw the old lady slap him on the back of the head once when he must've said something she didn't want to hear. It's just not right, when a woman intimidates a man like that."

"Thanks…."

"Glad to do business with you. Now I'd better get this boat unloaded before I pay penalties for late delivery." He turned and raised his hand, palm towards the workers, before sweeping it down in a rush and yelling, "Go!"

Arcon shook his head. *He's a few scales short of a dragon.*

He sent to Sinjenasta and Avruellen—Sinjenasta having stayed at the end of the pier to avoid causing havoc when Arcon was trying to find someone who would talk to him. *We have to leave now, Av. Morth has got her, and they've sailed into the distance. Will that captain of yours be ready to sail soon if you tell him it's urgent?*

Avruellen, who had been desperately waiting for some contact, answered immediately, *Dragons' balls! I wish you'd killed him when you had the chance. As for the captain, I'm sure for enough money he'll sing and dance the whole way too. We're coming down now.*

Blayke's loading our belongings on the horses, just in case. I'll be there shortly.

Arcon walked to where Sinjenasta waited. "This is my fault."

How so?

"First of all, I should have killed Morth when I had the chance. I should have hunted him down and finished it. And secondly, in all the excitement of seeing Avruellen, I stopped shielding. That's when Morth, or whoever he answers to, found us again. So, when Bronwyn rushed out from under your protection, they were already waiting nearby. You'd think I'd be a better realmist by now. I can't believe I made such stupid mistakes."

Sinjenasta's tail twitched. *We all make mistakes or bad calls in judgment. If I hadn't been so eager to please a god, I would be at peace by now.*

"So you regret your bargain?"

There are times, yes. I'm hoping Drakon sticks to his promise this time.

"What promise is that?"

Sinjenasta warded their conversation before he answered, *What would you want if you were me?*

With a melancholy smile, Arcon answered, "I'd want to be human again. If he's betrayed you once, he could do it again."

The bitter laugh Sinjenasta sent to Arcon sounded human enough. *Let's just say I've got something up my fur. I think for me, it might be worth sacrificing civilization as we know it.*

Arcon gasped. "You're waiting till the end to play your hand?" When he looked into Sinjenasta's eyes, he saw a new danger, but he couldn't blame him; all he could do was pray that Drakon kept his promise. *Stupid bloody gods,* he thought just before he felt a weight descend on his shoulder. He jumped and clutched his chest then realized it was Phantom, not Drakon smiting him on the spot. He laughed.

Someone's highly-strung this afternoon, said Phantom.

"Well, unlike someone I know, who's been sleeping all day, I've been trying to find Bronwyn. Morth has her, and even though he was using Blayke for bait last time, he might kill Bronwyn. I hate not knowing anything. I just wish I knew who he was working for."

The only way to find out is to catch him.

"Thanks for that intelligent conclusion. Ouch! What in Drakon's name was that for?" Arcon raised his hand to his ear and touched a drop of blood.

Phantom hooted a chuckle. *Stop complaining, Arcon; it was only a little nip. I'm here to make sure you focus and don't get lost in that silly human drama of self-pity. It helps no one.*

"There's not one day that goes by that I don't regret bonding you."

Why, thank you.

All banter ended when Avruellen swept to the end of the wharf. When Arcon saw the thunder in her eyes, he almost felt sorry for Morth—almost, but not quite. "The captain is gathering his men now. We should be ready to go within two hours. He said we should wait onboard. Follow me."

A deckhand escorted them aboard. As he walked up the gangplank, Arcon remembered something, and his heart sank. Oceans and the realmist didn't mix—the last time he had traveled on a boat, he was vomiting before they left the harbor. "If anyone needs me, I'll be in my cabin."

He cursed Drakon one last time and gritted his teeth.

Avruellen called out, "Wait." He stopped and she caught up to him. "We haven't had a chance to talk about retrieving the book. As soon as we kill Morth and get Bronny, we'll have to go straight to the Isle of the Dead Souls. Time's running out. If we don't find the information we need, we won't be able to unlock the quartz. Oh, and I forgot to tell you about some rumors floating around Carpus."

There were so many things Arcon could have said, but didn't. There was no point in stating the obvious—what if Bronwyn were already dead, what if the book wasn't there. "What rumors?"

He had a feeling he wasn't going to like what she had to say.

"I think I know where the gormons are."

Arcon huffed out a defeated sigh. "I thought you might say that. Haven't we got enough problems at the moment?"

"Apparently the gods think not. The townspeople have told me they've heard people have been going missing at Blaggard's Bay. They're not sure of numbers, but at this stage, it's around five. The only remains found of any of the victims is blood spatter."

"That doesn't mean there are any gormons there."

"No, but that true dream I had felt like somewhere around there. There have been sightings apparently, and the description sounds too close to be just a fantasy. 'An ugly type of dragon, twice the size of a man, with black skin that radiates a green glow.' It sounds as if it's attaining adult status already."

"Don't jump to conclusions. I still don't think we have enough to go on, and you know how things get distorted when people start panicking. Once we've found the book, we'll discuss going to Blaggard's Bay."

Avruellen put a hand on his arm. "They're there: I can feel it."

Arcon placed his other hand on hers. "One thing at a time."

She nodded, letting her arm drop when he walked away. It was time to find someone to talk to; she didn't want to wallow in the what-if's of whether Bronwyn was still alive. She went to find Flux and wished she had a better way of gaining luck than just crossing her fingers.

CHAPTER 15

Leon sat on the edge of the king's bed: his bed. He smiled and reached over to caress the face of his new bride as she slept, strands of golden hair splayed enticingly over her dark skin. So far his plans had gone better than he could have hoped—other than those two traitors escaping, but no matter; he had something more valuable now and would enjoy exacting his revenge.

He pulled a white shirt over his head, and then laced up knee-length boots before going to the thick crystal mantelpiece over the fireplace. It was unexpected—such a delicate decoration to have in the king's chambers, but Princess ... no, *Queen* Tusklar, he corrected himself, explained it was a portal of power. She didn't think it had been used since before the Gormon War, or so Inkra's history books said. In the hopes the palace's library would give him information on how he could use it, Leon was having the place turned upside down by scholars. A crystal stand, which appeared to grow out of the mantelpiece like a small tree with a trunk and two branches, held the crowns for the King and Queen of Inkra—one on each branch.

Leon picked the larger crown off the tree, placed it on his head and looked at himself in the gilt-framed mirror that hung above the mantle. Thin veins of gold filigree traced complicated runes just below the crown's surface. He surmised the only way to have put them there would be by using Second-Realm magic. Admiring the way the gold tracings complemented his yellow-flecked brown eyes and sandy-brown hair, Leon smiled a smile so devoid of warmth that even he noticed. *I am what they made me. Now it's time to show them who that is.*

Striding the black-tiled halls towards his captive, he contemplated his recent dreams. Ever since his marriage and coronation a week ago, when he had worn the crown for the first time, the dreams started. The first few nights he dreamt he was asleep in his new bed, shrouded in the black of night. In his dream he woke knowing something watched him. He stared into the darkness, feeling a summons and repulsion. As depraved as Leon was, he knew whoever or *whatever* watched could create suffering beyond his imaginings.

Last night, when his dream-self woke and looked into the gloom, he saw a hulking impression of a menace darker than the blackness—a space devoid of light, hope, and time. He smelled the rot and loneliness of death. A fear he had never known seeped from his pores, but there was nowhere to run. As the shape bred more detail with every dream, he knew that one night soon he would confront his future. For the first time since he was blessed with awareness, he questioned what he was getting into. He had a feeling it was already too late to go back.

He reached a heavily guarded door. The sentries bowed, eyes downcast while they opened the door. Leon's boots made no sound as he walked through the antechamber into a size-able room furnished with a large, gaudy bed, the head a slab of polished, white stone. Attached to the base, four thick, white pillars rose to the ceiling and supported a purple-fringed, black canopy. He didn't think he'd ever seen an uglier bed. The Inkrans seemed to equate taste with ostentation—something he would enjoy beating out of them.

On the other side of the bed, next to the fire, dozing on an armchair—the leather apparently dyed to match the purple fringing—was his niece, or was she his daughter? He crossed the room and studied her. Her pale skin was her mother's, but he knew her brown eyes and fair hair were his. Finally, he was taking back what was his. He would kill his brother and take Gabrielle for his own—how it should have been from the start. He would rule two kingdoms and have two wives. In fact, why not make it three? He would have as many as he damn-well pleased. It would be a shame his brother wouldn't be around to see Leon own everything that used to be his.

She must have sensed his presence, for she woke. As soon as she saw him, a scowl came over her face, lines of anger exaggerated by the dwindling fire's wavering light. She unfolded her legs and stood. "What is going on Uncle Leon? Those thugs you sent to get me let slip that you brought me here. Why? When my parents find out about this, you are going to be in so much trouble."

"What, no *hello, nice to see you, Uncle Leon*?" Verity crossed her arms in front of her chest. "I did it for your own good, Verity. Dangerous times are coming, and you'll be safer here. If I told Edmund about it, someone else may have found out, and then your life would be at risk."

"What danger?" She narrowed her eyes. She didn't trust her uncle—even though her mother never said anything, she could see her tense whenever he came into the room. Something wasn't right.

"The gormons are coming back to Talia, and the first thing they're going to do is kill any ruling families."

"Gormons? They're just a myth, or at least the stories don't sound real. Even if they were here before, that was so long ago no one can even say for sure they were here."

Leon laughed. "They're not a myth, my darling princess, any more than the dragons are a myth. I've been doing some research that suggests they might even be related to the dragons. Now get dressed. You'll find some clothes in the adjoining dressing room." He nodded at a door next to the one he had entered. "When you're dressed, you can come and meet my new wife, the queen."

At sixteen, Verity hadn't learned to school her features to neutral. Leon enjoyed seeing the surprise and questions in her eyes.

"You're married? But I thought Inkra already had a king." Understanding grabbed her by the shoulders and shook away her naiveté. This time she pretended she didn't think he was a murderer; surely he didn't, wouldn't, couldn't?

"*I* am Inkra's king now, and you are the heir to two thrones; at least until Queen Tusklar and I have children. What do you think about that?"

Verity didn't know what to think except that the fervor in her uncle's eyes was that of a dangerous man. She decided to play along, because even she could see that any resistance might mean she would never escape. It was important to work out why she was here. She had to let her father know what was going on. "I'm surprised, to be honest, but then you were always very clever and handsome. It's a good thing the princess agreed to marry you and form a stronger bond between our countries. I'm sure when father finds out, he will be pleased."

Her smile was the one she gave to unappealing suitors who attempted to woo her at dinners and balls—sufficiently pleasant without being overbearing, and since she'd had a lot of practice, it was believable.

Leon considered her for a moment. "I'm glad we're in agreement. Now choose what you wish to wear, and I'll send a servant to take you to bathe. I'm glad you're here and safe."

He kissed the top of her head and left. She loved him; of course she did—he was her uncle. Despite how he treated others, he had always been good to her, but something was off, like when your food had a subtle taste of strangeness but not enough to stop eating—a few hours later was when you paid the price. She ignored her fear and went to choose a dress, hoping the price they were all going to pay wouldn't be settled with blood.

CHAPTER 16

Bronwyn woke, the bitter taste of vetchus in her mouth—it felt like her tongue had been dried and coated in sand. Opening her eyes, she looked up to see the underside of a dark-timber bunk bed crowding over her. She heard breathing near her ear and turned her head, feeling the bed dip and rise. Slapping one hand over her mouth, she held her breath for a moment before she removed her hand. "Drakon's balls!"

"It's nice to see you too." Corrille, the best friend she hadn't seen since Sinjenasta had taken her away, leaned over and gave her a hug. "Are you okay? You've been unconscious for more than a day. Those bastards who kidnapped us gave you some kind of drug, I think."

Bronwyn slowly sat and shifted her legs over the side of the bunk so her feet touched the floor. With her elbows resting on her thighs, she buried her head in her hands. "I don't feel too well. Where are we, and how did you get here?"

"We're on a ship—the gods know where." Corrille sat next

to Bronwyn. "The day after that giant thing took you, I had a fight with your aunt. I went for a walk, and that's the last thing I remember before waking up in the back of a covered cart. Oh, my goodness, Bronny, I never thought I'd see you again." Corrille wiped her eyes with her palm.

"I never thought I'd see you again either, or Aunt Avruellen. But I did see her before I was kidnapped. Do you know who they are?"

"The man is called Morth, and the ugly woman is his mother. I think she looks like a man, and she's more scary than he is." Corrille whispered, "She bosses him around. Sometimes I don't know who's in charge."

"So now what do we do? I can't stay locked up here. I need to find everyone; we've got things we have to do."

"What things, and who's 'everyone?'"

As relieved as Bronwyn was to see her best friend, Avruellen's words sounded in her mind, and she was careful about how much she said. "Guess what? I have a brother!"

This was news she could genuinely smile about. She wondered if he was worried about her.

"What, a brother? That's wonderful news! How did you find out?" Corrille jumped up in excitement and hit her head on the bunk above. "Shit! Ow, that hurt."

She rubbed it with her hand.

"Are you okay? That sounded hard."

Corrille looked at her with a *what a stupid thing to say* look, and they both laughed.

"It's so good to see you again." Bronwyn stood carefully and hugged her friend. "Hmm, I think you'd like my brother; he's kinda cute."

"What does he look like?"

"A bit like me; we're twins. He's got dark hair, and he's tall with green eyes."

"Twins? This story just keeps getting more interesting. Do you think he'd like me?"

"Of course he would. What's not to like? Anyway, that's enough silly talk. We need to figure out how to get out of here."

A knock at the door interrupted their reunion. Bronwyn tensed, resisting the urge to reach for a corridor to the Second Realm. She was getting stronger and quicker at linking with the Realm but decided it would be better to be patient—she shouldn't to give her secret away to Corrille if she didn't have to.

A man, who Bronwyn recognized as the person who spoke to her by the sea, entered; his shoulder-length, curly, blond hair would have been more suitable on a woman, and his thin moustache ensured he looked more like a foppish noble than a kidnapper. Bronwyn wondered if the sword at his hip was for show, or if he could really use it.

"Ah, good to see you're awake. I'm Morth, and I'm here to insist you behave."

"Or what? And incidentally, why am I here?" Her plan had been to be quiet and watch, but she always felt impelled to act in confrontations, especially when she felt someone—in this case, her—was wronged. She took a step towards Morth.

"If you don't behave, we'll make sure you sleep the whole way to where we're going. As for why you're here, that's simple: Klazich has ordered it. Now there's to be no more questions."

Corrille grabbed her friend's arm. "Just listen to him. I tried to get away once, and his mother attacked me." Corrille lifted her hair and showed Bronwyn yellowed bruises around her neck.

"She tried to strangle you?" She really wanted to get her hands on Morth's mother. Deciding it didn't matter whether Corrille knew she was a realmist or not, she looked for the corridor to the Second Realm. As her speeding awareness reached the entry of the corridor, it crashed into nothing: an invisible barrier. Bronwyn fell to the ground, stunned.

Corrille bent over her. "Oh, gods, are you all right? Bronwyn, can you hear me? Bronwyn, talk to me."

She tapped Bronwyn's cheek with the ends of her fingers.

Morth laughed. "Didn't expect that, eh? What do you take us for, realmist? For that indiscretion, you two can go without food today. How do you like them apples? Ha, ha. Get it?"

He exited, shutting and bolting the door.

Bronwyn's eyes focused, and Corrille helped her sit up. "What happened?"

"I have something to tell you." Bronwyn hoped her friend wouldn't hate her for keeping such a big secret, or even for being a realmist. They had never discussed realmists before, and she had no idea whether Corrille hated them, liked them, or just didn't believe in what they could do. "I'm a realmist. I just tried to get to the Second Realm, but they've put a barrier up, and I crashed into it."

"What? What are you talking about? You can't be a realmist; they're old and have beards."

Despite the headache digging its fingers into her brain, Bronwyn giggled. "Some do, but not all. They start studying when they're young."

"I don't know if I believe you. How come you never told me before?"

"My aunt wanted it to be a secret. You don't have to

believe me—it doesn't change what I know." Bronwyn shrugged, disappointed. While glad that her friend didn't hate her for being a realmist, she was hoping Corrille would be impressed, or even surprised—but not believing her? And when had she ever lied to her friend? "I'm not feeling well. I'm going to lie down."

Corrille didn't say anything and Bronwyn watched as she climbed onto the top bunk. How was she going to get out of here without Second Realm power, and who, or what, was Klazich? Did Avruellen know where she was? She worried because they only had a certain amount of time to find the ancient book and figure out how to do the second unlocking of her amulet by the next full moon. With no ideas materializing, Bronwyn gave up thinking and, lulled by the roll of the ocean, fell asleep.

CHAPTER 17

Close to midnight, Bayerlon slept. Draped by night's dark pelt, the dragons, Agmunsten, and Arie prepared to leave. In a training field behind the castle, the realmists took to their saddles, excited. Riding on a dragon was rare and so invigorating that even Agmunsten enjoyed the rush of gliding through the cold, fresh heights, wind lifting his spirits and reminding him how amazing life could be.

"Is everyone ready?" asked Arcese.

"Yep," came the unanimous reply.

The dragons channeled earth magic, calling the heat from deep underneath Talia to come to the surface, thereby warming the air and creating additional lift. The dragons, heavy as they were, needed assistance to leave the ground—whether that was running off a cliff, jumping from a height, or invoking thermals. As they extended their wings, ready to take off, Queen Gabrielle ran out, yelling at them to wait. Both dragons stopped channeling and folded their massive wings.

Gabrielle reached them and spoke through winded breaths, "Boy's missing."

Agmunsten spoke, "How long has he been gone?"

"I don't know. I haven't been up to see him until now. I just wanted to check he was sleeping okay. I have a feeling he's gone after Edmund, thinking he can help. You have to stop him. If you find him, take him with you, but look after him, please? I would ask you to bring him back here, but I know you're in a hurry. If he runs away again, I can't afford to send soldiers to chase him."

"We'll find him. Don't worry. I forgot to mention I've also had a chat with The Academy, and I have a realmist coming to help you. Her name is Astra. She's originally from Zamahl but escaped across the sea on a trading ship when she was a teenager and found us, which was very lucky considering the rarity of Zamahlan ships coming this far west. She's been with The Academy for forty years and is one of our best teachers, especially when it comes to manipulating the power to create lightning."

"Lightning? What use am I going to have for that?"

"You'd be surprised how quickly it can cook food." He winked, but no one saw it in the dark. "Astra can do other things too. She'll keep you safe, and I can keep you updated through her."

"I'll take your word for it. Get going and stay safe." Gabrielle hurried back to the castle, and the dragons channeled again. Arcese flapped her giant wings. Arie felt the resistance as she tried to leave the ground. For a few seconds, it seemed as if they were held fast by stretchy fabric. After straining it as far as it would go, it snapped, and they were flung at a great speed, up and forward. Arie decided he much preferred the "jump off a cliff" approach.

Once the dragons settled into smooth flight, Zim sent part of his awareness to the Second Realm and scried for Boy's symbol. He soon found him—forty miles from the castle. "He's managed to get a fair way. His symbol is overlapped with another; I'm assuming he's on a horse. We'll be on him in less than an hour. I'll fly down while you go ahead. I'll catch up."

When they neared Boy, Zim descended, swooping low over him and landing in front of his plodding horse. Boy pulled hard on the reins and quickly pulled a dagger out of his belt with shaking hands.

Agmunsten jumped off Zim and reached Boy in a few large strides. "Boy, it's Agmunsten. Put the dagger away."

"Agmunsten?" His timid voice reminded the realmist that he was only ten. What sort of sabotage was he really capable of? He was just a child doing what his master told him. How could he know the consequences?

"Get down, lad. The queen is very worried. She sent us to find you. Climb up on Zim; you're coming with us."

Boy, stunned, slid off his pony and flinched as he walked past Agmunsten. "I'm not going to beat you, child. Just hop up on the dragon." He was disgusted at Boy's reaction—how many times had the child been abused that now he expected it? Agmunsten decided there were a few adults he wouldn't mind feeding to the gormons. He climbed up in front of the child. "Hang on around my waist, and whatever you do, don't let go. Okay, Zim, we're ready." Zim channeled, flapped, and they farewelled the ground.

When they had been flying for a while, Boy spoke. "Will the horse be okay?"

"Yes, lad. He'll find his way home, most likely. Even if a farmer finds him, the Laraulens brand their animals. Now tell me, what were you doing running from Bayerlon?"

"It's not that I wanted to leave Bayerlon; I just wanted to help the King get Verity back."

"And how do you think you were going to do that, eh?"

"I figured I'd think of something by the time we got there."

"You bloody kids think war is glorious or easy, or, I don't know. Chances are you would have died in the cold with no food before you even caught up to the king. You're with us now, and I expect to be obeyed. I won't think twice about using the Second Realm to make sure you can't move if you even think about going against what I say. Have I made myself clear?"

"Yes, sir."

They flew the remainder of the night; Boy snuggled against Agmunsten's back. Agmunsten thought ahead to what they had to do when they arrived at Klendar. Whatever they did had to be done quickly, before Leon knew they were coming; two dragons couldn't escape notice for long in the open—the terrain within one hundred miles of the castle was mildly hilly scrubland, thin forest with no caves or thick stands of trees to speak of. Pernus had filled them in on what to expect.

After a few hours flying northwest, Agmunsten noticed the black sky lightening to dark gray, the change so subtle it came without warning. "I think it's time to land. We're not far from the border, so there's still places to hide. I'm sure there's a cave around down there somewhere."

Zim answered, "When was the last time you were in Inkra, my friend?"

"Hmm, about forty years ago, but caves don't just get up and walk away."

"I was thinking more of how good your memory is, and you could have crossed the border anywhere."

"True, but it was west of Feldon, so I've narrowed it down."

"Yes, great. You've narrowed it down to within one-thousand miles."

There was nothing to say to that, so they descended in silence and searched for a place to hide. Two more nights of flying and they would reach Klendar. Agmunsten's heart beat faster as he imagined confronting Leon. As much as they wanted to arrest him, chances were he wouldn't come willingly. Someone would die, and the realmist didn't think it would be him. He had known Leon since he was born, and even though he hadn't turned out as he hoped, killing him was not something he was looking forward to. He would make sure it was quick. Maybe he should have brought Astra with him—delegating the job to someone who was good with lightning bolts sounded good to him right now.

Zim landed next to Arcese at the base of a small hill. There was enough light for Agmunsten to appreciate the mass of trees that would cloak them while they slept. They were far from any thoroughfare and were unlikely to be disturbed. Boy and Arie remained silent while they walked as far into the forest as they could—only stopping when the gaps between trees were too narrow for the dragons to pass. Zim spoke out loud since Boy didn't have the skill of listening with his mind. "Arie, I'd like you to take first watch, and Agmunsten will take the second. Arcese and I don't usually need a lot of sleep, but we've been flying all night and my wings ache. I could do with a good nap."

Boy and Agmunsten watched as both dragons curled into balls, their skin shimmering to a gray-brown imitation of large boulders.

"I didn't know they could do that." Boy was clearly impressed.

"You learn something new every day, hey lad?" Agmunsten and Boy lay down. Before too long, Arie could hear his teacher and one of the "boulders" snoring. He chuckled and hoped if anyone came near, they were hard of hearing. Settling in to watch for a few hours, he crossed his fingers and prayed they wouldn't be disturbed—Inkrans weren't renowned for their hospitality. The wait began.

CHAPTER 18

After dinner on the second night, they gathered in Arcon's room. Too sick to get out of bed, the realmist lay on his bunk, a bowl within easy reach. Avruellen commandeered the only chair in the room, so Blayke sat on the floor next to Sinjenasta. Out of habit, Avruellen spoke aloud. "I've warded our conversation. There's not much use shielding ourselves, as I'm sure whoever has been watching us knows we're after Bronwyn." The realmist waved her hand in front of her face. "For goodness sake! How does a squeeto get out here? The last thing I need is for tiny bugs to be hatching out of my skin." This time she brought her other hand up and clapped in the air. "Got it. Now, as I was saying … what was I saying? Oh, yes, I spoke to the captain this afternoon. His man in the crow's nest says the dot is getting bigger."

"By dot, do you mean the boat we're chasing?"

"Yes, Blayke. What other *dot* would I be talking about?"

"Just checking."

"So, as well as gaining distance on them, the captain said the only place he could be heading for is Aspurle and Blaggard's Bay. Apparently there are no other islands in that direction for at least two weeks, and if we can believe the talk around the docks, the ship only had supplies for a few days."

Arcon groaned, from feeling sick or dreading what that meant, no one could tell. "Are we grabbing Bronwyn and getting her out, or are we looking for the gormon too?"

Avruellen answered, "I think we stand a good chance of killing it, two against one."

"Hang on. I'm here too," Blayke said.

Arcon's voice, although low, was in a tone that forewarned against arguing. "I need you to help Sinjenasta get Bronwyn back to the boat. We can't afford to lose anyone. My sister and I might decide we have to retreat, and I don't want to have any extras to worry about. We're on limited time."

"Yes," interrupted Avruellen, "the captain said it's about five days from here to the Isle of the Dead Souls if the wind favours us, and even if we find the book straight away, it might take some time to find the part we're looking for. The full moon is in nine days: that's not a lot of time to waste."

"What happens if we miss the full moon? Can't we just wait for the next one?"

"No, Blayke. If we miss it, according to the prophecy, the gormons will be upon us before we do the last activation, and then it will be too late. The amulets are the key to defeating the gormons—without them there is no way. And don't ask me how because I don't know." Arcon propped himself up on one elbow and hovered his mouth over the bowl. Nothing came out. He dropped his head onto the pillow. "I hate boats."

Sinjenasta sat up and curled his sleek tail around his feet. "How far ahead are they? If they land too far ahead, they could do anything to Bronwyn before we get there. I'm blocked from feeling her, but surely I'd know if she died."

"They're about three hours ahead. It's not much," Avruellen answered.

"That's too far for my liking. I think I'm going to call up some extra wind, see if we can't speed this boat up."

"Be careful, panther, you don't want to tire yourself out. Who knows what's waiting for us. Now, I need to go to sleep; it's the only escape from this rotten ship I can find." Arcon rolled over, indicating the conversation was over.

The others climbed above deck. Avruellen stood with the captain, a squat man with dreadlocks and a cropped brown beard. Blayke, with Fang nestled in his shirt pocket, joined Sinjenasta at the prow of the timber vessel. The panther stood quietly, staring in the direction of where he thought Bronwyn must be. His stare glazed over as he concentrated. *Drakon, are you there?*

Yes. What is it?

What's waiting at Blaggard's Bay?

There is a gormon. He's preparing for the arrival of the horde. If you're going to ask me if you could kill him, I don't know. If I knew the future, by definition, it would be unchangeable. I do know the gormons will come through, with or without the one who is already there. And for you to fight thousands is still what will need to be done. Will one less make any difference?

So you're saying leave it? Drakon remained silent, and Sinjenasta realized the god had gone. The panther snarled, and Blayke, who had been watching him trance, pulled his sword out of its scabbard, anticipating an attack. *Put that away, cub.*

Blayke relaxed. "Why the growl?"

Just having a conversation with the dragon god. He has no concept of manners, which surprises me since his dragons are Talia's foremost author-

ities on etiquette. Sinjenasta swished his tail and sat down. He sent to Avruellen and Arcon. *Drakon says there is one gormon at Blaggard's Bay. He's hinted we shouldn't risk it because there are thousands about to get here.* Silence stretched until he spoke again. *Hello? Avruellen, Arcon?*

Sorry, I'm here, said Avruellen. *I just don't know how to answer. Thousands? When?*

He didn't say.

He might not know. Arcon's mind voice sounded just as ill as his real one.

He can't see into the Third Realm very well. When I was living with him and we tried, it was like looking through a heat wave that contained a dust storm. You can see shadows but nothing else, and hearing conversations is like listening to someone talk underwater. As you know, the gormons have black symbols and are invisible in the Second Realm.

Arcon paused before he answered. *If it's an easy kill, do it, but we can't afford to go chasing about the island. We have to get to the Isle of the Dead Souls. Getting Bronwyn might take all the realmists and time we have.* Sinjenasta cocked his head to the side and waited.

I'm not happy about this, but okay. Avruellen spoke with the voice she reserved for chastising people.

Whatever you want. Now excuse me while I throw up. Sinjenasta was glad Arcon broke the link before he had to listen to any more.

Can you watch me please, Blayke?

Blayke, who had re-sheathed his sword, nodded. "Do you need any help?"

No, but if I call you to the Second Realm, be ready to come.

"Okay." Blayke tensed.

Sinjenasta lay on the deck and shut his luminous eyes. He sped through the dark tunnel to the Second Realm, the sea breeze on his face mimicking what he might have felt had his body been hurtling through the space between realms. He became his symbol. The thought to absorb power automatic, his symbol immediately pulsated as he drew power from the space around him, which was pregnant with energy. When he collected what he needed, he carried it back with his awareness, attached by familiarity—the energy knew him because he had touched it, and it obeyed.

Sinjenasta threw the power out, mentally intoning a recipe for heat. Far in front of the ship, he blanketed the air with warmth. Within a few minutes the colder air behind and above them rushed in to sink under the warmer air. Blayke's ears popped as the air pressure changed and the wind increased, filling the sails to capacity and causing the two masts to creak. The ship leapt forward and ploughed through newly formed whitecaps. Salty spray spattered Blayke's face.

"What happened?" Avruellen, wearing a hooded cloak, appeared to materialize out of nowhere.

Sinjenasta answered. *I've given us a little help. It will only last about an hour because my reach wasn't as far as I'd like. It will be just enough so we can hopefully land just after Morth.*

"I hope you know what you're doing."

Sinjenasta raised one furry eyebrow; the back and forth sweep of his tail warned her to curb her rebuke. Avruellen sniffed and returned to her room. Blayke noted the exchange and realized Sinjenasta must have a lot more power than he originally thought. No one stood up to a realmist like that and got away with it, especially not one of The Circle. As the ship fell and rose with the swell, Blayke gripped the railing and hoped the big cat really was on their side. *We're coming, Bronwyn. Hang on; we're coming.*

CHAPTER 19

Bronwyn woke to the slosh of water lapping against the hull. Shouts of, "Throw the rope," and "Steady now," filtered down to her prison. The ship had docked. She reached out with her mind and gently prodded the barrier blocking her from the Second Realm. There were no gaps, nothing to squeeze her awareness through. She despaired at being cut off from her power, but then she remembered her natural magic.

Quietly she rolled out of bed and crouched, placing her hands on the floor. She sent vibrations of awareness into the timber but found no rivers of power. Dead timber really was dead, it turned out.

The realmist also thought of her weapons for the first time. She hoped they hadn't thrown away the sword and dagger Avruellen had given her. Feeling naked without them, she pretended she held her sword and practiced her forms in the cramped space, realizing how difficult it would be to fight in such confined quarters. Being told and experiencing it were two different things.

Hearing a key in the lock, Bronwyn turned to the door. When it opened, in barged a large woman, taller than Bronwyn, wearing a knee-length brown dress belted where her waist should have been, a dagger clutched in her masculine fingers. The light from the one porthole wasn't particularly good, but Bronwyn was sure the woman had a shadow of a moustache above her sour mouth. "Git up, yer lazy cow."

Corrille, who had woken when the door opened, jumped down and curtseyed.

"I'm sorry, madame."

The woman turned malicious, beady eyes on Bronwyn. "Where are your manners, girl? Curtsey when a lady enters the room."

Bronwyn coughed into her hand. "When is the lady getting here?"

As soon as she said it, she knew she should have kept her mouth shut.

For a large woman, she moved fast, pinning Bronwyn against the wall with the dagger pressing a white line across her throat. The woman spoke, her nose an inch from the realmist's. Fish-scented breath struck Bronwyn's face with every word. "Shut it. One more word from you, and I don't care what my orders are: you're dead." She emphasized her words by adjusting the point of the blade and pricking Bronwyn's skin, holding the knife up to her face to show her the fresh dewdrop of red. "Now, out!"

Corrille, who stood slack-jawed throughout Bronwyn's ordeal, hurried to obey. Bronwyn followed her out, stumbling from a shove in the back. The realmist was so angry she wanted to cry. As soon as she was on land, she would see if the Talian magic worked.

But what to do about Corrille? Her friend seemed so scared that she might not run when the time came, and she couldn't leave her, could she? *Okay, don't think about that now. Deal with it if it happens.* When they reached the dock, Morth waited. "Ah, Mother. I see you've met Bronwyn." The way he rolled the 'r' in her name almost made her laugh, which made her question her sanity. *How can I possibly want to laugh at a time like this?*

"Stop your talking and let's go. It's waiting."

Bronwyn surveyed the island as they walked. If she did escape, where would she go? And was Sinjenasta on her trail? Maybe she would just have to wait and see where they were going. Avruellen's constant reminder sounded in her head: be patient. If it was one thing she hated, it was waiting and being told to be patient.

The dock ended at a cobbled road, which rose gradually and disappeared behind the cliff in front of them. Instead of taking this road, Morth angled left and walked towards the base of a cliff where a narrow path wormed between boulders and twiggy bushes that would have looked dead if not for the brightest pink flowers Bronwyn had ever seen clinging to them.

Bronwyn didn't have time to check if the Talian magic worked here, because all her concentration was needed for the climb. Several times Corrille slipped on loose stones and slid backwards into Bronwyn. Each time, Morth's mother would yell, "Hurry up, clumsy! We haven't got all day."

After more than an hour, Bronwyn watched Morth disappear over the lip of the cliff. Corrille scrambled over, crying in relief, and as Bronwyn placed her feet on level ground once again, she froze. It was like she had walked face-first into a giant spiderweb. She wanted to brush at her skin, and adrenalin flooded her body. Bronwyn jumped when Morth's mother prodded her, none too gently, from behind. "Keep going."

Trying to ignore the disturbing sensation, Bronwyn, against all instinct, walked on but checked her hair for spiders, just in case. Not far from the top of the cliff, Morth turned left and travelled parallel with the coast. The closer they drew to their destination, the more jumpy Bronwyn became. It felt like spiders crawled over her body, hundreds of tiny, hairy feet prickling her skin, causing a surge of goose bumps to spring up, covering her arms and legs. She stopped.

Wherever they were going, Bronwyn knew once they got there, she would never leave. It was apparent no help was coming. It was time to help herself and do what Avruellen had trained her to do her whole life. If she got it wrong, well, at least she had tried. She burrowed her awareness into the ground and found what she was looking for: a thick stream of power just waiting to be tapped.

"Keep going." Bronwyn's least favorite person pushed her with a meaty fist.

"No." Bronwyn turned to face the tyrant. "This is where I tell you what a horse's ass you are and take my friend and leave."

"Bronwyn, no, don't! They'll kill you." Corrille and Morth stopped, while his mother readied her dagger, yet again, raising the tip to Bronwyn's face.

Without taking her eyes off Morth's mother, Bronwyn answered her friend, "Corrille, if we go wherever they're taking us, that's it. We're dead." To Morth's mother, she said, "I hope whatever you're getting paid is worth dying for."

With fury in her eyes, the older woman grabbed Bronwyn's arm and opened her mouth to deliver a threat, which

Bronwyn cut off. Holding as much of the power as she could, she opened both palms outward, towards Morth's mother. Staring into the depths of her depraved eyes, Bronwyn didn't flinch as she released the ball of white-hot energy flowing through her veins.

Bronwyn had never released that amount of power at one time and the force caused her to stumble backwards—the woman's grip on her arm ripped free. The realmist held her gaze and saw her face twist in pain and surprise as she felt the missile blast a hole right through her middle. The sizzling heat cauterized the wound: even after Morth's mother lay dead on the scattered rocks and stubs of gray grasses, no blood stained the ground; however, scented tendrils of burnt flesh lingered.

Satisfied she was dead, Bronwyn, overcome with dizziness, fell to her knees.

"No!" Morth ran to his mother. He caressed her face and kissed her cheek. Crouching, he turned wild eyes on Bronwyn. "You!" Not bothering to stand up, he crawled to her and grabbed a fistful of her long, dark hair. Yanking it back so her throat was exposed, he pulled his own dagger from a sheath strapped to his ankle. Bronwyn recognized the intricate patterns and thought how ironic that she would be killed with the blade given with love by her aunt. She tried to reach for more power but couldn't hold more than a trickle—maybe enough to sting him like a squeeto. *Oh well*, she thought as she directed it between his eyes. It was enough to surprise him, and he released her hair.

As soon as he let go, she brought the heel of her hand up and smashed him in the nose. Morth fell backwards, bleeding and drawing Second Realm power as he went. Bronwyn dragged herself to her feet and without looking back, shouted at Corrille to follow. Bronwyn forced her weak legs to move. She staggered past Morth, towards the cliff track. She heard crackling behind her and dropped flat to the ground. A bolt of lightning exploded a stunted tree three feet from where she lay, sparks showering the ground near her face.

"No!" Corrille screamed. Bronwyn rolled over to see Morth, energy radiating from his hands, gathering force.

"No one kills my mother and gets away with it." He prepared to release the next lightning bolt, and Bronwyn wished Corrille was braver—her friend could have pushed him, hit him, anything to give them a chance, but she stood still, mouth open wide in horror. Bronwyn felt wisps of hair rise with static and fought the temptation to shut her eyes. She wanted to leave this world in a way that would make her aunt proud, not cowering like a rabbit.

"Stop!" Bronwyn recognized the voice, relief flooding her. "Put your hands down, Morth." She looked up and saw her brother—he had come to save her! But then she panicked: what if Morth killed Blayke?

"Well, if it isn't my former kidnappee." Morth's mouth twisted up at one corner. Disheveled hair and dirt-smudged pants made him look crazy and almost pathetic, but Blayke made no mistake; the power coursing through Morth's body was lethal. Morth raised his arm, but Blayke was ready. He said not a word. Pupils dilating, he pushed away the nausea he felt at killing another person and freed the fingers of flame. Morth's beard and hair combusted, followed by his skin, which smoked and blistered. His demise smelt worse than his mother's. The onshore wind carried his haunting scream to nearby caves.

An answering shriek reached them as melting skin mixed with ash on the ground. Sinjenasta's voice sounded in the realmists' minds. *That's the gormon. We have to get out of here, now. Blayke, you get Bronwyn's friend. I'll help Bronwyn. Come on.*

"Wait. My dagger." Bronwyn ran past Blayke and threw herself at the mess on the ground, looking for the gleam of her weapon. Spying it, she swallowed down vomit and reached her fingers towards the dagger, shuddering when she touched the firming goo. She snatched it up and ran towards the cliff.

As they descended the steep slope, Bronwyn slid on her backside at times, thankful for the sturdy tufts of grass she grabbed to steady herself. "Where's Avruellen?" Bronwyn asked Sinjenasta.

She's with Arcon, minding the ship and making sure we have a clear getaway. We need to get to the Isle of the Dead Souls as fast as possible, and it wouldn't do to lose our boat while we're not looking.

Bronwyn swore as rocks and sharp fronds grazed and cut her palms. The trip down was quicker than the trip up, and it wasn't long before they reached the ship, Arcon and Avruellen standing on the wharf, smiling in relief. Avruellen snatched Bronwyn in a hug. "Okay," came Bronwyn's muffled voice, "you can let go now."

Avruellen reluctantly put her arms down and shooed Bronwyn towards the boat.

As she climbed aboard, Bronwyn looked back to check on Blayke and Corrille. He had his arm around her waist, helping her walk. She limped along and smiled up at him. *What? She didn't even get hurt. Give me a break.* Bronwyn knew she shouldn't be jealous, but Corrille was beginning to annoy her. Had she not learnt anything since she had been kidnapped? Wasn't it Bronwyn who was almost disintegrated?

Bronwyn didn't want to be confined again so stayed at the bow and watched the gray clouds gather in the distance. Avruellen stood quietly, reassuringly at her shoulder.

"Why didn't the gormon attack us?" Bronwyn hugged herself, rubbing her arms.

"Until their skin grows thick enough, the sun burns them. Infants rarely go outside during the day. Although that one should be almost mature by now. Maybe it didn't want to take on three realmists at once? What happened up there?"

"I killed Morth's mother, and Blayke killed Morth. I used Talian magic." Sinjenasta, who sat next to Bronwyn, leaned against her, his weight a calming touch.

"Talian magic. Where did you learn that?"

"At Vellonia. Arcese taught us. I burnt Morth's mother through the middle with a really, really hot ball of white energy. It wasn't pretty, but it was effective. She wasn't very nice. It did take everything I had, though. I couldn't draw any more power after that."

"I see. If it's anything like Second-Realm power, you have to build up your strength by using it. We'll have practice sessions every afternoon. When we battle the gormons, you'll need to be as strong as possible—there is no way one white-hot ball of anything will kill them all. Bronwyn?"

"Yes?"

"Look at me, please." Avruellen waited for her to turn around. "I'm sorry I wasn't honest with you about your parents. Sometimes we do what we think is best for the most people. Even when you were old enough, I was still scared to say anything because I thought you would hate me. I let my fear lead me to make a bad decision. I'm sorry. Can you forgive me?"

Bronwyn was surprised into silence. Her aunt never, ever apologized for anything. "I forgive you. I'm still a bit angry, but I know why you did it. I just wish you didn't have to." She briefly squeezed Avruellen's hand. "So, we're off to The Isle of the Dead Souls, I hear. Sounds interesting."

Avruellen returned her niece's smile.

"I remember a time, not too long ago, when you didn't want to go anywhere."

"Who, me? No way. That must have been some other girl."

As the crew lifted oars and hoisted sails, Bronwyn and Avruellen enjoyed a rare moment of peace. They had a small victory today. As Bronwyn looked over to Blayke, Corrille, and Arcon, she saw they were enjoying it too. She had quickly learnt you took what happiness you could get and didn't dwell on the stuff you couldn't change. But she couldn't help feeling left out as her best friend slipped her hand into Blayke's. She was just starting to get to know her brother, but she had a feeling he would run out of time to spend with her now.

Don't worry, Bronwyn. You have me. Sinjenasta broke her train of thought.

"Yes, I do, and I'm grateful." Leaning down, she hugged the panther and sneezed. "Can you do me a favor?"

"Anything."

"Do you mind if I shave you? Then I'd be able to cuddle you without sneezing."

What? I beg your pardon. No one shaves me. I refuse to go naked. What do you think this is? You women are never happy.

Bronwyn laughed. "Careful, Sinje. You're starting to sound like a man." Sinjenasta wanted to say something but thought she'd had enough shocks for one day. How could you tell the woman you loved that your relationship was based on lies? At least it wasn't hard for a panther to hide its feelings. She would never have to know.

The crew pulled in the oars as the sails filled, driving them ahead. The realmists withdrew to the low-ceilinged stateroom to discuss strategies before Arcon became too sick to participate.

Avruellen still mistrusted Corrille, so she sent the girl to be entertained by the captain, who had many stories of wild sea crossings and escapes from pirates. Bronwyn was happy she had her family to herself again, and even though she knew it was wrong, she wondered if she would have been happier if Blayke had not saved her friend. *What is wrong with you? She's your best friend.* Shaking her head free of such disloyal thoughts, she heard Arcon say, "The time is nearing when the gormons will arrive; we could have only a few days left. We can't afford to make any mistakes. We need to find the ancient tome, read the relevant parts and activate the quartz. Any questions?" When no one answered, he grabbed the bucket that had become his constant companion. "If you'll all excuse me, I'm going to bed."

As soon as Arcon passed through the door, they heard him expunge the contents of his stomach, hopefully, into the bucket. "Why me?" Arcon moaned as he staggered down the dark passageway and shut himself in his room. He wasn't sure what he dreaded more: being sick for five days or arriving at their destination. The time of action was upon them and he couldn't believe he was spending most of it vomiting. *Being a realmist had its perks indeed*, he thought sarcastically as he bent over the bucket one more time.

CHAPTER 20

Mirrors. Everywhere Leon looked, his reflection multiplied into infinity. This small dining room was anything but cozy. With mirrors on every wall, floor, and ceiling, the room and its contents appeared to shrink and repeat, shrink and repeat into a cold forever. *Is that where I'm heading?* thought Leon in a brief moment of self-reflection.

He tilted his head down to avoid seeing hundreds of himself spoon the spicy pudding into his mouth. Tusklar, who had finished eating, stood and walked around behind him. Kneading his shoulders, she spoke. "Why so tense, my love?"

He put the spoon down and closed his eyes, enjoying the feel of her manipulating fingers. "I just want everything to go as planned."

"It will. I have spoken with Klar. He has assured me that after the rites tonight, Verity will be blessed. She is to be elevated as are you and I. We will rule alongside the gormons. They have promised Klar they will leave many alive. We can be in charge of the breeding program." Her fingers worked harder into his flesh, and he groaned at the blissful pain.

"So, in a few hours we will all be initiated. Thank you for helping me." He held her hand and brought it to his lips, kissing her palm. He stood and faced her. "Once this happens, there will be no going back. The future is ours to control."

Tusklar's throaty laugh contained darkness. She now knew the voice inside her head was a gormon priest, but it served her to let Leon think this was all Klar's doing. Both she and High Priest Zuk had been surprised that Leon had not been shocked at the gormons' involvement—he, of course, didn't realize how closely they guided his wife, but he was happy to form an alliance, especially if it was in the name of a god.

High Priest Zuk salivated. What neither Leon nor Tusklar knew was how complete their indoctrination into gormon culture would be, and that soon Zuk would be free to take his own body—that of Verity. The gormon wondered, in passing, how Leon would react. He cackled in Tusklar's mind. Infected by the priest's mood, she laughed too.

❧

Verity had spent the past two days exploring the castle, getting to know as much about it as she could, just in case an opportunity for escape presented itself. Two black-clad guards followed her, but they were quiet and she soon forgot they were there.

The palace décor was macabre, with black-marble floors, tapestries on the walls that depicted violence and death, and sculptures twisted into surreal caricatures of people and animals sometimes both inhabiting the same body, Verity could not help but feel smothered by darkness. It was with relief she discovered the kitchen on the lower level. A gigantic room with several ovens, cream-colored flagstone floors, and three times more bench space than at Bayerlon, a plethora of cooks and their assistants labored at baking bread, chopping vegetables and seasoning stews. The aromas made her mouth water, and after she tentatively watched for a while, one of the head cooks, a plump woman with olive skin and almond-shaped, violet eyes, motioned her to come and taste something.

Outside the kitchen, in all other parts of the palace she had seen, Verity noticed that no one made eye contact—fear dictated everything. The kitchen seemed a safe haven where the staff saw her and tried to communicate. Even though they couldn't speak the same language, they sometimes made themselves understood, and Verity felt safe for the first time since being kidnapped. She wondered what the people of Inkra thought about Leon and Tusklar's coup.

Sitting on a stool, nibbling on a piece of freshly baked, crusty olive bread, Verity wondered how she could escape. The more of Leon she had seen, the more crazy he appeared. He had changed for the worse since coming here. The other night, when she had been introduced to the queen, looking into her cerulean eyes had been like looking through the sky into the Third Realm. Something dark dwelt just beyond sight, like an unseen hand ready to shoot out and grab an unsuspecting throat.

Verity knew by the meal being cooked that dinnertime neared. It was time for her to bathe and attend Leon and Tusklar in the dress that had been chosen for her. When the queen had laid it upon her bed this morning, Verity had been shocked at its lacy sheerness. The dress reached her feet; however, the delicate gaps in the black fabric allowed her skin to show through. It was scandalous. Her parents never would have allowed anyone to wear such a garment in their home.

She slid off the stool and waved goodbye to the closest thing she had to friends in this place and climbed three floors to her room. As she contemplated the humiliating garment on her bed, she suddenly feared it would be the last thing she ever wore. Since she had never been one for premonitions, Verity shook her head, banishing the thought. Grabbing her towel, she reluctantly made her way to the washroom.

To Verity's relief, dinner was held in the great hall, but it remained empty save for the king and queen, servants, and Tusklar's realmist, Orphael. Even with limited company, the young princess blushed through the entire dinner, finding her appetite diminished. While she was relieved the tight-fitting shame didn't expose her nipples, there was enough pale skin and curves showing that she felt like a prostitute. She resisted the urge to fold her arms in front of her chest or undo her hair, which formed an elegant bun at the back of her head, to let it fall and provide some protection—she didn't want them to gain any pleasure from her distress.

All through dinner, Queen Tusklar watched Verity with predatory eyes. Verity wished she wore looser clothes, something in which one could hide a knife. Verity felt like something was going to happen. No one spoke: unusual when small talk normally accompanied dinner. Leon seemed lost in his own thoughts, Orphael's lips moved at times, like he was repeating something in order to remember it, and Tusklar alternated between staring into space and staring at Verity.

Tusklar broke the silence with barely a whisper. "It is time."

Leon looked at Verity. "Our destiny awaits, Princess. Are you ready?"

"I'm not sure, Uncle. What's going to happen? Will I have to do anything? Will others watch?"

"You will see. Trust me."

Everyone stood, chairs squeaking on the black marble, sending shivers down Verity's back. Leon led the way up three flights of stairs, past the level that contained the bedrooms, to the level that contained the library, and now to a level she had not explored. Fewer torches lined the walls, throwing heavy shadows in the wake of their passage. As they continued, Verity felt the cool air flow against the exposed parts of her skin; she shivered. Muffled, booted steps of the men and the clicking of the queen's high heels the only sounds.

Their destination was a set of curved double doors at the end of the hall. The heavy black doors were tattooed with crimson symbols—it looked to Verity like blood written in the night sky. Orphael placed his palms on both doors and, in a flat voice that sounded to Verity devoid of life, intoned, *"Ishten abouklir fenemas kline."* He removed his hands from the doors, and the symbols oscillated before Verity heard a loud hiss and the doors swung slowly inward.

Orphael's dark robe fluttered behind him as he entered. Verity followed Leon and Tusklar in, two almost-invisible guards behind her. The vast, round room reminded Verity of the observatory in Bayerlon. She marveled at ornate columns, runes scratched into their surface, and the domed glass roof. In the center stood a circular table of russet marble, attached to the floor by a single, wide leg—like a flower growing out of stone, it appeared to sprout out of the floor. A thick book, covered in finely woven, golden threads, sat on the table, flanked by a ruby-encrusted dagger, three bowls, unlit candles, and the most grotesque skull Verity had ever seen.

Orphael lit the candles with an arrogant click of his fingers. As he leafed through the heavy tome, Verity scanned the room, noticing empty chairs in the shadows lining the walls. On the northern perimeter, two thrones hulked in the darkness—the princess caught intermittent glints, which suggested gold or jewels set in the timber.

Orphael looked up. "It is time, my king."

The lanky-haired realmist raised his hands to shoulder-height and rapidly clapped his hands twice in a gesture that in other circumstances would have had Verity laughing in a heap on the floor. Wall torches flared to life, and the shadows to the right of Verity disappeared as fire suddenly filled the previously unseen fireplace. Everyone's eyes were drawn to the mantel above the fireplace, which held the two crystal crowns from Leon's boudoir.

"King Leon, Queen Tusklar, please approach the table."

Leon took his wife's hand, and together they stood next to the table and faced the fire. With no warning, Verity was grabbed from behind, her wrists bound tight before she could move. "Uncle, help me!"

Turning his head towards her, his expression nonchalant, he smiled. "It's for your own good, my child."

"What? What's happening?" Verity struggled but it made no difference. The black-clad men seated her in one of the vacant thrones and tied her to it, looping rope around her waist to be knotted at the back of the chair. And what did Leon mean by "my child?" He had never called her that before, and the way he said it bothered her. It was almost as if he was insinuating that he was her father. *How ridiculous,* she thought. *He really is mad.* She tried to force her wrists free, but the rope didn't give. Orphael's chanting broke through her thoughts, and she looked up, mesmerized and terrified by what she saw.

The realmist held Leon's hand and sliced Leon's wrist, blood flowing freely into one bowl. Orphael then took Tusklar's hand and did the same. When both bowls were full, the black-clad sentries cauterized the flesh with an iron brand already heated in the fire. Leon groaned through clenched teeth, and Tusklar screamed. Within moments, the stench slithered to Verity. She coughed and gagged, doubly wishing her hands were free so she could cover her mouth and nose.

Orphael took both bowls to the fireplace. Leon and Tusklar followed, stopping behind him. The realmist raised both bowls above his head. *"Verthist arkrolmin chandar.* I summon the darkest spirit from the Forgotten Realm."

He threw both bowls into the flames.

Both crystal crowns, attached by an ethereal chord of silver, floated above their stands and sailed to Leon and Tusklar, hovering for a moment before alighting on their heads. The air around them darkened, and the pressure in the room dropped. Scalding power, sucked from somewhere Verity couldn't see, swarmed into the crystal. The crowns melted into the monarchs' heads. The air thickened, expanding with heat. A fissure, cracking like a graveyard of bones breaking one by one, rent the roof as if it were a thin sheet of ice.

Orphael ran, taking cover under the table. Leon and Tusklar were trapped in the sphere of darkness as deadly shards rained down, glancing off their near-invisible barrier and smashing on the stone floor. Verity, seated against the wall, escaped the worst of it but for one icicle-shaped spike, which impaled her foot through her flimsy slipper. She cried out and closed her eyes, but not for long. A roaring filled the void above, sounding to Verity like thousands of tortured spirits moaning, shrieking—a call from evil incarnate.

She watched the shadow around her uncle and his wife coalescing. As it did, the king and queen swelled and twisted, metamorphosing into an atrocity Verity could never have imagined. She shrank into her chair, tears falling unbidden. Absorbing the black atmosphere around it as it grew, the creature became as one; all traces of Leon and Tusklar were gone. When the noise ceased, the monstrosity stood at full height: twice as tall as a dragon.

Thick, pustulated, green skin, slick and dripping with a slimy membrane as if it had just hatched, covered the creature, from its thorny tail to its too-long, snouted face. Deep-set eyes, as red as a nightmare cliché, glowed under a flat forehead brimming with spikes. The creature appeared confused for a time before it focused on Orphael, who, head barely visible, peered out from under the table.

In a voice that whistled eerily, like the last breath escaping a dying man, a hint of Leon and Tusklar's voices overlaid a deeper, more sinister presence. "Orphael, stand and face us."

The realmist scrambled from under the table and bowed before standing to look up at the creature's face. "M . . . m . . . my king?"

"That's right. Your queen is here too, and we have a guest with us. But only for a short time." The creature—an amalgamation of a gormon, Leon, and Tusklar—looked at Verity. "Ah, there she is: right where we left her." Dizziness overcame Verity as she sat pinioned under its scrutiny.

"Orphael, bring her here, and we will bless her with a gift from our gormon brothers and sisters."

Upon reaching the princess, Orphael noticed her injured

foot. Mumbling an incantation, the glass dissolved into sand, which soon turned red as the tide of her blood seeped out. The realmist untied her hands, sensing she was too stunned to fight. Verity remained in the chair and held onto its arms so he couldn't drag her away, her pleading eyes begging him to help her.

"Come now, Princess. Your destiny cannot be avoided. It is a great destiny, to be sure." He grabbed her arm, pulling until her fingers tore loose of the throne.

"No, no. Please, no."

"Stop it. That is no way for royalty to act. Pull yourself together!"

He grabbed her shoulders and shook. Dazed, and seeing no sympathy in his eyes, she looked to the *thing* that used to be her uncle and swallowed against the bile in her throat. *If that happened to them, what in the Third Realm is about to happen to me?*

Orphael half-dragged Verity to stand on the opposite side of the table to where the creature stood. He addressed it. "What should I call you, masters?"

"The coming of us has been foretold in gormon legend. We are infused with the spirit of the most powerful gormon priest ever to have lived. His knowledge, his experience … his power—all ours. You will call us Kwaad." Kwaad reached down and, ever so lightly, touched the end of its claw to the priest's cheek. Blood emerged, sliding to his jaw. Kwaad leaned over the realmist and licked the morsel with a rough, acidic tongue. Orphael screamed as the saliva burnt his skin. "Mmm, tasty."

Kwaad laughed.

"And now it's time for High Priest Zuk to transform our lovely Verity." Kwaad's red eyes bored into Verity as if a mere look could move her to action against the very core of her being. "Take the skull in your hand."

Verity fought the terror that compelled her to obey. The skull had changed from when she had first seen it. A green light radiated from the long-empty eye sockets, reaching through the ruins of the roof to the night sky beyond. She didn't know what would happen when she touched the skull, but she knew it wouldn't be pretty. Caught between wanting to scream and disappear, she heard her dress rip as she fell to her knees. Fragments of glass sliced her hands and knees as she crawled frantically, trying to get away, blood smearing across the floor. Had her brain been capable of rational thought, she would have known she never could have escaped.

She felt, rather than heard, the creature. As Kwaad's rasping breath descended behind her, Verity's voice broke forth. She screamed.

CHAPTER 21

The Isle of the Dead Souls came into muffled view—a shadowed shape in the still, dark night. Bronwyn sat in a rowboat with Sinjenasta, Avruellen, and an oarsman. Sheltered bays were a scarcity on the island, and because of a lack of visitors, the only inhabitants of the island, the monks of the Sacred Realm, deemed wharves a low priority. The ship stayed anchored beyond the shallows.

Bronwyn listened in between the rhythmic splash of the oars, to Blayke and Corrille talking in the boat in front. It seemed they were getting along very well, *too* well. Blayke spoke to her friend more than he spoke to her, his own twin sister! When Bronwyn had tried to get into the boat with Blayke, Corrille had touched Bronwyn's arm and said, "I hope you don't mind if I go with Blayke. I just feel so much safer next to him."

At which point, she'd looked up through her lashes at him and giggled. His response was a stupid grin that Bronwyn wanted to rip off his face and beat him over the head with. In the end she had quietly retreated and joined Avruellen and Sinjenasta.

Why don't you trust her? Sinjenasta interrupted Bronwyn's thoughts.

I do trust her.

Hmm, if you say so; I know Avruellen doesn't.

Avruellen looked at Bronwyn, gauging how much to say. *He's right, Bronny. I know she's your friend, but there's something about her.*

Bronwyn thought about it and reluctantly came to a conclusion. *I love her; she's always been my best friend, but since she's joined us again, I don't trust her. Maybe it's because I'm jealous of the time she's spending with Blayke. I feel left out. They're so goggle-eyed at each other; it's pathetic.*

I think it's more than that, said Sinjenasta. *I think you're growing up and seeing some things for the first time. If there's one thing I know from being a panther, it's to always trust your instincts.*

He's right, Bronny. Some truths are hard to accept. Who knows? Maybe you'll work things out with her.

Mmm. Maybe. Bronwyn rested her hand on Sinjenasta's back and absently stroked his fur. His hearty purr made her feel a bit better. *At least you love me.*

Sinjenasta purred louder.

The boats crunched into the sand, and they stepped out. A dark shadow waited on the beach. They reached the robed man, and Arcon, with Phantom perched importantly on his shoulder, inclined his head. "Good evening. I'm Arcon of The Circle. We've come in search of a certain book, which I'm told can be found in your library."

The disciple of the Sacred Realm—the realm said to be

the home of all the gods—bowed. "Welcome to you, Realmist. We have waited many years for your arrival. Please follow me." Surprised at the ease with which they were accepted, Arcon and Avruellen breathed relieved sighs.

As they made their way to the monastery, Sinjenasta spoke to Fang. *How goes it, my little friend?*

Fang, surprised at the sudden attention from the usually aloof panther, nervously cleaned his whiskers as he peeked out of Blayke's bobbing pocket. He looked across at Sinjenasta who walked a few feet behind. *I'm well, thank you, Sinjenasta. To what do I owe the pleasure of this conversation?*

I wanted to get your opinion on something.

Yes?

What do you think about Blayke's new girlfriend?

Fang paused, wondering how much he should tell the panther and if there was any way he could use the information against him later. He decided it would be safe to confide—they were on the same side, after all. *She's certainly smitten with him, and I think the feeling is mutual….*

But?

But, there's something I don't trust.

That's the general consensus with everyone else. I think Blayke's the only one who can't see it. Have you seen anything in particular?

Not really, but I'll keep my eyes out. I'm glad it's not just me. I don't think it's wise to say anything to Blayke just yet—he wouldn't believe us without proof.

No, of course not.

Flux interrupted, *Sorry to butt in, but I'll give you my two whiskers' worth. I think she's a bit silly, but Avruellen hates her.*

Hates is a strong word, but I haven't known Avruellen to overreact about anything, mused Sinje.

Ha, you should see her when people don't do what she says. Flux joked, and the creaturas laughed.

Fang looked at Avruellen, knowing she couldn't hear, but worried nonetheless. *Okay then. I'll let you know as soon as I find out anything.*

He turned around to see they were almost at the entrance of a sprawling, squat complex that glowed white, even in the dim light. Several domes roofed the attached buildings, and timber shutters stood open at the many square windows, allowing the cool night air inside.

They entered a stone-paved courtyard through a creaking timber door, crossed the expanse, and entered another door that opened into a low-ceilinged foyer that barely held the large party. A woman waited. Standing taller than even Blayke, a brown robe covered her thin frame, and her white hair was twisted into a bun on the crown of her head. Their guide placed his hands together in front of his chin and dipped his torso in a slight bow. "Thank you, Steen. Please see that their rooms are ready." She turned to Arcon and Avruellen. "Welcome to our cloister. My name is Fiora. We've been expecting you."

"That's good to hear. I'm Avruellen, and this is Arcon." Avruellen gestured towards her brother. "Would I be able to bother you for a cup of tea?" Arcon looked at Avruellen as if she'd asked for a bucket of slops to be poured on her head. "Oh, don't look at me like that, old man! Discussions are always more palatable when enacted over a cup of tea and a biscuit; isn't that right, Bronwyn?"

Bronwyn nodded, remembering the last time she had eaten Avruellen's biscuits—the day they had left home. She sighed.

"Indeed, Avruellen. I'm sure the table has already been set for you to break your fast. Dawn is approaching. Please follow me." Her smile was warm, and Bronwyn admired her elegant movements as she glided out of the room.

They were shown to a modest dining room with two plain timber tables. Upon closer inspection, the low-backed chairs were speckled with signs of age: nicks and small flecks of different colored paints. Blayke noticed a subtle scent of musk under the stronger tang of the ocean. When they sat, Corrille sat next to him. He got a tingly feeling in his stomach when her arm brushed his. She edged her chair even closer, and he felt her hand rest on his leg. When he raised an eyebrow at her, she giggled. He shook his head and whispered in her ear, "You're going to get me into trouble."

"No one can see. Stop being such a spoilsport."

"I just feel uncomfortable. It's okay when we're alone, but not in front of everyone. Please?" She frowned but took her hand away. "Thank you."

Ever since he had rescued her and Bronwyn, she hadn't left his side. He liked how it felt to hold her small hand in his and although he had kissed a girl before, this was different—his heart raced and he felt like he was losing control. He'd had to go to the deck more than once for fresh air. He wondered if this is what it felt like to fall in love. Suddenly he wished her hand was still on his thigh.

A rattling of plates preceded the smell of bacon as two young, robed men entered with trays of food. Blayke saw Corrille smile at one of them. The black-haired acolyte blushed, and Blayke felt jealousy squash a heavy hand around the butterflies that had been playing in his stomach.

Bronwyn, sitting across from them, watched with interest.

She'd been busy admiring the dark-haired serving boy, thinking how vivid his blue eyes were, but when he had finally noticed Bronwyn, Corrille turned her attention on him. Bronwyn spoke into Sinjenasta's mind, *What is she playing at? Isn't one man enough?*

What are you talking about? He and Flux sat on the floor behind Bronwyn, waiting for their food.

Corrille. She's all over Blayke but now she has eyes for that other guy. Bronwyn folded her arms, wondering if Corrille was doing it just to annoy her, or if she was just desperate for everyone's attention. Corrille had suffered an awful childhood, but Bronwyn had always been nice to her and didn't deserve to be treated this way. *Is this how all friends behave?*

No, certainly not. I would tell you you're better off without her, but you probably won't listen.

But she's my friend; we've always done everything together. She's just upset because of everything that's been happening. I bet she'll go back to normal soon. Bronwyn spooned grilled tomatoes onto her plate.

If you say so, but I seem to recall having this conversation already. Now, where's my breakfast? I'm starving. Sinjenasta twitched his whiskers and sniffed the air.

The lad in question walked to Bronwyn's side of the table and offered her a plate with just-baked bread. The realmist took a piece and smiled, staring into his eyes: she knew it wasn't polite, but she couldn't help it. Shyly, she said, "Thank you."

His answering grin made her want to melt under the table. "My pleasure."

Suddenly she wasn't hungry. Her gaze accidentally met Corrille's over the expanse of the food-laden table, and her smile vanished: Corrille's eyes smoldered with hate. Blayke broke the spell by asking her a question, and Bronwyn had no doubt he remained oblivious to what had just happened. She hoped her brother wasn't lost to her; they had only just started to know each other, and family was something she had craved her whole life.

Bronwyn spoke to Sinjenasta, who was noisily tearing through two chickens. *This is all my fault. If I hadn't run off and been kidnapped, Corrille wouldn't be here now.*

Don't be like that, cub. She's not that bad. You can't be serious that you'd rather she was fed to the gormon?

No, I suppose not. She reddened and looked at her plate, realizing how ridiculous she sounded.

Now, do you mind? I'm trying to eat.

Bronwyn turned to look at him. Sinjenasta did his best *let me eat or you'll regret it* look, but Bronwyn burst out laughing.

What's so funny?

You have feathers on your nose. You are such a messy eater. Sinjenasta pawed at his nose in an attempt to dislodge the offending plumage. Bronwyn was sure if a panther could blush, he would have. He turned his back to her, and she heard a bone snap as he chomped down with purpose.

Arcon set his knife and fork down. "I think we'll need all hands on deck today. We have to find this book in a hurry and as much as I'd like to think we will, knowing our luck, we probably won't. No one knows the full name of the book, but we do know one word: *almanac*."

"One word?" asked Bronwyn.

"Yes, my dear," answered Avruellen. "Why do you think I've been trying to get you to learn patience all these years? I've found nothing worth doing is easy." Avruellen looked at Corrille. "And I think while we're searching, Corrille can help our hosts since we're a bit of a drain on their resources." Bronwyn suppressed a smile at Corrille's scowl—Corrille had been openly unfriendly to Avruellen since her return and wasn't about to start being subtle now. Blayke noticed his sister's reaction.

When they reached the library, Blayke, with Fang cozily ensconced in his pocket, spoke to his sister. "What was that smile about at breakfast?"

She looked at him. "What smile?"

"When Arcon said Corrille couldn't help us. Well?" His cranky expression was one Bronwyn had never seen.

"You really want to know?" He nodded. "Okay then. Ever since you and Corrille met, I've hardly spoken to you. She's always practically in your lap, and neither of you include me in anything. Is it wrong for me to want some time with my brother? We've practically only just met, and already I feel like you don't care. Didn't you ever want a brother or sister? I know I did."

"She's not practically in my lap."

Bronwyn raised an eyebrow, and Blayke was reminded of Avruellen. Blayke's cheeks and neck heated to red. "It's not my fault she's like that. Anyway, I like her; she's nice. I also feel sorry for her; she told me your aunt picked on her."

"She's your aunt too, and yes, they didn't get along, but it wasn't *all* Avruellen's fault. Look, I'm just asking to be included. Do you want me to be your sister or not?"

"Of course I do. I'm just used to being by myself. What do brothers and sisters do, anyway?"

"I'll tell you what they do," interrupted Arcon. "They argue, fight, and sometimes be nice to each other—and they stick together. The other thing they do is what their superiors ask them to." The young realmists rolled their eyes. "Well, there's something you two have in common. Now off you go. Blayke, you start in that corner, and Bronwyn, in that one." Arcon pointed to their respective corners. "When you find something that looks like it could be the book, add it to my pile over there." He nodded at a long, polished wooden table, which sat next to a thick support pillar in the middle of the room. Bronwyn looked up the length of the pillar to the high ceilings lined with dark, stately beams. She breathed in air that encompassed the slow decay of thousands of leather-bound books and wished that was enough to gain knowledge.

Bronwyn approached her corner of the green-carpeted room, sat on the floor, and ran her fingers along the spines of each dusty book on the bottom shelf. When she stretched her neck out by tipping her head back, she despaired at ever finding the right book: a wall of tomes rose to the ceiling— shelf upon shelf of red, green, black, orange, blue, engraved with gold, silver, sometimes black. Millions of words, stories, spells, histories, and futures—Bronwyn marveled at how so many worlds could be condensed into one room.

Trying to ignore the feeling of being overwhelmed, she leaned close and began what she hoped wouldn't be a fruitless search. Bronwyn could practically feel the gormons' hot breath on the back of her neck. She read as fast as she could.

Arcon leaned back in his chair, arms slumped by his side. If someone had told him how many books had the word "Almanac" in their titles, he never would have believed them. He had skimmed over one-hundred books using Second Realm magic. He envisaged the words *amulet, gormon,* and *activation.* The power highlighted each word with a yellow glow to make them easy to find, but he still had to leaf through every page of every book and read sentence after sentence wherever the highlighting occurred. If he ever wanted to cast a spell to make a gormon itchy, a burnt meal taste good (which would come in handy considering his culinary skills), or make an amulet for casting fertility over a flock of sheep, he was set—but he had yet to find the book he needed.

He rubbed the back of his aching neck. "What? Tired already?" Avruellen stood next to him with an armful of volumes. She dropped them onto the table, the thump startling Blayke and Bronwyn out of their searching trances. "I think we should have a break. We've forgotten about lunch, and I'm sure it's almost time for dinner. We won't last long if we don't eat."

She placed an encouraging hand on Arcon's arm.

"Yes, you're right, but we're really running out of time. We only have until tomorrow night." Adrenalin shot through his stomach as he considered the consequences of failing. He swallowed.

Before Arcon could refuse the break, Fiora swept in and announced dinner was being served in half an hour. "I've had baths drawn for the ladies; the men will have to wait until after dinner to clean up. I hope that's okay."

Avruellen nodded. "Thank you, Fiora. I'm sure the men don't mind being dirty; I, on the other hand, would love to be free of this oily coating of dust. Come on, Bronwyn."

Bronwyn climbed down from the ladder where she was inspecting the sixth-level shelf, brushed the dust off her pants and followed Avruellen out.

Arcon rose and called to Phantom who had been preening himself while perched on one of the beams, two stories above. The owl swooped down and alighted on Arcon's shoulder.

Do you think we'll make it? asked the creatura.

Arcon, afraid to answer, shrugged. "I think we have a long night ahead."

We? You mean you have a long night ahead. I'm going outside to catch some mice; all this waiting has made me quite peckish.

Blayke, who had also dusted himself off, joined the conversation. "So that's where that word comes from."

Which word? asked Phantom.

"Peckish. Birds get peckish, as in they get hungry enough to peck for food. If you say it enough, it sounds weird. Peckish, peckish, peckish."

"Will you shut up, Blayke? And that was a rhetorical question, in case you were wondering. Gods, now I have two idiots to put up with."

Hey, old man, who are you calling an idiot? I'm wiser than you, or hadn't you heard? Phantom thudded a wing into Arcon's ear.

"All right, all right. Go easy. That's no way to treat an old man." Arcon winked. "Come on, let's go and eat."

❧

Bronwyn, sick of watching Blayke and Corrille fawn all over each other at dinner, ate quickly and excused herself by saying she wanted to keep sorting through books. When she entered the hushed library, she didn't notice she had company. Reaching her section, she was about to climb the ladder-on-wheels and looked up to see a brown-robed person standing on the rungs. She was relieved to see he was wearing trousers underneath the robe. "So that's what monks wear under their dresses."

"Only on a work day. You're lucky you didn't get me on a

feast day." The dark-haired acolyte looked down at Bronwyn and grinned.

"So, what are you doing in here?"

"Fiora asked me to help. She said it's urgent and if you don't find what you need, we'll all be dead before too long."

"Wow. She's not into subtlety, is she?"

"Not really. I should be able to speed things up—I've been here for five years, and I've read a few of these books. I think I can narrow it down a bit."

Bronwyn looked around the room at the thousands of books. "I hope you're a fast reader; there's a lot of books here."

"There was one in particular I think would help. It may not be the book you have to have, but I think it sheds some light on what's going on. Give me a minute and I'll get it." He pulled the ladder along by grabbing the shelves and dragging it across its tracks. After checking a few covers, he said, "Here it is."

The book he grabbed had a linen cover, woven with threads of gold and fawn. He scrambled down awkwardly with the large volume and carried it to the table. "*A Complete History of the Realms*. It's got some interesting background on the gormons and what caused the war in the first place. Some here say it's true—others say it's myth."

"And what do you believe?" Arcon had quietly entered, his eyes shining in the subdued torchlight, bright with a hope Bronwyn hadn't seen for a while.

"I believe it's true."

"What's your name, lad?"

"Toran, sir."

"Well, Toran, let me have a read of this book: *A Complete History of the Realms*. I would have thought that would be one of a many-volume set. How will I find what I need in here?" Arcon ran a forefinger over the course surface.

"I think you'll find it's a special book. Everything you want to know about the history of Talia is in there. We're not allowed to talk about it to outsiders, except you of course. It's a book that would, what's the right word … *upset* a few people, and maybe some dragons too. This book could start wars."

"If it has everything you say it does, I wouldn't debate that." Arcon cautiously opened the cover, not sure what to expect. Phantom, sensing his partner's tension, flew in through one of the windows, and the realmist automatically put his arm up so the owl could land.

Bronwyn, Arcon, and Phantom crowded around the weighty tome. The front page declared *A Complete History of the Realms, commenced three centuries after the Gormon War.* "That's unusual," said Bronwyn. "That sounds like it hasn't been finished, but that's impossible."

"Just wait and see," said Toran, his sapphire-blue eyes meeting hers, lingering longer than necessary. Arcon turned to page one and saw the story started some five-thousand years before the Gormon War. He quickly read the page and flicked it over. "This doesn't match up!" he declared. "We've barely had an introduction and now we've jumped ten years."

"Let me show you." Toran stood next to Arcon, turned back to the first page, and placed his finger on the bottom of the page. He traced his finger up the page and the words followed.

"What in the Third Realm? You didn't use any power. How did you do that?" Arcon bent over until his nose almost touched the paper. "That's incredible. Okay; leave me to it. I have a lot of reading to do." He straightened and looked at the youngsters. "I need you to find the other book. As interesting as this one is, it won't save us if we can't activate those damn amulets tomorrow night. We're almost out of time."

Bronwyn hurried back to her ladder, a mix of excitement and dread warring in her mind. What kind of a book did that? She had never seen anything like it—and without any power. She looked at Toran, who had begun searching on the opposite wall. His knowledge had impressed her, not to mention his to-die-for eyes. When Avruellen and Blayke entered the room and exclaimed over Arcon's new book, Bronwyn realized she was daydreaming. With a determination born of desperation, she diligently combed the shelves. Time was in short supply.

❧

Bronwyn trudged another armload of books to Arcon's newly named *table of doom*. The pile of books to read depressed them —the reality was that they were probably going to end up on the wrong side of their deadline without the information they needed. This table held their fate on its four sturdy legs. As Bronwyn dumped the books, creating a new pile, Arcon exclaimed, "No! Are you kidding? Dragons' bollocks. This can't be true. Avruellen, come and look at this." He quickly pushed his chair back and made room for his sister to sit.

Avruellen read. Her hand came to her open mouth and through it, she spoke the muffled words, "Oh, gods. I can't believe it." She looked at Arcon, their expressions of shock mirroring each other.

"What is it?" asked Bronwyn. The kerfuffle had enticed Blayke and Toran to the table.

"Where's Sinjenasta?" Arcon asked.

"I don't know. I'll call him." Bronwyn called to her creatura, and within two minutes, he padded through the door.

This better be good: I was asleep.

In his agitation, Arcon spoke out loud. "Is this true? Are the gormons and dragons related? Is Drakon their god too?"

Sinjenasta stared past the realmist for a moment and drew a breath. *Yes.*

"Why didn't you tell us?"

I was oath-bound by Drakon not to say. It doesn't really change anything.

"It may not change anything, but it may give us an advantage, for the gods' sakes! Why did he cast them out? What in the Third Realm happened?"

Blayke, thinking this was information that needed to be kept quiet, dipped into the Second Realm and shielded the library. "Thank you, Blayke," said Avruellen.

"Well, panther, tell us. Now!" Arcon growled, doing nothing to hide his anger.

"Don't get angry at Sinje—it's not his fault." Bronwyn stood by her creatura, putting a hand on the back of his neck.

Arcon treated her to his angry glare before turning it back on the panther. "It may not be your fault, but you're supposed to be on our side, aren't you?"

Drakon is on Drakon's side, and I was sent here to represent him. He wants what's best for his precious dragons. You want to know why the gormons were cast out? Drakon preferred his dragons. He created the gormons first and after a while he designed, for want of a better word, the dragons. They were his artistic achievement. The gormons were ugly, less refined.

He started by refusing to answer their prayers; then he would put obstacles in their way, challenges. He would play the dragons off their gormon brothers—like when a parent plays one child against another. Eventually the gormons, tortured from many years of trying to gain favour from their god, rebelled. They enslaved whatever dragons they could catch and treated them abhorrently. Rejected by their god and goaded by hundreds of years of mistreatment, they set out to destroy the dragons and the world Drakon had created.

Drakon lied to the other gods about why he needed the gormons banished from Talia. It took over a thousand years to groom the humans and dragons to fight back, but when they did, they succeeded, with Drakon's help, to banish the gormons to the Third Realm. When the other gods learned the truth of how they had been used, they refused to have anything to do with The First Realm, or Talia, again. As far as your gods are concerned, they won't help you because they'll be helping Drakon. We're on our own.

They stood there: Bronwyn, Blayke (with Fang peeking out of his pocket), Flux, Avruellen, and Arcon. Phantom perched on a chair, staring at Sinjenasta, silent. The news beat against their sanity like a trapped bird against a window. Their war was a lie, their existence a lie. The humans had been created to help rid Talia of the gormons, who had every right to be there. Toran, who didn't know how to listen to mind speak, broke, what was for him, a long silence. "Who died? Seriously, what's wrong? Have you all gone into some kind of trance? Is this normal with realmists?"

He looked from one person to another, eyebrows drawn down in worry.

"Have you read this book, lad?" Arcon asked.

"Some of it."

"Do you remember the part about the gormons being related to the dragons and Drakon banishing them from Talia because he grew tired of them?"

"I didn't read all of it. Is it true?" Arcon nodded.

"So now what do we do?" Blayke asked his uncle.

Arcon shook his head. "Sinjenasta's right. As horrific as this is, it changes nothing. If the gormons win, we die, and even if they have every right to be here, I can't lie down and die without a fight, and I'll be damned if I'm going to see those I love die painful, horrific deaths. This is a lot to process. For now, we keep looking for that book." Phantom hooted in support, and they returned, albeit in a daze, to their task.

Sinjenasta joined Bronwyn while she scoured the shelves. *Do you hate me?*

Stopping what she was doing, she met his eyes. "No, I don't hate you, but I do like Drakon even less than I did before. And I can't trust you. I can't believe you kept such a big secret. What are Drakon's plans for me? Am I going to get thrown on a funeral pyre by the time this is done?"

She referred to Symbothial, the dragon they had killed. Sinjenasta hung his head.

I'm sorry, Bronwyn. He looked up again, searching her eyes. *We are bonded, and if anything happens to you, it happens to me. I couldn't tell you; Drakon would have killed me, or dragged me up to the Sacred Realm again to be endlessly punished. Besides, I didn't lie to you; I just didn't tell you something, and yes, I know it was something important, but I really didn't have a choice.*

"What about the poor gormons? Forsaken by their god! How is that supposed to make them feel? Drakon created them, then shat all over them. I don't feel right about fighting them and kicking them out again."

"Bronwyn." Avruellen had approached, knowing her niece would likely empathize with the gormons. "I know what happened wasn't fair, but the gormons have evolved into something different. They are creatures of blind hate, cunning, and revenge. They have evolved to be everything that's wrong with Drakon. I don't think the dragons are everything that's good, but they are balanced. When Drakon rejected his children, they became the monsters he labeled them as. We don't deserve to die because Drakon made a mistake thousands of years ago."

"But…." Bronwyn's eyes brimmed with tears.

"Oh, for goodness sake, Bronwyn, don't you dare cry for those … things. They will skin you and start chewing while you're still alive to feel it. Cry for the innocents they once were, but those gormons are gone. The gormons returning to Talia are nothing like the ones Drakon betrayed." She grabbed her niece's shoulders. "Look at me. Promise me you will fight with everything you have. If the gormons get control, it will not only be us who dies, but the dragons, the animals, and eventually, Talia. Promise me." Avruellen's voice strained with desperation. "Do you *want* to die?"

"No."

"Well, neither do I." Avruellen took hold of Bronwyn's hands and squeezed. "And since we're agreed on that point, you'd better keep looking or we won't get our wish."

Heart aching, Bronwyn reluctantly searched for the book that would give them a chance to live. She finally understood the saying, "Damned if you do, damned if you don't." Painfully aware of hours passing, she decided she would rather be damned and alive than damned and dead. By the time she finally laid her hands on *The Comprehensive Realmists' Almanac of Incantations,* she was ready to fight.

When she handed the find to Arcon, he grabbed it. Slamming it on the table and flinging the cover open, sending dust puffing into the air, he perused the index and smiled. Turning to page two-hundred fifty-four, his smile widened. "Dragons' balls, we've got it! Quick, Avruellen, come and see. We made it. We still have a chance!"

Despite her guilt, Bronwyn felt good. They weren't going to die just yet. Only too happy to oblige when Toran offered her a hug in celebration, she didn't notice Sinjenasta lift a black lip and expose one fang in a silent growl. Musing that today had certainly ended better than it started—from feeling left out, to being in the arms of one of the cutest young men she'd ever met, *Yes*, she thought, *life is definitely worth living. Okay, gormons, bring it on.*

CHAPTER 22

Rust-colored dirt swirled about his leathery, clawed feet. Sand grazed his snout, lodged in his eyes and throat, even through the cloth mask he wore—they would have invented something better to shield their faces from the sandstorms that were a regular occurrence in this god-forsaken realm, but access to any kind of power was limited, and what they could reach had been used to control the entrance to the gate. "So this is it?" Kalzich asked, careful to stay away from the edge of the circle of dark water that seemingly lay dead—not a ripple ruffled the mirror-like surface, despite the tormenting wind.

"Yes, master."

"And it's ready to go?"

Embrax knew if it wasn't, he would be dead. He had made sure. "Yes, master, and I have two surprises." Over the distant screams of the last gormons being sacrificed to feed the horde before they departed tomorrow, the priest answered, "I have worked out how to split the corridor."

He paused, giving Klazich time to be suitably impressed.

"How does it work?"

"We will send the first half through the corridor and when they are through, I have calculated how to use my limited power to close one door and open another. The rest will go through a different corridor."

"Door?"

"The liquid you see here is a corridor, the surface a door. Look closer. What do you see?"

Klazich hadn't noticed through the dusty air, but the still surface looked to be painted with the picture of a cave—a shadowy outline of rocks with mineral formations stabbing down from the ceiling. "It's a reflection, Master. That is the cave to which we will be transported. If I have my coordinates correct, the other door will take us to another place on Talia."

"And which place would that be, Embrax?"

"Inkra, Master." This time Embrax allowed his features to relax into a maniacal grin. He could afford to be proud of this.

"But won't we arrive as disembodied spirits?"

"That is my other surprise. I have made contact with Kwaad. He has melded with a king and queen and can help us, now that he is in mature form. Kwaad has the power to help us breathe in the corridor, so our awareness can travel with our bodies. The connection was not clear enough to get details, but I'm sure he said at least one hundred of us will arrive whole and mature. For the rest, he has a whole city of Inkrans for us to possess." Acidic saliva dripped from his smiling mouth.

"This is good news, Embrax. I will decide who will go through in adult form and let you know. Have everyone waiting for me tomorrow night. It is finally time." Klazich made his way back to what passed for his palace—a mud-brick building tacked onto the front of a network of caves. *So Drakon, it is not over. You will regret the day you cast us aside. It is our time now.* Klazich couldn't wait to tell his brother: they were one day from taking back their world. The thought of going home had never been sweeter. Tomorrow night they would finally celebrate like no gormons had for over one-thousand years. Oh, yes, tomorrow they were reclaiming what had been stolen so long ago, and he was the one to have made it happen. He allowed himself a small smile. He was certainly going to enjoy this.

CHAPTER 23

Zim's outstretched wings cut through the night sky. Agmunsten and Boy sat astride his back. Their journey, to this point, had been uneventful, but minutes from arriving at Klendar, the realmists had felt something: a surge in the fabric of the First Realm, almost a tear.

"What in Drakon's name was that?" Arie sent the thought to Zim and Agmunsten.

Zim spoke. "There is a strong presence in the First Realm that wasn't there before. Agmunsten, do you think the gormons have already broken through?"

"I don't know. Whatever it was, it felt close. Keep going. I'm going to look in the Second Realm and see what I can find." The head realmist sent half his awareness through the familiar corridor and felt the pull as he neared the Second Realm. His essence spilled into the symbol-studded expanse—the silence so complete that it could have been a vacuum. Finding his own symbol, he worked outwards, searching for anything different—he was not sure what, but knew he'd recognize it when he saw it.

And within moments, he did see it: a nauseating-green symbol. Two other symbols, trapped inside like an animal being swallowed by a snake, bulged out, distorting the symbol but barely glowing through the thick membrane. He swooped closer, trying to obtain a better sense of what it was. It couldn't be a gormon—their symbols were black. As he neared, an intense smell overcame his awareness, which should have been impossible: odors did not exist in the Second Realm. Agmunsten's awareness *felt* the sharpness of sulfur and the cloying putridity of death. In the First Realm, his body gagged.

Without warning, he was buffeted by a force and pushed back. Momentarily dazed, his awareness remained still. Refocusing his consciousness, he drew power from around him as a shield. Next time the energy shot at him, it gave his First-Realm body a headache, but his awareness held firm. He watched as the malicious symbol charged towards him, tentacles of energy formed on the being, writhing, reaching. Agmunsten had never encountered real danger in the Second Realm: until now. Death approached.

He wanted to stay and fight, but knew that thing, whatever it was, had enormous power. He willed his awareness back to his body. His symbol hurried to the passage. Pain gripped his First Realm body when the tentacles grabbed him, sinking etheric barbs into his energy. He heard distant laughter as the enemy drained his spirit, his essence, his life.

A distant voice came through. "Agmunsten, are you okay. Zim! Agmunsten is letting go. He's going to fall off. I can't hold on much longer!" Boy screamed to be heard through the rushing air.

Zim sent to Arcese, "I don't have to time to land. We're

losing Agmunsten; I'm going in. If I don't come back, send to Arcon and Father. Let them know. You need to try and save Verity. Please promise me you'll honor our pledge to King Edmund."

"I will, Brother, or die trying. May Drakon protect you, Zimapholous. Be careful." The last words uttered, she could tell Zim was already gone, his body on autopilot.

Boy held tight to Agmunsten's body; each violent twitch threatened to throw them off the dragon. The young boy clenched the saddle with his thighs and clutched the realmist's thick coat. Fear of hurtling through space, to be smashed into an incoherent mess on the ground, ignited the adrenalin in his body. He wanted to panic, to give in to his fear, but that would mean letting go, forgoing his existence. He didn't want to die.

His arms and legs ached.

Arcese sped up and flew next to him. "Boy," she yelled, "I'm going to lead Zim to Klendar. There's no time to waste. We'll try and land on the palace roof. Hang on!" Arcese noticed, in the distance, an unwelcoming, vertical beam of moss-green light. Too much of a coincidence to be unrelated, she knew it came from the palace. She increased speed and heard a chilling scream. Arcese turned her head and saw Zim plummeting towards the ground. Knowing she couldn't save him, already mourning his death, she flew on. She had a promise to keep.

Zim, as Agmunsten had done before him, started by finding his own symbol in the Second Realm. Then he spied the leech draining Agmunsten's symbol. What in the Third Realm was it? Rather than figure it out—caution would take too long—he drew power around himself and armed his awareness with his birthright: fire. He raced as fast as his energy would go, flames covering him, heating to a white-hot inferno as he flew.

Almost upon the twisted amalgamation that was his friend's symbol and the engorged abomination, Zim braced himself for impact. He aimed for the side of the creature farthest from Agmunsten's symbol, which appeared dull, the life being extracted, particle by precious particle. Agmunsten was almost dead.

Zim collided with the mass. Drawing more energy, he attempted to burn a hole in the near-translucent barrier. Immediately, the creature turned a tentacle on Zim, but the dragon was ready with singeing energy. The creature flinched, distracted, and turned its full attention on Zim. "You think to interrupt me? Who dares interfere with Kwaad?"

The dragon stayed silent, not wanting to give away his identity. He could see Agmunsten's symbol, drained and dangling from one tentacle, the others now twisted around Zim's symbol. He could feel the tug of the parasite as it fed off his life force. He needed to escape and take Agmunsten with him—but how?

Remembering a lesson from his days at The Academy, when they had learnt about dangers of the Second Realm, he sent his awareness to connect with Agmunsten's and hoped he was still alive. A glimmer of energy remained. Zim plugged his energy in, linking with his fellow realmist—there was strength in numbers, and now he had a second link to the creature through which he could feed. He willed the creature's essence through Agmunsten's essence and then to himself.

The creature howled and pulsed in anger. Zim felt it strain to cut him off—but it couldn't. The dragon could feel the pull on his own energy slow, and suddenly the creature winked out, leaving Zim and Agmunsten floating among the eerily quiet sea of other symbols.

Zim gathered Agmunsten and, weary, raced to the corridor. Even though time didn't pass here as it did in the First Realm, he could have plunged to his death by now. Once at the corridor, he released Agmunsten, knowing that if he were alive, he would be pulled to his body, and if he wasn't, there was nothing he could do. Letting his own body call him back, he submitted to the force and prayed he would get back in time.

❧

Arcese and Arie neared the pulsing green shaft of sickly luminescence. "What is it?" Arie asked.

"I don't know, lad, but I think we can assume it's dangerous." Arcese stopped talking for a moment before confirming: "Whatever it is, Verity is in there with it."

"Do you know if she's okay?"

"Her energy is strong, but there's another symbol near hers, which has the markings of a realmist. I hope we get there in time to stop whatever is happening." She stretched her neck down, head pointed sharply into the wind in an effort to streamline herself. Her great wings beat faster, and Arie leaned forward, trying to shrink as small as possible.

"We'll get there, Arcese; we have to. Come on. You can do it." The young realmist focused on the palace, which was now more than an outline in the night as Arcese descended. Arie anticipated what they would find and opened his link to the Second Realm in readiness to fight. He expected they would face soldiers and now a realmist. Surely they could beat them with Arcese's great power?

Arcese circled the palace, assessing the situation. The beam pulsed through a smashed roof whose naked, curved girders looked like a skeleton of a long-dead giant in the etheric glow. This close, the green light looked as if it contained a foul, screaming face: a face not of this world. As they banked around, Arie saw a sinewy body, apparently swimming in the light, trying to inch downwards into the large room.

Arie heard Arcese gasp and felt her shiver under him. "What is it, Princess?"

"I can see Verity, and a monstrosity I had hoped never to see. Fight as long as you can; we have a promise to keep." She dove down into the closest thing to an evil afterlife Arie had ever seen.

Arie gripped harder as Arcese dodged between the girders, leaning at such a precarious angle that Arie thought he would slide off. With frantic wing strokes, Arcese stopped suddenly and fell the last two feet to the debris-strewn floor. Arie hardly noticed the jolted landing when he saw what Arcese had understatedly called a *monstrosity*. "Steaming piles of dragon crap," he said, not dismounting.

Ten feet away, twice as tall as Arcese, in the center of the room next to a skull, which appeared to be the source of the green beacon, stood a creature with mottled green-and-black skin—the coloring reminding Arie of a tiger slug. Sinewy limbs attached to a strong, spike-covered torso; veined wings folded at its back. A large forehead presided over red eyes and a drawn-out snout filled with gray teeth, each one longer than he remembered Agmunsten's fingers to be, each one slightly wider at the base, thinning progressively until it ended in a point as fine as a needle. They gleamed in the green light, acidic saliva showing them to their best advantage.

Arie's breath came faster, and he bit his tongue to stop himself from begging Arcese to get out of there.

"What is that?" he asked. Arcese didn't answer, focused, as she was, on drawing as much earth power as she could.

"What am I?" It laughed, a discordant melding of different pitches. "I am Kwaad. Maybe I'll let one of you go so you can tell your king who is coming for him. I am the god the gormons have cried out for. I will lead them to victory. I am the one who will eat your dragon for dessert after I finish what we're doing here, which you have, most unfortunately, interrupted."

"Arie!" Verity shouted. Arie noticed her standing near the gormon, next to the table. Her delicate dress was ripped from one hip to ankle, and her hands and feet were stained with smears of red. Clumps of crimson-tinged hair had broken loose from her bun, and harsh lines of red lined her face where bloody fingers had brushed them back.

"Be silent!" Kwaad commanded. "Enough! Orphael, lay her hands upon the skull. Let it begin."

Arcese, who knew what grabbing the skull meant, woke from her trance. "No!" she screamed, and Arie winced. Arcese launched well-placed fireballs at Orphael. He reacted quickly, throwing up an invisible shield. Two flaming missiles hit the shield and spread out, dissipating in a harmless trail of smoke.

"Run, Verity, run!" Arie shouted, preparing to jump down and help the princess climb onto Arcese.

Behind the shield, they could see Orphael mouthing words. He dropped the shield and shot a sizzling bolt of lightning. Arcese countered with her own bolt—the sparking electricity meeting with a deafening thunderclap. The room shook and rolled like a ship at sea. Verity stumbled and tried to run towards them.

"Enough of these games." Kwaad's voice undercut the commotion the way a headsman's axe silenced the condemned. The creature stepped towards Arcese. She turned her head towards Kwaad and spoke into Arie's mind. *Stay on my back or you might get burned to a crisp.*

She opened her mouth, and a jet of fire shot out, reaching Kwaad. He jumped out of the way, ungainly but surprisingly quick. Warring indoors was not easy when you were twenty feet tall.

"Hurry, Verity." Arie wished he could use Second-Realm power to gather her up. He watched her limping run—torturously slow, Orphael behind her, catching up. In two more strides, he had her. Grabbing her around the waist, he dragged her back to the table as she clawed at his face, trying to gauge out his eyes.

Kwaad turned red eyes onto Arcese and lifted clawed hands. Arie felt the pressure change as power was sucked into the vortex that was Kwaad. Arcese, despite knowing something monumentally bad was about to occur, ran towards Verity—if they couldn't save her, and Zim was already dead, there wasn't much point going home anyway. She wove strands of power as she crossed the room, throwing a shield over Verity and immediately breathing another wave of fire over Orphael. The realmist was not quick enough. His screams stopped abruptly, amputated by roiling dragon flames that turned his body into ash that floated to settle amongst the shattered glass on the ground.

Before Arcese reached Verity, Kwaad attacked. Arie watched as the glass rose off the floor. It commenced a lazy circle around him and Arcese. Thousands of pieces of scalpel-like debris spun faster, creating a whirlpool of impending death around the dragon and the boy. Not knowing how much energy Arcese had in reserve, Arie constructed a shield. He had never made a shield before, and as it settled around them, he wondered if he had done a good job. *Oh well,* he thought, watching the swirling slivers, *if it hasn't worked, I'll find out soon enough.* When the first point made contact with the shield, it squealed in protest, scratching the surface in its rushed trajectory.

Arie felt a tickle of sweat run down from his temple as he waited for the shield to break. The cutting points made contact —a cacophony of corpses' fingernails scratching down his spine. He felt his protection waver as a crack formed in the energy. As the shield collapsed, he squeezed his eyes shut: he never had liked the sight of blood.

It had taken no time at all for everything to go wrong. Boy had been enjoying riding on Zim, snuggled up behind Agmunsten —even though it was cold, it was invigoratingly so. But then Agmunsten had slumped forward, almost sliding off Zim. Boy's arms had burned with fatigue while trying to stop the old man from falling, and then Arcese had flown next to them and, after communicating with her brother, shouted at him to hang on and flown off.

Her words had given him momentary encouragement. He could see, when he risked a look past the realmist's limp body, a green shaft of light marking their landing place. But they never reached it.

Not far from their destination, Zim stopped the graceful rise and fall of his wings, and now they plummeted to Talia, Boy's arms linked under Agmunsten's arms, near his shoulders. The young man's legs pointed to the sky, his body in a clumsy dive: the only thing holding them onto Zim's back was Agmunsten's foot, which was caught in the stirrup. One of the images Boy's brain presented to him as they fell—and his life paraded in front of his eyes—was a day he had watched as an abusive patron was chased out of the brothel where his mother worked. He saw the overweight man fall from his horse and be dragged behind, foot caught as Agmunsten's was now, body grinding through the dirt, leaving a trail of dust in his wake.

Up here there was no dust, just cold air, and even though Boy felt like he had time to count every scale on Zim and taste every breath he inhaled, the speed of the air hurt his cheeks and dragged him dangerously close to letting go of his anchor, although he wondered what it mattered whether he died on his own spot on the ground or whether his remains were mushed in with an old man and a dragon—death was death, after all.

There was no one to talk to, so he said a silent goodbye to his life. *I'm sorry I didn't make up for my mistake, Verity. I hope you and Queen Gabrielle can forgive me. Goodbye.* His tears dried as soon as they emerged, buffeted by the wind.

But then…. Had he imagined that Zim's limp body was not as limp as it had been? Were his wings moving? As the ground neared, and Arie could make out tufts of leaves on the tops of trees, Zim beat his mighty wings and employed Second-Realm energy to lift him back into the sky. Boy landed in the saddle with a thud.

Collapsing against Agmunsten's body, he tried to brace himself to stop from falling off again, but his strength was depleted. His thighs, trying to grip the saddle, shook with exhaustion and shock—they hadn't died! *Oh, my gods, I'm alive.* He sobbed into the realmist's back and waited for the jolt that would signal the next catastrophe. But it never came. Boy felt the realmist's muscles tense under his coat, and he lifted his head.

Agmunsten blinked, surprised he still lived. He flexed fingers in his gloves, savoring the feeling of feeling. "Welcome back," said Zim, loud enough for Boy to hear.

"It's good to be back. What happened while we were gone, lad?" Agmunsten's weakened voice carried back to Boy with the wind.

"Nothing much, except almost dying. You almost fell off and I tried to hold you on and then Zim stopped flying and we were plunging to the ground and I didn't think I could hold on but then Zim woke up and started flying again."

"Take a breath, lad," Agmunsten said with a laugh. "So you're saying we had a close call?"

"Very close."

"Well, we survived this one, eh?" In his mind he spoke to Zim, *Thank you, my friend. You saved me from being an ugly symbol's dinner. I very much appreciate it.*

It was nothing. I didn't fancy having to explain to an irate Avruellen and Arcon why their head realmist didn't make it back. Anyway, enough chitchat; I think we're here.

I'm afraid I won't be much good if there's a problem: I can barely hold on as it is.

Well, whatever you do, don't get off, and tell Boy to stay put too.

Will do. They stopped talking as they descended into Kwaad's domain. Agmunsten involuntarily pinched Zim's scales between tense fingers at what he saw: *Klar's balls! We're too late.*

CHAPTER 24

Gabrielle yawned as Sarah bustled about the room. The queen heard the clink of her breakfast tray being deposited on a table and the soft creak of opening shutters. Crisp morning air cooled Gabrielle's face, and sunlight streamed through the windows, illuminating the dust motes Sarah had set dancing with her activity. The queen rolled over, burying her face into the pillow.

"Come on, my queen. There's a lot to do today, and Hermas has been hanging around the kitchen all morning pestering the cook for leftovers he can feed the ducks. I think he's just waiting to see you." Sarah tilted her head to the side and smiled.

Gabrielle's muffled voice came through the pillow. "But I'm tired. I had trouble falling asleep with Edmund gone. Can't I have just a few more minutes?"

Sarah gathered the queen's gown and stood at the foot of the bed. "I'm patient, my lady, but I don't think the rest of the court will be so forgiving."

Gabrielle sighed and rolled over, swinging her legs over the edge of the bed. Looking at the tray, she shook her head. "I won't be having breakfast today. I'm not in the mood to eat."

She managed a stern look at Sarah to ensure there would be no argument, before rinsing her face at the vanity in the corner of the room and undressing. As Sarah placed the peacock-blue dress over her head, the queen yawned again. "Excuse me. Oh, today is going to be so long. I wonder how they're going. I wonder how Verity is. You don't think that horrible pig of a man would hurt his own dau … niece, do you?"

The familiar weight of dread settled like a mantle of iron around her shoulders, and she lowered her head.

"I know it's hard, but try not to think about it. King Edmund, the realmists, and the dragons are doing everything they can. We'll get her back soon; you'll see." She squeezed the queen's shoulder before tightening and tying the golden ribbon that laced the back of the queen's dress. "Come and sit so we can make you presentable."

"I'm afraid with the bags under my eyes, you'll have quite the job." Gabrielle sat on her stool in front of the mirror and waited while her maid brushed and braided her long, dark hair before tying it with another golden ribbon. Sarah looked into the mirror at the queen. "Okay, done. You always look beautiful, even with dark circles under your eyes."

Gabrielle stood and checked her reflection. "Thank you, Sarah. I guess it's time to pretend I don't want to jump off the battlements. I hate having to set a good example all the time. Hmm, maybe tonight you could bring copious amounts of gozzleberry wine to my room. Two bottles should be enough."

"My lady!"

"Oh don't sound so shocked. You can stay and drink with

me if you like. I could so do with some company." Gabrielle didn't wait for an answer, since it was more of an order. She shrugged off any outward sign of sadness and marched towards the kitchens. Hopefully Hermas would have some good news for a change.

Gabrielle didn't notice as the kitchen staff curtseyed, her eyes on Hermas. The old man sat upon a chair eating warm, buttered bread, strands of wispy, white hair floating whimsically above his scalp. Upon seeing the queen, he grinned and stood, stiffly executing as much of a bow as his arthritic body allowed. He took her hand and kissed it.

A smile slipped through the queen's sorrow. "So nice to see you, Hermas. I've just risen and wouldn't mind a walk in the garden. Would you like to join me?"

"Oh, thank you, Your Majesty. I like walking."

Gabrielle turned to Sarah, saying, "Please, arrange to have those extra rooms made up. We have the realmist, Astra, arriving in the next few days, not to mention King Fernis of Brenland, Queen Alaine from Wyrdon, and Elphus, the other member of The Circle. Things are going to get very busy around here."

"Of course, Your Majesty." Sarah curtseyed and hurried to work while Gabrielle and Hermas strolled to the garden.

Hermas led them to a formal garden about a five-minute walk from the castle. There they sat on a stone bench amongst the birdsong and surveyed the low-cut hedges and gravel walks that threaded a geometric path through emerald-green shrubs. The morning sun warmed their backs, and they could see clearly in every direction: no one would be able to eavesdrop.

"So, my queen, I think we can talk." Hermas cast quick glances in every direction.

Gabrielle placed a hand on his arm. "It's okay, Hermas. We won't be bothered here, unless the trees or birds are spies."

Her laugh made him smile.

"You never know, these days. Ah, what strange times we're coming to, and dangerous ones. I'm sorry to hear about Verity." His eyes glistened, and Gabrielle clasped his wrinkled hand between her smooth palms.

"I know. I'm only just managing. There are days—in fact, every daythat I don't want to get out of bed, although when I am awake all I want to do is kill that evil, egotistical, lying bastard." She clenched her teeth, murder in her eyes.

"If there's any justice in the world, he'll get his; you'll see."

"Unfortunately we both know the world doesn't always work like that, my dear friend. Anyway, I assume you didn't just come here to offer your condolences."

"How perceptive." He smiled. "I have received a message that Astra, the realmist Agmunsten promised you, will be here sooner than we thought. King Valdorryn wants to help as much as he can and has sent Warrimonious to fetch her. They may arrive as early as tomorrow."

"Well, that's a relief. Since Edmund left, the burden has been much harder to carry. War is such an unsavory thing."

Hermas laughed heartily. "You have such a way with understatement, my queen." He paused and looked at Gabrielle. "There is something you're not telling me. Care to share?"

"Do you remember Boy, Leon's lackey?" Hermas nodded, and she continued. "He's taken Verity's disappearance almost as hard as I. He decided to take matters into his own hands and ran away yesterday, after everyone left. Agmunsten assured me they would find him and keep him safe, but it's just another child I have to worry about."

She stared at her hands, which still held the old man's.

"If I hear anything, I'll let you know. At least tomorrow you'll have your own, personal communications expert on hand."

"That's right. I'll feel much better when Astra arrives. Well, if there's nothing more you have to tell me, I'd best get back. The young woman from Inkra, Karin, is homesick, and I know my company makes her feel better, plus I like her, and I could do with a distraction right now. She knows how to play scorpa. Would you believe they have that card game in Inkra too?"

"Let's hope empathy is something else our races have in common."

Gabrielle gave him a wan smile as they stood. Walking back to the castle, she tried to appreciate the sun on her face, but it wasn't easy.

Gabrielle and Karin spent the day playing cards and sketching —the Inkran was more than proficient at drawing still life and portraits, a pastime the queen also enjoyed. Conversation was limited, although Karin was picking up Veresian quicker than the queen expected. After dinner, when they retired to the queen's private sitting room, Sarah joined them and brought the wine they had spoken of that morning.

Leaning back into her silk-covered armchair, Gabrielle sipped red wine out of a crystal goblet. The wine heated her tongue with its spice and she swallowed, savoring the warmth. The room was quiet, save for the low trilling of the crickets—the fire remained unlit in the unusually warm night. Gabrielle spoke, her words as smooth as the wine. "So,

Karin, tell us more about your home. Did you live with your parents?"

"Mama and Papa?"

"Yes."

Karin hesitated, attempting to formulate her answer. Her speech was slow and her accent clipped, but they understood her words. "I lived with Mama. My father was not with us. Now he is dead."

She bowed her head, hiding any emotion, as was the Inkran way.

"I'm sorry, Karin," said Sarah. "Do you have any sisters or brothers?"

Head down, she answered, "One brother. He is smaller, but taller."

"Oh, you mean younger. How old are you, if I may ask?" the queen ventured. Karin's almond-shaped brown eyes met the queen's and were no less captivating for the resignation clouding them.

"I am twenty-winters old."

"Oh, you look so much younger. I thought you might be sixteen," said Sarah, who reached down and scooped a handful of sweet, dried frocus berries from the plate next to the wine bottle. "Have you tried these? They're good."

The queen's maid did her best to lighten the mood, but it seemed a night for suffering suffocating emotions, facing what one would rather walk away from, and secrets.

Gabrielle stared at Karin, wondering why the girl, of all people, had ended up here. She wanted to get to the heart of who this girl was. Karin, so unreadable, her Inkran heritage the master of all teachers in that respect, but the queen still sensed there was something important yet to discover. And she planned to unearth it tonight. Gabrielle opened her mouth to speak, but a chaotic flapping at the window startled her. She turned to see a blue feather floating to the ground—the same sky blue as the family crest. A harvel perched on the thick stone sill, black eyes staring out of a midnight-blue face. The predator's curved beak preened at the lighter breast feathers, dislodging another one.

Karin rose calmly and padded to the window, careful not to startle the visitor. She cooed an impressive imitation of the bird's tongue. Fixing its gaze on her, it tilted its head to one side, listening. When Karin fell silent, the bird nodded once then flew away. Gabrielle and Sarah looked at each other and back at Karin.

The queen stood and joined the Inkran at the window. "Karin, what just happened? Who are you?"

The girl's eyes met the queen's. Without flinching, and with the calm air of royalty, she answered, "My father is King Suklar. I am second in line to the Inkran throne. Ashander is my pet. I talk to her. She will let my mother know I am all right."

Gabrielle was too stunned to hide her shock. She returned to her chair. "Sarah, be a dear and pour me another drink, please. And just when I thought my day couldn't get any worse. Please come here, Karin. We have much to discuss."

"Yes, Your Highness."

Gabrielle gulped down her wine. Why the honorific? What was she trying to say? Did she have the girl's support? It was a long night. Gabrielle sent Sarah to bed some time before dawn while she spent the night learning about Karin, her country, and family. As they rose to seek their beds, a rap on the door interrupted them.

"Yes?"

The muffled voice on the other side of the door answered,

"It's your guard, Philip, my lady. I've come to let you know a dragon and a realmist await you downstairs."

Before Gabrielle opened the door, she turned to Karin. "You do know I can't possibly let you go now. Our countries are at war. I will have to post two guards to accompany you for the duration of your stay until my husband says otherwise. I wouldn't let the truth of who you are get out either; there are, unfortunately, some Varesians who would sooner kill you than see you returned to your homeland. Now go and get some sleep. I'm afraid I've kept you up all night."

Karin curtseyed, her face unreadable. "Yes, Your Majesty. I understand."

Gabrielle let the girl out and gave instructions to her guards. After attempting to fix her hair, which she was not used to doing, she hurried to meet the new arrivals. Even with strands of dark tendrils escaping her braid and the shadowed ridges under her eyes, no one could mistake her for anyone but the queen as she strode into the king's reception rooms with the elegance and straight-backed assuredness she had practiced since childhood. Gabrielle hoped the new arrivals could be trusted because she needed their help.

Suffering the continual torture of not knowing if her child was alive or dead, revenge was her primary motive, but Gabrielle also had a plan. Talia needed to go to the final war united. What the queen proposed might be their only hope. Putting on her friendliest smile, she appeared in front of Warrimonious, the imposing, gray dragon; and Astra, the diminutive realmist from across the ocean. Astra wore a loose-fitting purple dress and her chocolate-brown hair fell in tight ringlets to her shoulders—violet, cat-like eyes watched Gabrielle with a serene stare. The queen almost felt naked in front of the woman's knowing gaze.

"Welcome to Bayerlon. I'm so glad you're both here."

The dragon bowed his massive head, and Astra dipped a curtsey. Warrimonious spoke; his deep, confident voice wrapped Gabrielle in security—she definitely felt safer now than she had in a long while. "It is our pleasure, Your Majesty. I will be staying until my wife returns. Have you heard any news?"

The queen hesitated and realized he must mean Arcese. "Oh, she's your wife? Congratulations; she's an extraordinary dragon."

Gabrielle felt strange, as she wasn't used to having polite conversation with dragon captains, or dragons in general, come to think of it.

Warrimonious smiled—a sight Gabrielle was trying to get used to. "Have you heard anything?"

"No, I'm sorry. They only left yesterday, so they wouldn't have reached Klendar yet. Don't worry. Zim and Agmunsten are quite capable of looking after her, and to be honest, she seems able to look after herself."

"I wouldn't normally worry about her, but…."

"But what, Sir Dragon?"

"My beloved wife is with child."

"Oh, congratulations again, it seems. Have you tried contacting her?"

"I'm unable. Normally we can speak mind-to-mind, but it's like shouting over such a long distance, and anyone else with the ability would be able to hear us. It is imperative that her mission not be compromised. The enemy mustn't know we are coming."

"I understand. Why don't we discuss this later?" Gabrielle now stood close to the dragon, and she placed a soft palm on his thigh, patting it in a calming gesture. "You must both be hungry, and I have so many questions to ask Astra—I want to hear all about where you come from."

"The Academy?" the woman asked, purposefully being obtuse.

Gabrielle smiled and pretended her question had not been fended off. She enjoyed being direct, and if others were reluctant to follow her lead, she would wrangle them to her way with stubbornness renown throughout Bayerlon. "No, Astra. I would like you to tell me about Zamahl."

"As you wish, Your Majesty." Astra inclined her head and Gabrielle noticed the twitch of a smile on her lips.

"Please follow me to the dining hall." Gabrielle walked with purpose. Her husband was away doing what he could for Talia; now it was her turn.

CHAPTER 25

Zim landed with a thud, any grace forgotten in his urgency. He spoke into Arcese's mind. "Sister of mine! Put up a fire shield. I shall melt the glass. Arie's shield will not hold much longer."

"Zimapholous!" She resisted the desire to embrace her brother. Her joyful exclamation was all she allowed herself before dredging what power she could hold from the Second Realm and creating a protective bubble inside Arie's. As she tied the power off, hairline cracks slithered haphazardly over the original shield, and just before it shattered into the ether, Zim breathed scalding flame. The attacking shards melted and fell to the floor—glowing, red slag pooling on the stone.

Kwaad turned to survey the new arrivals. "What? More of you to have fun with? Oh, this really is my night. I get to kill so many."

Its laughter, harsh and devoid of mirth, pricked goose bumps on Agmunsten's skin before echoing into the night sky.

The monster reached sharp-boned arms out and gathered Second-Realm power.

Zim flinched at the amount of energy he could sense being siphoned and knew if he didn't act now, they would all be dead. He summoned natural power and shot razor-sharp slices of energy to each side of a steel beam in the roof frame. The blue laser cut both ends of the weighty beam, and before Kwaad could release his spell, a shrill groan pierced the air. Steel fell.

Arie and Boy screamed, as it appeared that Verity might be crushed, but Zim's aim was true, and Kwaad suffered the blow. The creature was pushed to the floor but lay under the wreckage for only seconds before the beam shook and rolled to the ground, crushing stone tiles to sand as Kwaad stood. Arcese and Zim drew more energy, fearful that none of them would escape. This monster was stronger than anything they had anticipated.

"What about Verity?" Boy whispered to Agmunsten. He had looked for her as soon as they landed and had not taken his eyes from her since. Agmunsten didn't answer, and Boy realized the realmist was channeling, something he had seen him do a few times. It seemed everyone was intent on fighting the monster, but who was going to save Verity? He had to try.

As Boy slid off Zim's back, both dragons loosed their power. A crack rent the air as Kwaad's returning energy met the dragons' in the center of the room. Fluorescent green pushed against pure white, death edging closer to the dragons. Arcese shook with the effort, and Arie could hear her panting. The young realmist also drew energy and fed it into their stream, knowing if they were hit by Kwaad's power, he would suffer the same fate as the dragons: swift death.

Boy snuck across the floor, unnoticed by the warring

parties. Verity watched him come and stood. "Oh, Boy. You came! Oh gods, thank you, thank you." Her tears flowed freely, and she flung her arms around his neck.

"We don't have time now. You can thank me later, Princess." As much as he wanted to prolong the embrace, he knew there was no time. "We need to get out of here. Which way?" He gently disengaged himself from her arms. "If the dragons can't hold on, we need to find another way out."

Verity looked at the double doors she had entered what seemed like a lifetime ago. Boy's gaze followed hers and he grabbed her hand, pulling her towards them.

Kwaad's life-ending energy continued to creep towards the dragons. Zim stooped, Arcese breathed heavily, and two divots of concentration pitted the skin between Arie's eyes. They were losing, even though it was three against one. Agmunsten saw what was happening and reached through the corridor too —if he overextended himself, he would die, but if he didn't try to help they were dead anyway.

And then the energy stopped encroaching on the dragons. Movement near the doors had captured Kwaad's attention. "Where do you think you're going?"

Verity and Boy froze under the red-eyed stare; both teens could feel their hearts pounding against their chests, and the princess squeezed Boy's hand.

Zim called out, "Over here: both of you. Now!"

Boy wanted to run out the door—it was right there, a foot away—but if they could get on Zim, maybe they could fly away and escape. Then Boy realized Kwaad would not let that happen, and shook his head at his foolishness; he actually thought he might be able to save Verity by running some-where. They could never run fast enough, not from that. Boy knew what he had to do. "Go, Verity. I'm right behind you."

She looked at him: fear and hope, appreciation—a collage of emotions in her eyes. He quickly kissed her cheek and pushed her towards Zim. "Hurry; your mother is waiting."

She tripped over her torn dress but managed to stay on her feet. Not daring to look behind to see if Kwaad was after her, she sprinted for the black dragon. Kwaad looked at Boy as if to say *I'll deal with you later* before taking measured, calm strides towards Zim.

"Get her and go, Zim. I'm right behind you, Brother," Arcese urged.

Zim wanted to argue but knew if he hesitated, they would all die. Maybe they had a chance to get the princess and Agmunsten to safety. The Circle needed to be whole, but Arcese and Arie weren't members—Talia could win the coming war without them if they had to ... so the prophecies said. Drawing what power he could, he held it and waited.

As Verity reached the dragon, Agmunsten leaned down to help her on, but Kwaad was almost upon them. *We can't fail now,* Agmunsten thought. *Gods, not now:* he stretched further.

Boy saw how close the evil creature was to those he cared about and knew this was all his fault. He didn't want everyone to die, not because of him. Needing to do what he had set out to when he ran away from Bayerlon, he trotted behind Kwaad, spying a thick shard of glass—as long as his forearm—on the floor. He picked it up and ran, the glass slicing where he gripped, pain screaming up his arm. He grunted but kept going, seeing his target.

Kwaad reached for Verity, claws extended, ready to rip her from safety. Again Arie willed her to hurry. She scrambled on Zim's back, sweaty palms slipping on the saddle. Kwaad's talons grazed her back.

Remembering his mother one last time and the day in the

forest when he had betrayed Verity for Leon, Boy struck, plunging the glass into the back of Kwaad's leg. The shard sunk deep, and Boy screamed as his palm split wide, slick fluid drenching his hand. The creature faltered: it was not immune to pain. "Fly!" Boy shouted, "Fly!"

Zim released his power, pushing force against the floor, giving him an accelerated takeoff. Arcese did the same. Both dragons launched into the air, furiously beating leathery wings.

Verity, Agmunsten, and Arie watched as Kwaad bellowed, turning instinctively to rake Boy's chest with bladed fingers. Verity cried out, "No!" and Arie turned his face away, shaking with violent sobs. *Not my friend. No. Please, no.* Agmunsten's tears, something he thought he had out-aged, came as they hadn't for two-hundred years. *You've done us proud, Son. I'll make sure they know you're a hero.*

Skin parted like butter, and Boy felt pain and warmth as blood flooded from his chest. Boy smiled through the agony and metallic crimson bubbling through his grimace. "You … didn't … win." He collapsed to the floor, and Kwaad howled into the space where the dragons had escaped. Fury hazing its vision, Kwaad gave into its gormon lust. Plunging its mouth into the child, the thing that was Kwaad fed and thought through the satisfying crunch of human bone: *They won't be so lucky next time. The horde is coming. Soon. So very, very soon.* It laughed, blood dribbling down its chin.

CHAPTER 26

Waking in the afternoon from a fitful sleep, after going to bed near dawn, Bronwyn saw Avru-ellen's bed was vacated and made. Her aunt never needed as much sleep as she did, and Bronwyn always tired first. It was frustrating being bested by an older person all the time. Bronwyn dressed and hurried to the kitchen, hoping food would be available between lunch and dinner, as she was light-headed from hunger. Entering the warm, flagstone-floored space, she saw Corrille chopping vegetables.

Hoping they could get over their recent troubles, Bronwyn approached her. "Hi."

Her stomach clenched in fear of rejection. Corrille, after a time, looked up but didn't smile. "Hi."

"How are you?" Bronwyn almost cringed at the awkwardness of the conversation. How had they gone from telling each other their most intimate secrets to hardly speaking?

"I'm chopping vegetables in a kitchen. How do you think I

am?" she hissed through closed teeth. "Your aunt has managed to make my life miserable ... again."

"I'm sorry. I'm sure she didn't mean it to be torture. I guess she just thought we should try and help some way since we've practically invaded their monastery."

"Trust you to defend her. I thought we were friends, but I was wrong." Corrille pounded the blade on the chopping board as she dissected a carrot, causing the supervising cook to raise an eyebrow.

Bronwyn sighed, blinking back tears. "But we *are* friends; at least I want us to be. What did I do wrong? Since I woke up on that ship, you seem ... different. I feel like, well, like there's some invisible barrier between us. I don't know. Can you tell me why?"

Corrille looked up. Hate burned in her eyes. Bronwyn stepped back, feeling as if the other had stabbed her with the knife she held. "You abandoned me, Bronwyn. When you left with that panther, you left me to that evil woman's mercy and then worse. Do you know what I've been through since I last saw you? Blayke is the only one I can trust now; he loves me; he saved me. You showed what a true friend you were when you abandoned me without a second thought. Now, if you don't mind, I have work to do."

Corrille's face was flushed with anger, and Bronwyn felt the heat of her hate radiating in waves. Bronwyn swallowed, her appetite gone. She had lost her childhood friend, and it wasn't even her own fault. There was nothing she could say to make Corrille listen.

Wiping a palm across her eyes to clear away the tears, Bronwyn searched out Avruellen; there was a lot to do before the ritual tonight, and it was going to be dangerous. None of them knew what to expect. The day the gormons invaded en masse was nearing. Bronwyn shuddered as she walked the halls. "Drakon, you bastard, don't fail us now," she growled under her breath.

Unsurprisingly, Bronwyn found Avruellen, Arcon, Blayke, and the creaturas sitting around the central table, discussing procedures for the coming amulet activation. She sat, trying to keep her sadness from showing.

"So, you're finally up? Did you sleep well?" Avruellen asked.

Bronwyn forced a smile. "Yes, thanks. So what's happening?"

Arcon answered. "According to *The Comprehensive Realmists' Almanac of Incantations*, both amulets have to be activated together—they need to get to know each other, so to speak."

"Why?" asked Bronwyn.

"Because they will work together. The battle with the gormons is where the final activation will take place. During this final activation, the amulets will not only be dangerous but will change you and Blayke, although it doesn't say how. Whatever it is, it doesn't sound like something you are going to come out of unscathed."

"What do you mean? Will it kill us?" Bronwyn place her palms on the table and stared in fear at Arcon.

His neutral expression gave nothing away. "I don't think so, but there is a warning at the end of the section. It was supposedly written by a realmist dreamer channeling Tokim, the god of what will be." Arcon cleared his throat and read.

During a time of darkness
Fierce battle will they see
Against murderous gormons
And Kwaad, their enemy,
Who will bear the might of Three.

When blood doth run
Rivulets around their legs,
Victory Drakon will not find
Unless the keepers of the halves
Have sacrificed to make it One.
And having burnt away
All that they are
In dragons' cleansing fire,
Know themselves they must—
For only if they do
Will the hordes be overcome.
But, be that so, even in victory
Two must die to make them free.

Blayke rubbed the back of his neck. "That gives me the creeps. It reminds me of my dragon dream. You know the one."

Arcon nodded.

"What dragon dream?" asked Bronwyn.

"I used to have it all the time but didn't have it for ages. Actually, I started having it again after we came down out of the mountains, on the beginning of this—what would you call it—adventure."

Bronwyn looked at him and saw he was reluctant to continue. "Would you say it's more of a nightmare?"

He nodded.

"Well, I have one too, and I guess that's no surprise since we're twins. In my nightmare I'm standing in a storm, and the rain is falling so hard it hurts my skin. There's an awful, deep scream. I shut my eyes tight, and it's all I can do not to die from fright. When I open my eyes, there's a dragon standing in front of me, but not a normal dragon. This dragon is three times the size of Zim and it...." Bronwyn took a deep breath.

Blayke interrupted before she could continue. "And it opens its mouth and eats you alive?" She nodded. They both looked to Arcon for an explanation. Arcon looked at Avruellen, and she gave a slight nod. Sinjenasta hung his head: he knew what the dream meant, but he wasn't able to tell them. Drakon would probably strike him dead before he'd let that happen.

Arcon spoke. "That dream is a true dream. But before you go screaming down the hall, it may not mean what you think it means. Your life is not necessarily going to end in the belly of a dragon."

"But it might?" asked Bronwyn.

Arcon pursed his lips. "Well, there are no guarantees, of course. From what this prophecy says, you and Blayke will join the amulet so it becomes one. What happens after that involves fire, but who and even *if* someone dies is another matter. I'm sure those prophesy writers got a kick out of knowing they were going to scare some poor realmists one day in the future."

Blayke spoke, the words rushing out in a single breath. "But someone does die."

Everyone looked at him.

"You don't know that, lad," said Arcon.

Blayke stood up. He couldn't believe he'd almost given away the painful secret he'd been keeping since the last activation. Not wanting to alarm his family, he sat back down, took some calming breaths and lied. "No, I suppose I don't. But what if I am right? Isn't there another way to fight the gormons and win?"

Arcon shook his head. "That's enough speculation. I only

read the prophesy out so you had some expectation of what might happen. I didn't want to scare everyone. We can all do this. We have the strength to fight. After we finish the second activation tonight, we'll head back to Bayerlon: I'm sure King Edmund will need us, and it's the perfect place to plan a war. The other thing we need to think about is initiating you two into The Circle."

Bronwyn and Blayke let their mouths hang open. They had been working their whole lives just so they could become members of The Circle, but neither really believed they'd ever be good enough. "Okay," continued Arcon, "it's time for dinner; then we have some amulets to bless."

Instead of going to the dining hall, Bronwyn thought she'd help serve the meal: maybe she could get Corrille to see she really did care. Entering the bustling space, she approached the head cook. "What can I do to help?"

The chubby woman smoothed her white apron with work-worn fingers. "You can take any full bowls to the table. You'll find everything that's to be served over there." She pointed to the timber table in the middle of the room that doubled as the dining table for kitchen staff. Bronwyn almost walked into Corrille, who held a hot terrine filled with roast potatoes, baked pumpkin slices, and eggplant, with cloths to protect her fingers.

"You want to help? Here." She shoved the dish at Bronwyn, who grabbed it—without the cloths. Bronwyn, not near the table, dropped to her knees, hurriedly thumped the terrine on the floor and looked at her blistered, red hands. Concentrating through tears, she channeled a trickle of power from the Second Realm—not enough that anyone would be alerted —and sped up the growth of new skin cells until her hands were a healthy pink, the pain gone.

By the time she looked up, Corrille had left. The cook stood over her. "Are you all right? That will leave a nasty burn. Here: use this wet cloth to cool the skin."

"No. It's okay. I took care of it." Bronwyn held up her hands to show the woman, then grabbed the cloths Corrille had dropped on the floor beside the dish. Bronwyn wasn't usually vindictive, but this had to stop. She seethed. *How dare she! What in The Third Realm was she thinking? That bitch. She'll think Avruellen is a docile milkmaid by the time I'm done with her. Just you wait, Corrille. When you least expect it, expect it.*

When Bronwyn finally sat down, Sinjenasta, tearing at a shoulder of venison in the corner, spoke, *What happened? Are you all right?*

Trying to be obtuse, she said, *What do you mean? Oh, yes.* Bronwyn remembered feelings carried through the bond. There were times you could mask emotions or pain, but she hadn't been thinking when it happened, and Sinjenasta was in such close proximity that of course he would have felt it. *Corrille happened. She handed me a hot plate on purpose and I burnt my fingers.*

Bronwyn spooned some of the vegetables onto her plate, stabbing a potato forcefully before shoving it in her mouth.

She's proving to be a real little troublemaker. Would you like me to take care of her?

Bronwyn turned to look at the panther. *You can't kill her!*

Sinjenasta laughed. *I wasn't going to kill her, just scare her a bit.*

No, it's okay. I think I should take care of this myself.

Okay, but if you need any help, just call out. He winked.

You're a bad, bad panther, but thanks, Sinje. I'll be sure to let you know if anyone needs scaring. Bronwyn turned to Avruellen. "When will we start? Will it be straight after dinner?"

"No. We'll start just before midnight. I'll call you before it's time, and you can meet us outside the library. From there we're going to a special room they have here for prayer and rituals. In the meantime, I suggest you relax and get yourself focused. What we're going to do will be very dangerous."

Bronwyn almost rolled her eyes. "Really? You don't say."

"No need to get clever, young lady. The time I don't say it will be the time something happens."

"Stop worrying, Auntie. I know it's dangerous, but if something's going to happen, it will, whether you warned me beforehand or not." Bronwyn wondered how old she would be before Avruellen stopped treating her like a child.

"One day you'll wish you had been more careful or more prepared: it's happened to me before. If we had been more prepared, Augustine wouldn't have died." Avruellen suddenly looked all of her hundreds of years. Bronwyn hadn't realized her aunt still thought about that disaster. She'd assumed Avruellen would have suffered many such losses and would have put it aside, but apparently she hadn't.

"Sorry. I'll be careful—don't worry." Bronwyn leaned over and squeezed Avruellen's shoulder. Bronwyn finished dinner and decided to spend some time outside, where she could relax by listening to the water caressing the shore. Bronwyn took her boots off and walked barefoot through the scratchy coastal grass. Reaching the cool sand, she sighed. Rolling up her tight-fitting trousers, she waded into the water until she was shin-deep.

The light from the monastery didn't reach the water and Bronwyn gazed up at an uninterrupted view of the night sky. It looked to her like glass had shattered into a billion tiny fragments on a black marble floor, catching the light and reflecting cold, stark beauty. Although reminded of the symbols in the Second Realm, Bronwyn felt alone—a miniscule spectator unnoticed by the vastness of the realms. She wondered where her mother was and if she missed her.

"What are you doing?"

Bronwyn jumped and turned, warmth spreading through her when she saw Toran. "Oh, for the gods' sakes. You scared me. I was just taking some time to get myself together before the thing we have to do."

"The activation, you mean? Don't worry; Arcon told me all about it."

"Why would he do that? Everything we've done so far has been super secret. I wasn't even allowed to tell Corrille."

"Maybe he trusts me, and maybe he thinks I can help." Toran waded in to stand beside Bronwyn, close enough that he could have reached out and held her hand.

"Hmm, maybe. Anyway, what are you doing out here?" Bronwyn looked straight ahead at the moonlight shining a shimmering path to the horizon. She wished he would reach over and take her hand.

"I have some exciting news I wanted to share."

"Ooh, I love exciting news. What is it?"

"I told Arcon I wanted to learn how to be a realmist. He placed his hands over my ears, and I felt a warm tingling in my head, and then he said yes. I'm coming with you when you leave."

When Bronwyn turned to smile, he was looking at her with a large grin. "It will be so great to have company! Corrille and Blayke have been keeping to themselves lately. It'll be nice to have someone my age to talk to. I'm glad you're coming."

Bronwyn was happy it was dark and he couldn't see her blush.

"Me too."

So, what's going on here?

Bronwyn jumped for the second time that night. A large shadowy shape—Sinjenasta—stood two feet behind her. She spoke aloud. "Toran has some good news, Sinje. He's coming with us when we leave." Toran turned to see who Bronwyn was talking to.

Sinjenasta's mind voice was dry. "That's good news? Hmph. Anyway, it's time to come in now; I don't think Avru-ellen would like it if she knew you were out here, alone, with a strange boy."

"He's not strange!"

"Who's not strange?"

"Sorry, Toran; I was talking to Sinjenasta. He says my aunt wouldn't like it if I was alone out here with a strange boy, and unfortunately, he's right. Um, not the strange part. I don't think you're strange."

"It's okay," he said with a laugh, "I've been called worse. Come on. I'd hate to get you into trouble."

Bronwyn retreated to the library, and the panther followed. A pile of silky, gold-fringed cushions in the corner attracted Bronwyn, and she fell into their softness and folded her arms, glaring at Sinjenasta. "So, spoilsport, what have you been up to?"

What do you mean 'spoilsport?' Sinjenasta sat elegantly in front of her, curling his tail around to lie on his front paws.

"Don't pretend you don't know. Toran's nice and it's the first time I've had someone my own age—and species—to talk to for a while." Bronwyn looked in her creatura's eyes. "I feel lonely sometimes."

Lonely? How can you be lonely with the bond we have, with your aunt here and now your brother?

"Well, I like knowing you're around, and I would miss you if you weren't, but it's just not the same. I mean, you're way older than me and you're a panther. Oh, don't look so offended!" Bronwyn kneeled and stroked his head. "Sometimes I need a human to talk to—one that isn't going to tell me what to do and judge me. I know Avruellen loves me, but it's hard to have fun conversations with her, and Blayke's busy with my former best friend, in case you'd forgotten."

Do I look old?

"What? No. It's not like you have gray fur or anything, but I'm figuring you have to be at least a few hundred-years old. Do you want to tell me how old you are?" Sinjenasta shook his head. "I didn't think so. Anyway, I like Toran; he's really nice and he's cute, and I don't want you messing things up for me. Okay?"

Sinjenasta narrowed his eyes and let the silence settle for a moment. *Hmm, okay, but I'll be keeping an eye on him. Trust me: you can't trust young men—they're all after one thing.*

"And what would that be?" Bronwyn's raised an eyebrow.

Hasn't Avruellen had the talk with you? Never mind. The panther grumbled.

"Oh, *that* talk. Can we change the subject?"

Gladly. Are you ready for tonight?

"As ready as I could ever be for something unknown." Bronwyn pushed down the nervousness bubbling inside. "I'm a bit scared, actually. Does that make me a bad realmist?"

Fear is normal. It means you'll be careful. Just don't let it interfere with what you have to do. You must be focused and strong, and make sure you're not easily distracted. I have a feeling you'll be tested tonight in a way you haven't been before. The amulet won't want to be controlled by a person who is not worthy. Tonight is about proving yourself as much as it's about surviving the activation.

"*Surviving* the activation? Thanks for reminding me." Another tide of adrenalin washed through her body. "Sinje, if you're going to stay, do you think you could distract me? Tell me about your family."

The panther's ears twitched while he thought. *My family's long-dead. I can hardly remember them.*

"Was there ever a *Missus* Panther?"

Sinjenasta laughed. *You could call her that. We had three cubs. They were young when Drakon took me away, but I was able to keep an eye on them as they grew. They had children of their own and so on, but the descendants who are left are so far removed from me that I don't feel anything towards them.*

"Oh. That's sad. What was your wife's name?"

Arabella. I do think of her sometimes, but not often. It was so long ago.

"Do you ever get lonely?"

The panther didn't answer. He lay down and rested his head on his paws. Bronwyn snuggled next to him and sneezed. "Damn allergy," she complained and sneezed again. She found comfort next to her big cat so weathered the sneezing. By the time Avruellen came looking for them, they had fallen asleep.

Sinjenasta sensed the realmist and sat up. Avruellen had to gently shake Bronwyn's shoulder. "Hey, sleepyhead. It's time."

Bronwyn yawned and rose from her position against the panther.

"Oh, wow. That time already? Are you sure I'll be able to do it?"

"Bronwyn, I'm as sure as I can be. You're intelligent, you've worked hard, and I know you're determined. I've taught you as much as I could, and now you have to trust that we've done the work. I think you'll do fine. Follow me."

Bronwyn scrambled to her feet and had to jog to catch Avruellen as she left the library and turned left down a narrow corridor. At the end of the corridor, they followed another left turn. When they reached a staircase, Avruellen walked up. Bronwyn was surprised because she had assumed they would activate the amulets somewhere safe, like a basement.

A pair of wall torches lit the landing at the top of the stairs, low flames reflected off the polished-gold door handle. Without hesitation, Avruellen opened the door, and they stepped out into a rooftop garden unlike anything Bronwyn had seen before. A lush carpet of grass spread out before them, fringed with topiary fruit trees, flowering vines twined around their trunks. The full moon gifted silvery light to the scene, highlighting buxom lemons, apples, and dark, ripe plomes.

"Take your boots off, dear," Avruellen instructed. Bronwyn sat and undid her laces, leaving her shoes next to the door. Standing, Bronwyn felt the coolness of spongy grass under her feet. The musty odor of dirt dampened her nostrils, and the usually-crimson petals of the armin flower—on a vine adorning an apple tree—leached to rust in the cool, empty light. A strange sense of timelessness and decay settled over her, and when she looked at Blayke, Avruellen, and Arcon, who all stood in the center of the otherworldly park, their images shimmered—healthy bodies overlaid with phantoms of bloody carcasses, their waxen skin peeling away like milky scum scraped from a diseased cave wall. Hoping this was not a vision of their futures, she took her position with them and waited.

Sinjenasta, Flux, and Fang sat together—a few feet from the realmists—and watched.

Why can't we help? asked Fang.

It must be those four. Anyone else and the energies would not be balanced. They would risk failure, answered Flux.

How do you know? Fang licked his tummy, a nervous habit.

He's right, Fang, said Sinjenasta. *I lived with Drakon for centuries.* He looked down at the brown and white rat. *I spent my time there wisely.*

Do you think they'll do it? Fang asked.

I don't know, but we'll soon find out. Look: they're starting. Flux wished he could do more to help.

Avruellen stepped out the perimeter of the ward and took her place at the eastern point of their square, opposite Arcon. Blayke stood at the south point opposite his sister—a balance of blood on every corner. Through the ages, their family had borne the burden of The Circle, and now they were the last hope for Talia. Avruellen had sometimes wondered why, but knowing she would likely never find out, she accepted it and moved on. Although the moving on was harder now: the lives of her niece and nephew stood in offering before her. Talia's fate walked a precarious road, and tonight, if the amulets didn't undergo their second activations, Talia would be headed for an inevitable end—at the mouths of hungry gormons.

"Take off your amulets and hold them," instructed Arcon.

Blayke fumbled his fingers into his shirt and pulled the necklace over his head. He looked up to the stars and squinted at the brightness of the moon. The quartz in his open hand absorbed the hoary light and glowed, the sweat on his palm sparkling like a scattering of gold dust in the sun. Blayke raised his head and met Bronwyn's eyes. His closed-mouth smile was meant to be reassuring. *We can do this, Bronny,* he said mind-to-mind. She returned his tempered smile and nodded.

As Avruellen began the incantation, Blayke swallowed against his fear. He focused on the crystal in his hand and searched for the Second Realm. Bronwyn whispered, "Mum and Dad, wherever you are, I love you"—before she stared at her amulet and sent her thoughts through the darkness. Both young realmists were vaguely aware that Avruellen and Arcon now spoke in unison: a different incantation to the first activation, their voices rising and falling, gathering power as Blayke and Bronwyn, their energies side by side, seeking the corridor.

Bronwyn felt her brother's energy as a warmth and a subtle tug—similar to the awareness she had of Sinjenasta. It reminded her of the day they bonded. When she had climbed out of the lake, she knew where he was with her eyes closed. Now she could see the mouth of the tunnel as a darkness blacker than their black surroundings. Just as they approached, Avruellen and Arcon spoke into their minds, *Stop!*

What? What's wrong? Blayke asked, halting, his awareness floating next to his sister's.

Wait a moment. When Arcon and I have finished what we're doing, another tunnel will open. This is the one through which you must travel. The connection cut off.

Where are they sending us?

You know as much as I do, Bronny. I don't want to be negative, but if we don't make it through this, I want you to know I'm glad we found each other. If I have to have a sister, I'm glad it's you.

Um, thanks, I think. I'm sorry if I've been cranky. I want you to know that finding you has been the best thing that's ever happened to me. I wish we could've met our parents, but….

You never know. If we do survive, I'll help you find them, okay? Blayke felt Bronwyn's energy pulse with happiness for a moment before it changed to fear.

What's that? Bronwyn watched as a small dot of white light turned into a circle, growing larger and larger until it was all they could see. Engulfed by the incandescence, they felt themselves sucked farther in. In the distance, Bronwyn saw another dot—a dark spec, which expanded as they neared. *This must be the other tunnel,* she reasoned. Forgetting she was in spirit form, she tried to reach out and grab Blayke's hand, but there was nothing to grab. Struggling not to panic as the darkness coalesced into moving shapes, Bronwyn reached her awareness towards her brother's. Reassured he was there, she focused on what she wanted: to get through this and whatever was coming. *I am a realmist. We have to save Talia. I want to live to meet my parents.*

The shadowed vista jumped forward until it was all they could see. A rush of warm, dusty air pushed into their faces. Blayke grunted as they were spat onto the hard, red ground. Bronwyn, on her stomach, lifted her face to look around, spitting dirt out of her mouth. She saw Blayke lying dazed next to a boulder. Tufts of silver-green grass interrupted the otherwise desolate soil, and white-barked trees stood at intervals, their crowning domes of jade-green leaves ignoring the midday sun.

She rolled over, sat up, and clamped her hand over her mouth to stop from screaming: Bronwyn was staring at a leather-clad pair of muscled legs. She looked up, past the sword that sat in the scabbard at the man's waist, past the arrow in his strong, brown hand, past the fitted white shirt and into a sun-bronzed, black-bearded face. The wrinkles around his dark eyes were not earned from laughing. He spoke to someone behind him, someone Bronwyn couldn't see. "Well, Sandar, it looks like our prayers have been answered. Although, call me skeptical, but I have no idea how these two children are going to defeat Devorum."

The man who must be Sandar walked around his comrade to get a better look at Bronwyn. Bronwyn gasped when she saw his face. *It can't be. Not again.* He spoke in a familiar, soothing voice that caused her heart to race. It was the young man from the realm she had been to when bonding with Sinjenasta. She was torn between staring into his blue-green eyes and looking away—she didn't want him to know the effect he had on her.

"Princess! Is it really you?" He held out a hand to help her up, but she ignored him, standing by herself and slapping the dust off her clothes. She finished by wiping a forearm across her mouth to clear the last of the dirt.

"I told you before: I'm not a princess. My name is Bronwyn, and that's my brother, Blayke." She walked over to help him up and whispered in his ear, "Are you okay? I don't know what we've gotten ourselves into, but we need to be careful."

Blayke leaned on her as he rose. "I'm okay. I headbutted that damn rock when I came through. I don't think anything's permanently damaged." He rubbed his head. "Where the hell are we?" The two men had followed Bronwyn over, and the older one spoke.

"Sorry to interrupt. I'm Korden, and this is my cousin, Sander. You're in the Sacred Realm. Please forgive me, Bronwyn, but you do look like Princess Tawin."

Bronwyn rolled her eyes. "Okay, Korden, great. Now that's settled, what do you want from us? We must be here for a reason, and whatever it is, I'd like to know as soon as possible." She looked around. "Oh, bugger, the corridor's gone. How are we going to get back?" When she had found herself here the first time, she knew the lake was her way home. Were they going to have to find the lake again? Even if they did, they would end up back in Vellonia, not where they needed to be.

"You're right." Blayke turned in a circle, hoping to see the hole in the air from which they had dropped. He faced the men. "Where in the Third Realm are we? Where exactly, or what exactly, is the Sacred Realm?"

Sander answered, "It's the realm from where all other

realms come, the perfect realm that gods plunder from to create other, inferior versions. It is said there are mirrors of our realm, although I've never seen them."

"So," Blayke asked, "if the First Realm, where we come from, is a mirror of this one, then there should be another one of me here and one of you there?"

"I don't know if it works exactly like that, but it is possible. Maybe that's why Bronwyn looks like the princess."

"Oh, for the gods' sakes, can we please just get on with what we have to do and stop talking nonsense? In case you haven't forgotten, Blayke, if we don't activate the amulets properly, there won't be any First Realm to worry about." Bronwyn turned to Korden. "What do you want us to do?"

"We've been ordered by our king to capture Devorum. But we can't kill him; we need him alive."

"Who, or what, is Devorum?" Blayke asked.

"Devorum is a dragon: an enormous, black dragon—the most feared creature in this realm."

"Why does he want to catch this dragon, and why would you think we could help? Surely you have realmists here who can do the job?" Bronwyn didn't want to die fighting someone else's battles when she had enough of her own.

"What's a realmist?"

Blayke and Bronwyn looked at Sander, their mouths open in disbelief. "You don't know?" Both men shook their heads, so Blayke continued, "Bronwyn and I are realmists—we can draw power from the Second Realm to *do* things. Although I don't know if we can get access from here. Hang on a minute."

Blayke concentrated and searched for the corridor.

"What's the Second Realm?" Sander asked.

Bronwyn, sensing that Blayke was busy, answered, "It's a

place where you can't physically go, but you can send your spirit there, to gather power. It reminds me of the night sky. You do have a night sky, don't you?"

Sander looked at Bronwyn, cocking his head to one side. "Ha, ha, very funny. Yes, we have a night sky."

"Thank the gods; I was beginning to worry for a minute there." Bronwyn grinned.

"Yep, Bronny, we can get to the Second Realm." Bronwyn let out a relieved breath. Blayke turned to Korden. "So, why do you need us to catch this dragon?"

Korden and Sander exchanged glances, the younger man giving a small nod. Korden answered, "The gods have spoken to our king. Even though other realms mirror ours, we know nothing about them: we are not permitted to see. But, if any other realms are threatened, the balance here is affected. There is an island in the Verren Sea; well, there was an island. It is now a whirlpool of black—nothing comes in, nothing goes out, but the island—and all its people—were sucked into that black hole when it formed. The gods have told us it's because of an imbalance that occurred fifty years ago, and the next one will have a much greater impact."

"Where did it go?" asked Bronwyn.

"We don't know. Please tell us you'll help us?" Sander stared into Bronwyn's eyes, hoping she liked him enough to agree.

Blayke stepped between Bronwyn and Sander. "My sister and I need to discuss this … in private. We'll be back when we're ready." Blayke grabbed Bronwyn's arm and dragged her out of hearing range of the men. "What do you think?"

"I have no idea how we're supposed to catch a dragon without killing him, but maybe we don't have a choice. Maybe this is what we've been sent here to do. This could be what activates the amulets. I mean, think about it: there's a threat because of another realm. Do you really think it's a coincidence that Talia's about to be overrun by gormons?"

Blayke sighed. "No. No, I don't. But we need a plan if we have any chance of doing what they're asking. I'm not feeling too confident."

"Neither am I, but think of it this way: if we're the future of Talia and The Circle and we can't do this, who in the Third Realm can? Let's go and get this over with."

CHAPTER 27

Sarah finished braiding her queen's hair and stood back, assessing the result. "I think you're ready for the day, Queen Gabrielle."

"Thank you, Sarah. I wonder if we'll hear from Edmund today. They've all been too quiet for too long. I'm worried."

Sarah looked at Gabrielle, her eyebrow raised. "I never would have guessed." She shook her head. "I think you have every right to be. I do hope they're on their way back with Verity."

"But why haven't we heard anything? Maybe Leon killed them all."

"Surely he would have sent a gloating message to us if he had."

"Oh, I don't know. If this goes on much longer, I'm going to grab a horse and go and find out for myself. I can't stand it." Smoothing her violet skirts with impatient hands, Gabrielle opened the door. On the other side was a guard, his hand raised, about to knock. Gabrielle startled, her hand clapping on her heart. "Oh, my goodness. Are you trying to give me a heart attack? What is it?"

The young guard blushed and bowed. "Sorry, Your Majesty. I've been ordered to tell you that two dragons have been seen flying towards the castle. Astra thinks it is Prince Zimapholous Accorterroza."

Gabrielle paled and swayed with a sudden rush of dizziness. Sarah held her arm. "Are you okay, Your Majesty?"

The queen swallowed, drew a deep breath, and nodded. Her eyes swam in waiting tears. Not trusting herself to speak, she hurried down the hallway, stairs, and into the front courtyard. The rising sun shone in her eyes: she shielded her face with her hand. Two dragons stood, backlit in the morning light, but she couldn't make out who they were. Wanting to vomit, scared to ask what news they carried, fearing her world was about to end if they told her Verity was dead, she stood silent, and waiting.

"Mother!" And then Verity was in her mother's arms, trembling, crying, trying to talk through grief and happiness—so much to say, but so much she didn't want to remember. Gabrielle breathed in, smelling Verity's windswept hair, convincing herself this wasn't a dream. Sarah clapped her arms around them, the three staying so for a time before Zim approached.

He bowed, not that anyone noticed. "Queen Gabrielle." He waited for her acknowledgement. "There is much to tell you. Can we retire somewhere private?"

Gabrielle looked at the dragon over Verity's shoulder. Reluctantly disengaging from her daughter, she hugged Zim, managing to reach her arms around part of the front of his belly. "Thank you, Zimapholous. You've brought my baby home. We owe you much. Anything you or your sister need, just ask."

He patted her back gently, awkwardly, and when Gabrielle was ready, they walked inside to Edmund's private meeting room. They arranged themselves around the table, the dragons sitting on the floor. "I'm so sorry, Arcese and Zim. We should probably have permanent bench seats installed; these meetings are becoming rather frequent. Before we start, you might want to call Warrimonious to join us. He arrived a few days ago."

Arcese sat up straight and set her jaw, giving Gabrielle the impression she was bracing for a confrontation. She hoped she was wrong: two dragons fighting in the meeting room would likely end in the destruction of said meeting room. Zim sent a mind message, and within minutes, Warrimonious and Astra arrived, Warrimonious rushing over to rub noses with his wife before embracing her.

Gabrielle took a seat next to Verity and held her hand. The princess would not usually sit in on sensitive meetings; however, she had information to give, and as painful as it would be, Gabrielle knew it was important: her daughter was becoming an adult before her time. There was nothing she could do to stop it now. She clenched her teeth and wished Leon was here so she could make him pay. "I'm afraid to ask, but where are Agmunsten, Arie, and Boy?"

Zim hesitated before replying. Gabrielle tensed, dreading the answer. "We left Agmunsten and Arie with Edmund and the army. We thought it best they fill Edmund in on everything we know. They should be here in a couple of days."

Gabrielle shut her eyes. "Oh, thank the gods." She opened them again. "And?" She heard Verity's sobs behind her, felt the sudden warmth in her own eyes.

Zim's eyes held a depth of sadness Gabrielle had never

seen on a dragon, and it surprised her that a human's life could elicit that reaction. "Boy was slain while saving Verity. He died a hero. His bravery, on more than one occasion, was something many grown men lack. I'm sorry we couldn't save him. Please forgive us, Your Majesty."

Zim knelt on one knee, his head bowed.

Gabrielle shook her head, mouthing, "No, no, no. Not sweet Boy." Rising, she approached Zim and placed a hand on his snout. She spoke through tears. "There is nothing to forgive. I know you did your best. I will never forget him: such a tragic life for such a beautiful boy. I'm sorry we all failed him."

She knelt too and sobbed, leaning against the dragon until Astra whispered in her ear and led her back to her chair.

Astra took the lead. "I'm Astra. Pleased to meet you, Prince Zimapholous and Princess Arcese." Astra gave an elegant half curtsey. "It is clear we have a lot to get through, and I know Edmund and Agmunsten would appreciate it if we formulated some plans before they return. The gormons will break through soon, and Talia is still a world divided. We all know the consequences of that. We need to act now." She turned violet eyes on Verity. "I know this may not be easy on you, but we need to know everything that happened while you were with Leon. Don't leave anything out, no matter how unimportant it seems."

Brushing her sleeve across her nose, she stopped crying. Leon used to be her uncle, but no more. He had killed her friend and turned into the physical form of what he was inside: a monster. The vehemence in her voice surprised her. She did as instructed, and left nothing out. When she finished, it was clear: if it were up to all those in the room, Leon would not survive for another second.

Gabrielle called Sarah in to take Verity to bathe and eat. When she left, Gabrielle shared Karin's story and her own plan. By the time the meeting ended, they felt hope. They weren't done for yet.

CHAPTER 28

After agreeing to help, Korden led Bronwyn and Blayke to where two horses were tethered. Blayke mounted behind Korden, and Bronwyn rode with Sander. She sat behind him, too shy to touch him, even though she wanted nothing more than to snuggle against his back. *Oh, for goodness sake, you're not here to meet men: you're here to save Talia. Focus.* She hoped talking to herself would be enough of a distraction to stop her mind wandering where she didn't want it to go.

Sander laughed. "I won't bite, you know. You can hold on to my waist. I would hate for you to fall off."

"But my hands are all dirty. I don't want to ruin your lovely white shirt."

He turned in the saddle, looking at Bronwyn out of the corner of his eye. Setting the reins on the horse's neck, he reached behind and grabbed both of her hands, setting them on his waist. "Don't worry—I have plenty of shirts, but there's only one Bronwyn, and I really don't want anything to happen to her: she has to help me save the Sacred Realm."

Bronwyn dropped her head down, wrinkled her nose, and squinted her eyes shut, smiling, trying not to giggle. His muscled waist felt pleasant under her hands: warm and firm. *Focus, idiot, focus. No, not on him.* She breathed in as the horse started walking, the thud of his hooves stirring up puffs of red dust. "So, you're saying that if you didn't need me to save your world, you wouldn't care if I fell off?"

She was happy he couldn't see her cheeky grin.

He snorted. "You women always turn everything around. It seems women are all the same, no matter what realm they come from."

"You mean fabulous and smarter than men? Yes we are."

"Oh, boy. Hmm, I wonder if Korden wants to swap. I don't know if I can take a whole day of this."

Bronwyn took her hands off his waist. "I'd be happy to swap, since all you men are the same."

"Hey, I was only joking."

"I know. Sorry. I'm just not in the mood. It's easy for you to ask Blayke and I to go and catch a deadly dragon, but now we have to figure out how to do it without getting ourselves killed. You do know that if we die, Talia dies and so, I guess, a whole lot of people from somewhere in this realm will die too. It's not much fun to have that much pressure, you know. Who are you, anyway? Where do you live, what do you do, other than accosting realmists from other realms to save your hide?"

"I'll only tell you if you put your hands back where they belong." He stayed quiet until Bronwyn placed her hands on his waist. "Okay then. Where to start? Korden is chief of the King's Guards, and I'm second-in-charge. My parents live in the main city, Arethene. I have two brothers and a sister. That's all there is to tell."

"How old are you?"

"Well, assuming your years are the same as ours, I'm twenty-four."

"Can you tell me about the dragon?"

"He's the last greater dragon in our realm. There are lots of lesser dragons, but they're not as fierce and they're much smaller. Devorum breathes fire, of course, but he can also sway you with his mind. He can make men kill themselves, or each other, by invading their thoughts. See that tree over there?" He pointed to a tree that stood thirty-feet tall. "He's about that big."

Bronwyn swallowed, eyes wide. "Shit."

That marked the end of their conversation for the next two hours, until they rode into a village and stopped for lunch. Bronwyn and Blayke dismounted, Blayke trotting to her.

"Are you okay?"

"Yeah, why?"

"You look, well, not happy I suppose."

"I'm wracking my brain, trying to figure out what we can do to beat this dragon. Sander told me a bit about it. Did Korden tell you anything?"

"Enough that I'm preparing to die." A tired smile rested on his face. "After lunch we're going to set off for the base of some mountains, Ishkatar I think he said. We'll summon the dragon there."

"How?"

"They have a whistle that screams at a frequency that travels long distances. Apparently only dogs and dragons can hear it. It mimics the call of the dragons' ancient foe."

"What? Is that wise? I mean, why would you call the

dragon with a signal that will have it being totally angry by the time it reaches us? They haven't thought this through very well."

"It's the only way they can get it to come out, or so the gods have told them."

"So, have you got any ideas?" Bronwyn looked at her brother expectantly.

"I have a few ideas, but the problem is we don't know what power this dragon has, what he's capable of. We could make a net out of Second-Realm power, which could catch him, but would it be enough to stop the dragon performing magic on us? Korden says the dragon can hypnotize people and make them do as he wishes."

"We'll need to shield our thoughts. Avruellen has taught me a couple that could work. Don't forget about the dragons breathing fire thing. We'll have to think of some kind of physical shield. This is all going to take a lot of power. I know we've been practicing, but are we strong enough? We might end up like Arcon did after shielding your symbols, especially if we have to hold a Second-Realm net over the dragon until we get it to wherever it has to go."

"You're right. Could we do it with earth magic? I wonder if we can combine the different power sources? I know I don't feel as tired after using the earth energy."

Korden had tied up the horses and, tired of trying to get their attention by waving, approached the realmists. "Come on, there's lots to do. We're hungry and then, after lunch, we have to get you two some horses."

They followed him into a nearby tavern. Men and women sat around expensive-looking stone tables on cushioned chairs. Near the clean hearth, which remained unlit in the warm weather, slouched padded armchairs arranged around a low table. Bronwyn thought if she were to design a tavern, it would look like this. Small vases on the tables cradled small, white flowers that gave off an intense, caramel scent. Bronwyn was reminded of Avruellen's garden at home. Not for the first time, she wondered if she would ever see it again.

Sander pulled out a chair for Bronwyn. "Oh, thank you." She hesitated before sitting: no one had ever pulled out a chair for her before. One dimple appeared on Blayke's cheek as he gave in to a small smile. He'd have to have a word with Sander later. Bronwyn was also happy to discover Sander was a vegetarian too; then she thought of Sinjenasta. Last time they'd met, they both thought Sander had killed the panther. "Sander, do you remember the last time I was here, you shot my panther?"

He blushed and looked at her, guilt in his eyes. "Yes. How could I forget? I'm truly sorry."

"It's okay. When I got back to the First Realm, he was alive. I don't think everything that happens here, happens there. Don't ask me how or why, but Sinjenasta was fine." She smiled.

"I'm so glad to hear it. That panther must mean the world to you."

"He does. If anything happened to him, I don't know what I'd do." Sander grinned, and Bronwyn thought he must be relieved he didn't have to feel guilty anymore. After lunch, which passed in jovial banter, Korden took them to the local saleyards and they picked out two stallions. Blayke rode the black one, Bronwyn the bay.

Shortly after leaving the town, Blayke rode alongside Sander while Bronwyn chatted with Korden. Blayke cleared his throat, not used to having conversations like the one he was about to have. "I couldn't help noticing, Sander, that you have an interest in my sister." Sander looked across at him but said nothing. "I just want you to know that she's a good kid and doesn't have a lot of experience with men. Do anything to hurt her and I'll kill you. Understood?"

Blayke straightened in his seat and scowled, trying to look as menacing as possible.

Sander kept the smile from his face, knowing Blayke was trying to be a good brother. He might have told Bronwyn he was only twenty-four but he had lived a lot longer than that and had many secrets, most of which he hoped to tell Bronwyn one day. He knew they would be together, and until that time, he would be patient. "Understood." Sander shouted over to Korden. "I think we'd better pick up the pace. It will be dark in three hours and we want to be there before Vertem is in the sky."

"Vertem?" asked Bronwyn.

"A blue planet that rises two hours after the sun sets. It's at this time that the dragon has the least power." Bronwyn opened her mouth to speak. "Don't ask me why; it just is. If you have any plans to finalize, I suggest you do it while we ride. You will face Devorum soon." He drew his sword out of its scabbard and thrust it above his head.

"To war!" he shouted and dug his heels in. Bronwyn and Blayke followed, galloping towards their fates.

❧

The sun slipped below the horizon to their left, the last slanting rays piercing the dusty air and coloring their horses' hooves with bloody light. A dark mass of mountains rose in front of them, rocky outcrops a jagged black outline against the dusk sky. The trees and grass were thicker here, although there was still not as much protection from above as Bronwyn would have liked. She shivered and breathed the damp night air.

Blayke dismounted. "Korden, what are you two going to do after you blow the whistle? Have you got somewhere to hide?"

"We're not going to run away like cowards. You'll need our help."

"I hate to say this, but if we have to protect you with our power, it will be more of a distraction than a help. I'm thinking this dragon will be breathing fire and trying to get into your heads. What if it talked you into killing one of us?"

Korden swung off his horse, his feet thumping on the ground. "Sander and I have dueled with this dragon before and out of two hundred soldiers, we were two of the eleven survivors. We are immune to its mind speak."

"How?"

"There is a trial our soldiers endure when they wish to enter the top three ranks of the King's Army. During the trial, which some do not survive, we are bestowed with a gift from Drakon, god of the dragons."

Bronwyn butted in. "Oh, we know him. He's the reason we're in this mess now."

"Don't blaspheme against a god." Korden shot a look to the heavens and from left to right. "They're always listening. You don't want to invite their wrath."

"I wouldn't worry, Korden," said Bronwyn. "Drakon needs us alive if we're to help save his precious dragons. I daresay he'll keep us alive until we're not needed anymore."

Sander said quietly, "He's not as bad as you think. He has his faults, but he wouldn't kill you without a good reason."

Bronwyn wanted to ask why, but Kalden held the whistle up.

"In approximately one hour, I will blow this. What's your plan?" Bronwyn and Blayke looked at each other and shrugged. *You tell them,* Bronwyn spoke into Blayke's mind. *I need to go relieve myself. I'll be back in a minute.*

That's right: leave the hard work to me. Go on. Go pee. I'll still be here when you get back. He laughed.

Thanks, Brother; I knew I could count on you. She giggled and went to find a large tree to hide behind.

Sander listened to Blayke. Their scheme was simple, and even though they would likely fail, it had its merits, and nothing he had run through his head had been as good as what Blayke had just suggested. He watched Bronwyn's dark shape emerge from the trees. He hadn't been in love for a very long time, and as much as he wanted to sweep her into his arms, she could do without the distraction before facing Devorum. If they lived after this night, maybe he would tell her his secret … if he had the courage.

Bronwyn returned to the men. Their silence was solemn, almost defeated. "Are we all ready?" When she realized no answers were forthcoming, she continued, "There's one dragon and four of us. They're quite good odds. You guys haven't seen what Blayke and I can do. Seriously, you want us on your side." They looked at her, and although she couldn't see their expressions, she could feel them. "Oh, for goodness sake, ladies, work with me here. Every day, for the past few months, I wake up wondering if today is the day I die, or tomorrow, or when the gormons get to Talia. I'm sick of stressing about it. I'm going into this with the belief that we'll win, because I don't like the alternative."

"Who are you calling a lady?" asked Sander. He turned to Blayke. "Can we throw her to the dragon as a distraction?"

"I have a feeling if the dragon ate my sister, he would end up with a severe case of indigestion."

"That's the spirit." Bronwyn laughed; then a blue glint caught her eye. She caught her breath. "Is that Vertem?"

Korden mounted his horse; the others did the same. "It's time. Ready?"

They answered "yes" in unison. Sander's sword hissed as he released it from his scabbard. Blayke had already reached the Second Realm and was searching for their symbols. Thankfully they were in a remote, unpopulated area. Any symbols that came near them would stand out—it was an early-warning beacon Blayke was happy to have.

Bronwyn rode her horse to a nearby tree, dismounted, and placed her palms on the trunk, drawing power from the rivers beneath the ground. She carefully wove a net with the power, which stayed in the trunk of the tree and could not be seen unless one was touching the tree. If she had made the net out of Second-Realm power, it would have been visible to the dragon, or so she assumed. They were leaving nothing to chance.

When the dragon flew above the tree, she would release the net—to shoot up and, hopefully, snag the dragon. Once the dragon was safely secured in the net, Blayke would release a containment spell, which would stop the dragon from accessing the Second Realm or breathing fire on anyone. It sounded simple, but the dragon would have to fly where they wanted it to, and Bronwyn's timing would have to be perfect. Setting a trap was something she had never done before.

Korden put the whistle to his lips and blew. Blayke sat on his horse, watching in the Second Realm. Sander, unwilling to observe from a distance, rode to Bronwyn's side, ready to protect her if a mere sword was needed. She looked up and was about to say something when an echoing shriek rent the night, and another, then another. Blayke yelled into Bronwyn's mind, *There are four symbols. It looks like Korden's whistle called all dragons within hearing distance! One looks bigger than the rest, so he's our target, but we may need to kill the rest. Try not to die, Bronny.*

I'll do my best. Good luck. I love you. She felt strange saying it, but now might be the only time she got.

I … love you too. I know I haven't said it before, but you're an awesome sister. I couldn't have asked for better.

Thanks. You're the best too. They cut off the connection, and Bronwyn relayed the information to Sander.

"Shit. Why do things have to get complicated?" He drew his bow and arrow. "Dragons are endangered, so I don't want to kill them. Is there anything you can do to my arrow to make it put them to sleep for a while, instead of killing them?"

"Hmm, I've never done that before, but I'm sure it can be done. We don't have much time. Maybe you should have thought of that before. Here, give me all your arrows." Bronwyn took them and closed her eyes. She remembered a sleep intonation Avruellen had used on a horse. Farmer Smilton's best breeding mare had broken her leg. Avruellen had put her to sleep so she could mend the leg without the horse feeling pain. Bronwyn mouthed the words and directed fluorescent flows of power into the shafts. Sander saw the arrows glow then fade.

"Wow! That's pretty impressive."

"Thanks. I also added a little something to make the arrows more accurate and fly further." Screams claimed the night, and Bronwyn ran from beneath the tree to see what was happening. Blayke and Korden galloped towards her, dark, winged shapes close behind. "Oh, gods, they're coming. Get ready!"

Sander walked his horse from beneath the protective canopy to get a clear shot. Bronwyn ran back to the tree and placed her palms on the cool bark. She sent to Blayke, *Tell me when to let it go.*

Adrenalin thrummed in tune with the power in her blood, and her breaths quickened, barely reaching her lungs before rushing out.

Bow in hand, arrow shaft between competent fingers, Sander inhaled the cool air. Blayke and Korden neared, but so did the dragons, one swooping low—mere feet from the men.

"Come on, come on." Sander breathed. He cocked an arrow, his aim following the dragon as it approached.

Blayke huddled over the neck of his horse, trying to make himself as streamlined as possible. The symbols were almost melded with his, and the tree was so far away. He looked up and behind, confirming with his physical sight what his other sight told him: one of the dragons was almost upon them. His heartbeat raced in time to the pounding hooves on the hard-packed dirt. He faced forward again, and in the Second Realm, the symbol closest to his glowed—the dragon was drawing power. Blayke hastily formed a shield over himself and Korden, whose horse sprinted next to his.

A fireball descended, exploding as it contacted the shield. Both men flinched, and the horses rolled their eyes, Blayke's whinnying through labored breaths. "Come on, boy. Not much further now." He sent a mental caress to his animal. A second fireball exploded on the ground, centimeters behind them. The part of Blayke's mind drawing the power fatigued, like an overused muscle. He released the energy—a bright rope slipping rapidly through his symbol, back to the Second Realm. The shield disappeared.

Korden and Blayke were one-hundred feet away. Sander had seen the fireballs exploding, relieved when one disintegrated in a shower of sparks above his friends' heads. The next one barely missed its mark. He couldn't watch from this distance any longer. His horse bucked when he kicked his heels to her flanks—she smelled fire and dragons. He kicked again, and she surged forward, tossing her head in protest. When the two groups were fifty-feet apart, Sander aimed, his arrow flying straighter and faster than he could have hoped. It pierced the dragon in the chest, flaring. The sizzle of contact reached his ears. One dragon dropped to the ground, narrowly missing Blayke and Korden.

Sander stopped his horse, her hooves skidding over scattered stones. He nocked another arrow ... aimed ... shot. Caressed by the wind of Blayke and Korden's passing, he turned his horse and bolted for leafy shelter, trusting from the squeal and brief glow gracing the night that he had found his target.

Blayke reached Bronwyn and spoke into her mind. *I'm exhausted. Shields take up more energy than I thought. I have enough to subdue the dragon, I hope, but there's still two breathing fire at us. The dragon we want is staying too high. It's assessing the situation, I would imagine. Do you know how high the net will fly?*

I have absolutely no bloody idea. It would have been good to get some practice shots in first.

Sander called out, "Three of them left. They're circling, probably planning the next attack. I'm going to stay here, and I'll let you know when they're coming."

"Thanks." Korden replied. "So, what now, Realmists?"

"We wait, unless you have any ideas?" Blayke dismounted.

"What if the dragon decides we're not worth the trouble and leaves?" Korden asked.

"They're coming!" Sander yelled.

"Looks like that won't be a problem," said Bronwyn. "Let me know when, Blayke."

Concentrating, sweat speckling his face, Blayke watched, but it was hard to estimate height in the Second Realm; distance was easy, but height didn't translate. "It's no good. I'm going to have to go out there." Blayke ran to stand next to Sander, out in the open, leagues of sky above, death hurtling towards them.

Sander spoke, "Blayke, you worry about the big momma and I'll worry about the other two." He nocked another arrow and spied his desired trajectory.

Diving, speeding, dark masses, the dragons resembled kites with long tails. Each time Blayke breathed in, they had jumped closer: one-hundred feet, eighty feet, sixty feet, forty feet: their eyes glowed red, barbed tails outlined against the moon. "NOW!"

Bronwyn ripped the "lid" off the stored energy in the tree. Her net erupted like the first rock out of a volcano. Blue, spider-webbed power flung skywards towards Devorum. The creature's scream as it tangled in the net pierced their sanity. Blayke fell to his knees, hands clapped over his ears. Bronwyn drew Second-Realm power and shielded their ears and minds.

Blayke recovered and, straining, drew his own Second-Realm power over the net and pulled it towards them. The dragon should be shielded, but since he had not performed this particular weave before, he had no idea if it would do what it was supposed to. His stomach clenched as he wrestled the enormous creature to the ground.

Bronwyn saw Blayke struggling and ran to him. Grabbing

his hand, she opened up a stream to the Second Realm to link to his. "Is that better?"

"Yes, thank you."

A rush of air whipped Bronwyn and Blayke's hair across their faces as one of the smaller dragons swooped near, pulling its head back to launch fire. Sander loaded the bow, drawing the shaft in one graceful movement. His fingers released another energy-infused arrow. The dragon parted its jaws.

Sander's missile imprinted a trail of light in the darkness on its way to plunging a bloody wound into the dragon. The dragon's eyes closed, and it crashed to the ground. Korden dug his heels into his horse and shouted, "Watch out!" as the fourth dragon came from behind Sander, fire roiling from its maw. Sander jumped off his horse and tried to roll out of the way, flames singeing his hair and incinerating his horse. Korden, helpless to do anything but wave his sword in the air, stood his horse between Sander and the dragon, who had circled around the tree and was returning for another go.

Sander scrabbled at his back and pulled another arrow, knelt and, with the dragon blocking out the moon above him, shot. This was the one chance he had. The goddess of luck, Afrail, smiled on him. Squealing like an overgrown pig, the winged creature fell to land next to the unfortunate horse.

Blayke blocked out the commotion, trying to ignore the plight of his friends as he set Devorum down. The dragon that was, as Blayke had been warned, at least three times larger than any other dragons he'd seen, fixed his burning stare onto the two realmists. It stood inside the net, towering over them. Blayke's stomach felt like it was somersaulting; he kept hold of his sister's hand.

"I ... think we did it, Bronny. We actually did it!"

Heart still racing, she wiped a sweaty hand on her hip. "I think we did."

Her smile, somewhere between pride and relief, lit up her face; Sander thought she looked like a goddess, radiating with an aura of the power she had employed to catch the dragon, a circlet of moonlight reflecting off her hair like a crown. She turned to see him patting a lock of scorched hair. "Nice hair. I hear well-done is in right now." She giggled. "So, now what? Do we drag this thing all the way to your king?"

Korden wiped his arm across his brow. "That could take some time. I was hoping you could use your power to hover it along."

"Hover it? Dragons' balls, Korden, who do you think we are?" Blayke frowned. "I don't have enough power to hover an ant right now. I'm done for today. If you need any dragons hovered, call someone else."

Bronwyn touched Blayke's arm. "Um, guys ... call me pessimistic, but I don't think we're as good as we thought."

They turned to see Devorum slash his claws vertically, opening a hole in the net. The net dissolved with a fizzle of blue sparks. Blayke, abandoning the elation of but a moment ago, spoke, "Shit. Now what do we do?"

Bronwyn wanted to scream, but her voice came out as a hoarse whisper. "I don't know."

She looked around to where they could run, but there was no way they would escape this beast. Reaching for Second-Realm power, she was too weak to hold even a drop—it was like trying to make a fist on waking.

The dragon took a giant, clawed step towards them. "Oh, gods, Blayke, it's him: it's ... it's the dragon from our nightmares."

Her hand covered her mouth.

The roaring reply vibrated in their bones. "Yes. It is I, Devorum."

He lunged at the realmists, his great mouth stretched wide. With nothing left to do, Blayke threw himself at his sister, shoving her to the ground. Covering and protecting her, Blayke shut his eyes tight. Waiting for the stab of teeth into his exposed back, he wondered: *Why is it only the bad dreams come true?*

CHAPTER 29

Through the haze, Klazich admired the perfection of the reflective surface. Waiting in its depths lay home. Collective memories, stories, and the images he had seen when linked to High Priest Kerchex were the only way he had to see his ancestors' birthplace. The longing burned in his veins. Even stronger than the longing was the desire for revenge. Contained within their race for over a thousand years, it would finally be given freedom to consume all in its path. Klazich wanted to bathe in the blood of Talia and wipe its ashes over his barbed crust.

He surveyed the gormons on the opposite bank of the gate. A row of four stood at the lip of the large pond; behind them, lines of thousands faded out of sight. "How much longer, Embrax?"

"Not long, Master. The moon is almost at its zenith. I will count it down in a couple of minutes." Embrax's rasping voice came as close to excitement as Klazich had ever heard it.

Klazich turned to face the other way, to look at the uncertain view of the gritty plain that stretched out indefinitely. He had explored his world, walking in that direction for weeks, only to find nothing. As each new sector of desolate territory solidified into tangibility, his disappointment grew—nothing changed; no ways to escape presented themselves. The Third Realm truly was a realm devoid of sustenance: visual, visceral, and victual.

In the muted Third-Realm atmosphere, Embrax's metallic voice sounded like steel chain chinking together as he shouted the countdown into the dead haze. "Get ready to go. In *dex, neen, echt, sevet, simt, fev, felm, tre, durt, ens.* Now!"

The spikes on the back of Klazich's neck and head hardened in excitement as the first of the gormons bravely dove into the gate. None of them knew what would happen: would they die instantly, bob about in water that was, literally, a pond, or would they race through to the world they'd been promised? Claws, hides, and heads broke through the slick membrane and continued on. Klazich watched as they slipped beyond sight, then the next row, and the next, his brother Feldich gone now. Klazich needed someone he could trust at the other end, and his brother was his best choice.

Three hours passed, and Klazich swayed just as Embrax counted sixty thousand through the gate. Talia was quickly becoming overrun with the horde. Embrax allowed himself to feel satisfaction. "Halt!" The gormons obeyed. Embrax turned to Klazich. "It is time to change the destination. Wait one moment, Revered One. Then we will continue."

Klazich clenched his jaw and scratched a forearm. He had never been nervous before, but this was taking too long—what if he had missed his chance? Klazich had wanted to be among the first wave through, to ensure he escaped this no-place, but he didn't want to reach Talia and find only one thousand had made the journey with him. Returning to lose was not what he had envisaged for his rule.

Embrax opened his eyes. "It is done, Master. After you."

The picture on the gate had changed to a dark room. The only thing Klazich could see was a table with three candles, the light beckoning him. Without saying goodbye to the world where he crawled had out of the egg—he possessed no love for this place—he nodded to the priest and dove in, the liquid closing over his rough skin. This was his triumphant rebirth into a life that would be worth living. He grinned, the warm fluid rushing into his mouth, salty and sweet bathing his tongue as he was sucked through the tunnel. But then: water rushed into his lungs, and he wondered if it had all gone wrong before shooting pain knifed through his chest.

⁂

Leon floated in Kwaad's consciousness, wondering where his body was. Once he had adjusted to the depravity of Kwaad's thoughts, he settled in, happy enough to be there, but there were moments when he wanted to be his old self and to control the body in which he resided. Occasionally Kwaad would have a rest and Leon would take turns with Tusklar controlling where they went.

Kwaad had assured the Talians that they could have their bodies back if they wanted, but they would have to wait until the other gormons came through and it would require another ceremony. They would also have to agree to be reabsorbed when Kwaad desired: if Kwaad were by himself, he would become the size of a normal gormon. Neither the king nor his wife had any objections, and now they waited in Leon's throne room, in the middle of the night, the only light a trio of candles on a small table near his throne.

The moon had passed full some thirty minutes before. So far, the disc that hung in the center of the room, which was almost as tall as Kwaad but wider, had remained silent and black. They were expecting forty-thousand gormons to come rushing through at any moment. Scores of ebony-clad Inkrans waited, thinking they were supposed to escort the newcomers to their quarters, and in a way, they were ... just not how they thought. Some one-hundred gormons would come through as adults, but the rest would need homes. Stripped of their flesh, they would settle into the Inkrans and subvert their bodies.

Leon sensed that Tusklar was not entirely happy about this, but her craving for power was greater: she remained silent. The king and queen waited while Kwaad concentrated. Apparently he was helping some of the gormons through the corridor so they could arrive fully formed. Leon's awareness filled with satisfaction as he imagined how Edmund would react when confronted with these creatures. *Not long now, and I will have my revenge.*

The Inkrans, alert, were the first to notice the black disc was bulging. Despite their training, they collectively stepped back a pace as Klazich and Embrax spilled through onto the floor, struggling to breathe, writhing in pain. Two other spindly, thorny creatures followed, then four, and another four, and another. The slimy creatures formed a writhing, growing mass on the floor as more were thrown through the gate to land on their brothers.

Klazich, not able to draw a breath with his altered lungs, fought for air as his sight darkened. Without warning, the stabbing feeling returned, tearing through his chest until, mercifully, air rushed in when he opened his mouth. He heaved, expelling a gush of putrid fluid.

Recovered somewhat, he pushed against the throng of his brothers and stood. A small, dark-robed person beckoned at him to move out of the way, and he obliged, fighting the urge to tear into him and taste warm, sweet blood. Klazich knew these people were necessary for his brothers to take their places on this world.

Soon, Klazich stood shoulder to evil shoulder with ninety-nine of his kin in a dark corner of the vast chamber wherein the gate changed, excreting green bile: the spirits of the gormons. Klazich and Embrax watched as one after another, sinuous, lichen-green tendrils drifted to the Inkrans. The first spirit reached its host and slithered into the man's nostrils. The other Inkrans panicked when they heard his shrieks, breaking ranks and running for the door. They were not quick enough. Persistent smoky threads, like ghostly tapeworms, chased the men and pervaded their nasal cavities with ease. When there were no men left to possess, the gormon spirits floated into the corridor where unsuspecting Inkrans waited.

A noise, similar to the wind rushing through reeds, whistled through the throne room until it became a roar. The gate started shrinking, seemed to suck into itself until it disappeared, imploding and trapping the last ten-thousand gormons in the Third Realm. Klazich bowed his head in a final farewell and revelled in the fact that he was among the ones who had made it to Talia.

Kwaad waited until the final screams died. "Welcome, brothers. How glad we are you have come through. Klazich, much planning has gone into today. We hope you are pleased."

"I am, indeed, Kwaad. It is an honor to meet one of our most eminent priests. My forefathers have sung your name for generations, and you have kept your promise." Klazich dropped to one knee. "I am here to serve."

He stood.

"Excellent. Now, we must show you around your new home and get ready for the coming war. The gormons may take up to eight weeks to gain their adult status, so we are vulnerable until then, but the kings of this world are ill-prepared to move at this time. We have ninety-thousand gormons: a formidable force equivalent to one-million humans."

Klazich laughed and gestured Embrax to his side. "I trust you've met Embrax, at least in spirit."

"Ah yes, a most competent priest. You have done well and followed my instructions without fault. You will be most useful." Kwaad turned and climbed the dais where the thrones were mounted. "Come. We have waited a long time for this. You can start by feeding. I have rounded up a herd of Inkrans; they have a certain pleasing spice to their flavor. When you have eaten, we will decide how best to crush King Edmund of Veresia and the rest of his dragon-loving heathens."

Klazich, Embrax, and the other adult gormons followed Kwaad through a door behind the thrones. Klazich salivated. He called out to Drakon in his mind. *We're back, and we've brought one hell of a present for your children. You will never be free of us Drakon. Never.*

CHAPTER 30

Bayerlon was more crowded than Sarah had ever seen. Walking back to the castle with great bunches of red timeswald blooms to adorn the royal dining table at tonight's feast, the petite queen's maid was jostled by aproned army cooks, muscled soldiers with the brown vests of Wyrden and green vests of Brenland, not to mention the questionable women, wearing tight-fitting, knee-length dresses, who slunk the streets, eager to secure their share of the new business. Not only were the avenues and lanes bustling with color, activity, and noise, but makeshift shelters were being constructed outside the city walls to house citizens from nearby villages who feared an attack from Inkra and Leon at any moment.

Edmund had returned a few days ago, and this morning King Fernis of Brenland, Queen Alaine from Wyrdon, and Elphus had arrived, with soldiers, lackeys, and, in some cases, wives, in tow. Rumors of the impending war had spread to the outer reaches of Vellonia faster than a rumor about the queen dressing in unfashionable clothes spread at court. To cope with the extra food that would be needed, Fendill and Astra were spending time at farms up to a day's ride from Bayerlon, coaxing plants to grow and ripen faster than normal using Second-Realm power.

Sarah hurried, wanting to get out of the crush of unwashed bodies. Relieved, she entered the inner city walls and the courtyard before reaching the castle. Passing through the kitchen, Sarah gathered Arnita, a young castle maid, to carry two vases. The maids almost ran into Queen Gabrielle as they approached the dining hall. "Oh, wonderful! Those flowers are just perfect, Sarah. Thank you so much."

Arnita and Sarah curtseyed. "My pleasure, Highness."

Gabrielle watched as the girls hurried to complete their task. The castle had not seen so much activity in decades. Tonight's welcome dinner was also a celebration of Verity's homecoming, and although the day was shadowed by the death of Boy and the looming war, everyone was keen to take time out to enjoy a festive banquet while they could. After tonight, serious planning for the war would be well underway.

After checking in the kitchen to make sure the food preparation was progressing as she wanted, Gabrielle hurried to her husband's meeting room, where the visiting royalty, realmists, and dragons were discussing the logistics of having a reliable information network operating.

Guarding the entry were two tall, wide-shouldered men: one with the Laraulen family crest on his blue vest, the other a Wyrdenese soldier wearing his country's brown vest. Both men bowed, the Veresian opening the door. The queen swept in, and the room suddenly went quiet, all in attendance rising to bow or curtsey. Gabrielle rested her fingers delicately on her throat. "Why, thank you. Sorry I'm late. Please, continue."

She took her place, sitting in a small throne next to King

Edmund at the head of the table, satisfied to see that Perculus, Edmund's advisor, was absent.

Zim, his black frame hunched, trying to avoid hitting his head on the ceiling, continued. "So, after contacting Vellonia, my father confirmed that the realmists Agmunsten promised had arrived. We are deploying pairs of dragons and realmists. Two pairs will travel to Zamahl."

"Zamahl! Are you sure that's wise?" asked King Edmund.

"We have no choice. If we don't have their help, Talia will fall to the gormons."

"I know, but…. What if they kill our emissaries?"

Zim shrugged.

Gabrielle spoke, her voice loud, positive. "Okay, so that's Zamahl taken care of. I think you would do well to position two pairs of dragons and realmists outside Klendar and another pair at our border with Inkra. That takes care of 'the betrayer.'"

"Good idea, my queen," said Agmunsten. "I also propose a pair be stationed at the castles of Queen Alaine in Wyrdon and King Fernis in Brenland. Do we have your permission, Your Highnesses?"

The raven-haired queen blinked slowly, showing her long lashes and blue eyes to greatest effect and played with the gold chain at her throat. "That is a splendid idea. I feel so much better knowing the dragons and your people are looking after things, Agmunsten. I am ever grateful." Dipping her head slightly, she looked up through her lashes at the realmist, who coughed.

"I am also happy with the arrangement, Agmunsten," said King Fernis as he patted his portly belly. "But don't expect me to be as grateful as Alaine."

He winked. Queen Alaine laughed.

"Hmm, if everyone's done, can we continue?" Agmunsten was good at making jokes, but not so good at taking ones aimed at him. "I had a short communication from Arcon. They found the book they needed and are activating the amulets tonight."

"It's good to have some positive news for a change. How are they?" King Edmund asked.

"I'm assuming they're okay. We didn't talk long; you can understand the dangers of being overheard. It *is* good news, but it means I also have extremely *bad* news as well." The realmist made eye contact with everyone in the room, which suddenly seemed less safe. Zim, obese Elphus, and Arcese, being realmists, knew what the bad news was. Arcese shut her eyes, resisting the urge to put her clawed hands over her ears.

"The second activation of the amulets takes place at the full moon, but so does the gormon invasion." He spoke quickly, to finish before panicked commotion drowned out his words. "I don't know how many are coming, but they will be coming tonight, and from what Arcon tells me, they will be landing at Blaggard's Bay, off the west coast of Talia: between Brenland and Zamahl."

Agmunsten was smothered with a blanket of questions, from: "Will they come for us straight away?" to "Are you sure they won't come through somewhere else?" He held his hands up for silence. When no one obliged, he drew Second-Realm power and slapped his hands together. A thunderclap shook the spiderwood table, and the chandelier clinked overhead like a wind chime.

The guards outside the door burst in, and saw not danger but a room full of shocked dignitaries: faces pale, eyes opened so wide that they looked like they would never shut again. "Everything's fine. You may leave us," managed King

Edmund. "Ever do that to me again, Agmunsten, and I will find a not-so-cozy cell in the dungeon for you to spend some time."

"Thank you, King Edmund, but next time everyone is that unruly, I'll take myself to the dungeon; at least it will be quiet. Now that I have everyone's attention again, I will continue. We are in a position I hoped never to see. Talia is divided, Leon is planning to attack us and is in league with the gormons, as evidenced by the information we have from Princess Verity and what I have seen with my own eyes. Possibly thousands of gormons will arrive tonight. We have no time to lose.

"Tonight I want to plan our patrol rosters, army placement in the event of an invasion from the north, west, or south. I'm trusting Queen Gabrielle to manage our information network and pass on everything she feels is important." He turned to Gabrielle. "Thank you for volunteering, my queen."

"It was my pleasure. It's about time I stopped leaving everything to Edmund. I quite enjoy being involved." Gabrielle folded her hands in her lap and smiled.

"I know I'm going to regret asking this, but does anyone have any questions?" Agmunsten braced himself for a tiring afternoon.

❧

Perculus sat in the kitchen of a two-bedroom terracehouse near the bottom of Bayerlon and tried not to breathe through his nose. Since Verity had returned, his nights were spent trapped in nightmares sent by Leon and whatever evil being he had become involved with, and his days were spent running around the city seeing that Leon's orders were complied with. He had lost some weight as a result, his large trousers held up with a newly purchased belt. It was true that he could delegate, but he didn't trust anyone to do the job properly. If he failed, Leon had threatened to gather up his spirit and hold it for eternity, meting out punishment on a regular basis. Perculus didn't care if it happened to someone else, but he valued his own life.

The gormons would arrive tonight, on the full moon. It was Perculus's job to ensure that the underground tunnels would be available so the monstrosities could sneak in. Opposite him at the table were two criminals: a thief and a murderer. The thief looked as all good ones do: small, agile, and nondescript. The murderer's hulking shoulders and arms bulged out of his woven hessian shirt. He acted with the confidence of one who knew how to use the many knives concealed about his person.

Perculus had explained what he needed, and after the thief, Chork, and the cutthroat, Lunts, had agreed, Perculus slid the money across the table. Lunts slammed his thick hand on the coins, intending to see to their distribution, but the smaller man, with speed obviously outpacing Lunts's expectations, already held his share—snatched from the jaws of death, so to speak.

"I'll be back to see you in two days," said Perculus as he rose and wiped down his trousers with a flick of his pudgy hand, just in case. Deciding it was time to eat, he followed the main street until he found one of his favorite inns—The Gatekeeper. Perculus liked it because those considered "unworthy" were kept out. It ensured he could eat his meal surrounded by like-minded men, those considered in the upper echelons of society—it didn't matter if they talked about the same old things all the time; they were an exclusive group, and it made them feel important.

After ordering, he didn't have long to wait before his haunch of venison arrived, swathed in gravy and wreathed with roast potatoes and carrots. Perculus sighed in pleasure as he filled his mouth and chewed, letting the gravy dribble down his chin. Mid-chew, a stabbing pain sliced through his head.

Leon's voice echoed through his brain, overlaid with another hissing, rasping voice. *Hello, Perculus. Glad to see you're doing as we've asked. The time has come, and there's something else we require of you.* His already pasty complexion paled as Kwaad detailed Perculus's role in the coming destruction of Talia. His slack mouth fell open, and mush that used to be food tumbled out to land in a gelatinous heap on his lap, where its damp warmth soaked through his pants. The fear he held for Leon before was naught compared to this. His hand trembled as he set the fork down on his plate. He doubted he would ever be hungry again.

A three-piece band played. Agmunsten sipped his bitter ale and hummed along with the haunting combination of flute, lyre, and harp. Midnight neared, and although the banquet was meant to be a diversion from the current unsavory circumstances, Agmunsten's thoughts rode on the wave of the melancholy melody.

Queen Alaine sat to his left, enchanting in a low-cut, red velvet dress, which showed her figure to its best advantage. She was a pleasing neighbor to have at dinner, and they had chatted most of the night, but now, as time fast approached to the gormons' arrival and Bronwyn and Blayke's dangerous second activations of the amulets, Agmunsten could think of nothing else. He chewed his fingernails and gulped more ale.

Looking around at his friends, he wondered who would survive the coming war, or if, indeed, any of them would. He threw the tankard to his lips and tilted his head back to be rewarded with the last mouthful of alcohol. He held out his cup for some more and was promptly attended by a serving man.

Zim, who sat across from Agmunsten, spoke into his mind, "Don't you think you've had enough?"

"No. Since when did you become my mother?"

"We need you to be awake tomorrow and not stuck with your head over the privy."

"Let a man enjoy his last moments on a gormon-free Talia, would you?" Agmunsten closed his eyes and took another swig. As he placed his tankard on the table, he felt a vibration and a mild pressure change. Agmunsten looked at Zim. The dragon nodded. Agmunsten surveyed the room and wondered how everyone could still be enjoying the night when the worst thing that had happened in over one-thousand years had just occurred. Shouldn't the gormons' arrival be more obvious? He envied the celebrating people their ignorance.

So, that's it then, Agmunsten spoke into Zim's mind. *Do you want to tell Edmund, or shall I?*

Let's not ruin their fun—like you said: it's the last time they'll enjoy anything like this for a while. There will be plenty of time to worry about it tomorrow.

And the day after, and the day after, thought the realmist. He nodded and drained his cup, holding it out for another refill. An hour later, as Agmunsten slid under the table and his vision blacked out, his last thought was of the prophecy: *A time of darkness is here. May the gods help us all.*

… ACKNOWLEDGMENTS

This is where I get to thank all the people who help me every day. To all my author friends—your humor, understanding and encouraging words always get me back on track when I'm having a crap author day. Thanks to Robert Baird who does the most awesome covers in the universe. Many, many thanks to Chryse Wymer—without you my punctuation would be pathetic and my awkward sentences would be torturous and to Tonya Cannariato for proof-reading. Finally, to the readers who take a chance on indie authors, and in particular, me. Thank you for purchasing and taking the time to read my book, and a special thanks to those readers who tell me how much they enjoyed my writing—you guys make my day, every day.

If you would like to connect with me, you can find me on twitter @DionneLister or my website **www. dionnelisterwriter.wordpress.com**. Ciao!

ABOUT THE AUTHOR

USA Today bestselling author, Dionne Lister is a Sydneysider with a degree in creative writing, two Siamese cats, and is a member of the Science Fiction and Fantasy Writers of America. Daydreaming has always been her passion, so writing was a natural progression from staring out the window in primary school, and being an author was a dream she held since childhood.

Unfortunately, writing was only a hobby while Dionne worked as a property valuer in Sydney, until her mid-thirties when she returned to study and completed her creative writing degree. Since then, she has indulged her passion for writing while raising two children with her husband. Her books have attracted praise from Apple Books and have reached #1 on Amazon and Apple Books charts worldwide, frequently occupying top 100 lists in fantasy and mystery. She's excited to add cozy mystery to the list of genres she writes. Magic and danger are always a heady combination.

Tempering the Rose